This Large Print Book carries the
Seal of Approval of N.A.V.H.

A COUNTY CORK MYSTERY

MANY A TWIST

SHEILA CONNOLLY

WHEELER PUBLISHING
A part of Gale, a Cengage Company

Farmington Hills, Mich • San Francisco • New York • Waterville, Maine
Meriden, Conn • Mason, Ohio • Chicago

Copyright © 2018 by Sheila Connolly
Wheeler Publishing, a part of Gale, a Cengage Company.

LIBRARY OF CONGRESS CIP DATA ON FILE.
CATALOGUING IN PUBLICATION FOR THIS BOOK
IS AVAILABLE FROM THE LIBRARY OF CONGRESS

ISBN-13: 978-1-4328-5472-0 (softcover)

Published in 2018 by arrangement with The Quick Brown Fox & Company LLC

Printed in Mexico
1 2 3 4 5 6 7 22 21 20 19 18

Is iomaí cor sa tsaol.
There is many a twist in life.

ONE

"What do you think?" Gillian Callanan asked nervously. "It's not been easy for me to do much lately, what with the baby coming. And Harry's been so busy trying to sort out clients that he hasn't been around as often as I'd like. He'd like to be, I think."

Maura Donovan looked at her obviously pregnant friend and wondered whether it was the very unfinished home or the impending birth of her and Harry's child that had made her so frazzled. Probably both, Maura guessed — not that she had any real experience with either pregnancy or home decoration. But Gillian had asked for her opinion, and she wasn't going to weasel out of answering it.

"I think it's a great place. It's got the right amount of space for the three of you, and the view of Ballinlough is terrific. It's all on one floor. It's close to where you'll be working —"

Gillian interrupted with a snort. "If ever I work again. We still haven't touched the studio space, and it's filthy."

"We'll round up a bunch of the regulars from Sullivan's and scrub the place down for you. I'll offer them some free pints. Location: great. Size: perfect. Access: easy. You've got a decent road right in front, but it'll be quiet because whatever cars go by, the studio in front will block the noise."

"If I ignore the fisherman swarming about six months out of the year."

"I thought fishing was quiet."

"Once you're out on the lake, it is. But it's the getting there that's noisy, and once the men are done for the day, they've been known to lift a few bottles on the way in."

"Is that legal?"

Gillian shrugged. "Live and let live, we say. But this place has been empty for so long that those who fish here often have forgotten that it's a home."

"Maybe I can ask Sean Murphy to keep an eye on things."

"Your faithful garda — what is he these days? Friend? Or more than friend?"

"I don't know," Maura muttered. "But I'm sure he'd help."

"Don't trouble yourself. Harry and I will work things out. Harry can always offer

them his services as an accountant, which might hurry up their exit."

"Is he having any luck?" Maura asked, feeling a bit anxious. Harry Townsend had been a modestly successful accountant in Dublin, but then his great-aunt Eveline, who'd lived in the local manor house near Maura's pub, had passed away not long ago, and Gillian had turned up pregnant. Gillian and Harry had been on-again, off-again for years, but now they seemed to be firmly on, and Eveline's passing had provided just enough funds to buy the decrepit house and former creamery overlooking a small lake, Ballinlough. Harry had given up his apartment in Dublin and was trying to make a go of his business locally, but he'd been struggling. Maura knew in theory that a lot could be done by computer these days, but she had no idea what the timeline might be for setting himself up and finding clients in West Cork. The baby, on the other hand, had a very definite timeline.

And no matter how Maura tried to re-assure Gillian, the house was still just short of livable. Being so close to the water, there were damp problems, and little maintenance had been done for at least the past ten years. Maura really was going to have to step up her game, corral some of her patrons, and make sure the essential things got done on time.

"Okay, Gillian, tell me this: What absolutely, positively has to be done before the baby comes?"

Gillian gave some thought to the question before answering. "I've little experience with infants, but I'm going to guess the child should be warm and dry, so at least his or her room should be finished and done right. You know, heating, double-pane windows, proper ventilation. And I'm told they soil their clothes every time you turn around, so there'd best be a washer and a place to dry clothes. Something like a basic kitchen, so I can keep Harry and myself fed without too much work. A place to sit, and somewhere to sleep. God help us, there's next to no furniture — I've been living in rented flats in Dublin for years with none of my own. Harry's been promised a few bits and pieces from the manor house, but I'd feel terrible watching black mold creeping up eighteenth-century end tables. You're lucky, up the hill there — you get more of a breeze."

"Has your family come around yet?"

"Do you mean, have they forgiven me, or have they actually visited here?"

"Either one. Does anyone on your side

have any baby things they can recycle?"

"I doubt it," Gillian told her, looking resigned. "My ma's still not speaking to me, and my sisters resent me because I'm the one who got away, took myself off to Dublin, and called myself an artist, while they were stuck here having babies and going to Mass with Ma. You'd think they'd be eager to come lord it over me now, wouldn't you?"

"And Harry has no one on his side, right?"

"Exactly. And you've seen the attic at Mycroft House — there are no discarded cribs lurking in the shadows there."

"What do we need to do right now? Heck, didn't people use to put new babies in a laundry basket to sleep? It's not like they need fancy furniture and matching sheets."

"Good point. The kid won't mind, at least not for a few months." Gillian hauled her bulk out of the chair she'd been sitting in. "Come on, I need to move. Let's go out the back and admire the view. We've got a couple of very used plastic chairs out there."

"Fine," Maura said and followed her to the back of the house.

It was a view worth admiring. The lake was, in Maura's Boston-raised opinion, just the right size: not so large as to be intimidating but large enough that sound didn't carry off the water. Gillian's house ran north-

11

south, so the back view looked west, toward the setting sun. There were few houses in sight, only the gentle hills beyond the lake. Maura could hear the distant lowing of a cow — but then, she could hear that from almost anywhere in West Cork. Still, it was pretty and peaceful and surprisingly soothing.

Gillian shut her eyes and leaned back in the rickety chair. "I suppose I should enjoy this as long as I can. I expect this child might have other ideas."

"I'm told they do sleep sometimes," Maura replied. "You have any idea if it's a boy or a girl?"

"None. Harry would prefer a boy, I think. Someone to carry on the line, not that it matters anymore. But that's a male thing, I think. I'll be happy either way."

Maura wondered to herself whether Harry would stay the course. He'd been something of a — heck, what did they call it these days? Player? — for most of his adult life. He'd shown no signs of settling down until recently, although he was in his midthirties, as was Gillian. The two of them had danced around the idea of marriage, but it still hadn't happened, child or not.

"You have a doctor and all that?" Maura asked.

"I've been to the clinic, and there's a visiting nurse who comes around. Since I'm not exactly young for a first-time mother, I'm told I should have this child in hospital, although there are midwives around. And midwives in hospitals, for that matter. Don't worry. It's taken care of."

"And when do you have to be out of Mycroft House?"

"The National Trust has been very kind to let us stay while we get things sorted out, but I think they'd like to have the place open for tours by the summer. We've already inventoried who gets what. And the O'Briens left in a huff as soon as Eveline died. As you might guess, I'm not exactly keeping up with the housecleaning these days."

"I'm told there's a service you can hire to clean for you," Maura volunteered.

"Yes, over at Union Hall — I know a couple of the people there — but I'm not sure what money we have, and I'd rather save it for more important things."

Maura was feeling more and more useless. She really wanted to be able to help Gillian, but all this baby stuff was completely foreign to her. She'd never had any brothers or sisters since her father had died and then her mother had vanished when she was young, leaving Maura with her grandmother. She'd never done any babysitting in her Boston neighborhood because nobody paid for that there, calling on relatives most of the time, and Maura had needed to work to bring in some income, even when she was in high school. She knew which end of a baby was up and that they needed constant feeding and cleaning, but that was about all.

Gillian laughed, startling her. "Ah, Maura — if only you could see your face! I know you want to help, and I'm glad to have your company."

Maura smiled in spite of herself. "Okay, but let me do what I can, will you? The least I can do is paint or move furniture around."

"Don't fret. I'll ask. I know — we can't do this alone. Shouldn't you be off about now?"

"I told Mick I'd be in by five and cover the evening shift. So I guess I should be going. Is Harry picking you up, or should I drop you off at Mycroft House?"

"A ride would be grand. Let me check in with Harry." Gillian managed to get up, then made her way carefully into the house. She was back in under a minute. "Harry said he'd be eternally grateful if you would see me home."

"No problem. You ready to go?"

"Let me pee once more. Thank goodness the plumbing here works."

Waiting for Gillian, Maura turned back to the view. The days were growing longer, but the sun was already hanging low. She'd meant it when she said it was a lovely place. A good place to raise a child. But she was still having trouble seeing Harry settling in here. Maybe he'd be able to find a small office he could afford in Skibbereen or even Cork city. Someplace he could set up a desk and files and a computer connection, away from the interruptions of a squalling baby.

Gillian came out the door on the side. "Ready?"

"Let's go."

TWO

It was nearly dark as Maura drove along the Ballinlough road toward the village of Leap, where Sullivan's occupied a central place on the village's only main street. The building had stood there for centuries, leaning against a rock face behind, and its former owner, Mick Sullivan — usually known as Old Mick — had done his best not to change anything at all in the decades he'd managed it. In a way, Maura could understand that: if there was an Irish equivalent of "if it ain't broke, don't fix it," the shabby dark pub fit the bill. She had followed the same rule when she'd found out that Old Mick had left her the pub in his will, thanks to an agreement he and her grandmother had come to without ever bothering to mention it to her. Maura had always been wary of new situations, so she'd taken her time sizing up the place before deciding on any changes — or whether any changes were needed.

The staff had already been in place, and all had stayed, much to Maura's relief. "Young" Mick, in his midthirties, was the quiet mainstay of the place. Jimmy was less dependable, but he came as a package deal with his young daughter, Rose, barely seventeen, a sweet kid who was pretty enough to draw in some customers. Then there was Old Billy Sheahan, a longtime friend of Mick's who, thanks to a deal with Old Mick, enjoyed free rent in his tiny rooms at the end of the old building, not to mention a steady supply of fresh pints of Guinness. But Maura had quickly recognized that Billy was an asset: he knew everybody and everything about them and the region and its history, and Maura wasn't sure she would have survived the first few months without his steady guiding hand. Along the way, he had become the grandfather she had never had, and he was welcome to keep his warm corner by the pub's fire as long as he wanted it.

The pub was a small place with room for no more than two hundred people (which was also about the total population of the village) if they crowded together and used all the available space in the pub, but the people kept coming, first out of curiosity to see what the new young American girl would do with the place, and then because it seemed that they actually liked her — and because she hadn't changed things much. The only real change was that Maura had brought back Irish music to the place, a long-standing tradition that Old Mick had let lapse in his later years. The music attracted a few younger faces and a greater number of women, but it didn't really change the feeling of the place. And that was fine.

Maura parked her car on the street and walked into Sullivan's, drawn by the warm glow of the windows facing the street. She was greeted by the familiar odor of smoke — a heady mixture of burning peat and wood — topped off with a bit of stale beer, a dollop of woolens that hadn't been washed since fall, and a dash of cow. She raised a hand to Billy in his accustomed seat, and he smiled at her before going back to his conversation with two men she didn't recognize. She made her way to the bar, where Rose and Mick were keeping moderately busy filling pints and making coffee from the gleaming stainless-steel machine — it had been languishing in the cellar under Old Mick, and bringing it upstairs and getting it running was another positive change she'd made.

"How's Gillian?" Rose asked, watching her row of pints settle with an experienced eye.

"Large. Kind of overwhelmed with all the stuff that has to be done at the house, and she can't begin to do most of it in her current condition."

"And where's Harry, then?" Rose asked.

"Drumming up work, she says."

"Is he serious, do yeh think?"

"About staying around? Staying with Gillian? I hope so, to both. I think they're still kind of feeling their way along with all these changes. Are you too busy to talk for a minute?"

Rose checked out the room. It looked like most of the men held glasses that were at least half full. "I've time enough, I'd say. Can I make you a coffee?"

"Please." Maura watched for a few moments as Rose set the machine to brewing a single cup for her.

After a couple of minutes, Rose slid it in front of where Maura was perched on a barstool. "Yeh wanted to talk about something? Yeh're not thinkin' of firin' me, are yeh?"

"Good heavens, no!" Maura protested, laughing. "Not unless I know you've got something better lined up, or you decide to leave your da to Judith and head for the big city. Why don't we move to that corner? It's a little more private."

Once they were settled, it was Rose who picked up the thread. "I've been thinkin' . . . No, that's fer another time. What were you after talking about?"

"Gillian. And Harry. There are things that have to be done, since they've got to leave Mycroft Hall and move into their new place soon, and even together they don't have the time or energy to get everything done. And not enough money to hire people. So, when I was driving back down here, I was wondering if we could put together some sort of shower for them."

Rose cocked her head, looking curious. "A baby shower, are yeh thinkin'? That's pretty much an American thing. Here there's some that still hold it's bad luck to bring any baby things into the house before the child is born."

"What, the poor kid has to come home with not a thing to wear? That doesn't seem right. And I'm thinking not just a baby shower but more. Sure, Gillian needs stuff for the baby, and she won't mind hand-me-downs, but Harry's not very handy around the house. He's never had to be. You think it might be possible to put together a shower with the guys, maybe out at the house, where they do some of the heavier work? I mean, we don't have to call it a shower. It's like another American custom: a barn-raising. All the neighbors get together and help build the frame for a new barn. It takes a lot of people to raise it and nail it together. Or so I'm told — I don't know of many barns in Boston."

"I've not heard of that, but I like it. And instead of tea and little cakes, you give 'em a keg and bread and cheese?" Rose grinned. "Maybe an all-day thing, where they could drop by and put in a couple of hours each. *Ní neart go cur le chéile,* right?"

"Huh? Is that Irish?"

"It is. They made us learn a bit of it in school. The words mean something like 'there is strength in unity,' but the idea is that yeh're better off workin' together."

"That's exactly what I was thinking. When would be a good time? We've got to get the place warm and dry before they bring the baby home."

"More important, when's the baby due?"

"I don't know the exact date, but probably too soon. So we should jump on this ASAP?"

"I'd say so. And the men'll get caught up in their spring chores soon enough. Shall I

21

ask Judith what she thinks?"

"Please! How're she and your dad getting on?"

Rose laughed. "I'd say she has him well in hand."

"Have they set a date yet, or don't they plan to?"

"Judith won't let him slip away that easy. Before summer, I'd say."

"Where is he, by the way?"

"She has him out today looking at cows to add to her herd."

Maura laughed. "That I'd like to see. Well, think about the shower idea, will you? Do you need a break, now that I'm here?"

"Let me run over the road and pick up a bite fer me supper. Judith will feed me da."

After Rose slipped out on her errand, there was a brief lull, and Mick came over to talk to Maura. "There was a call fer yeh while yeh were gone."

"On the pub phone, you mean? Who was it?" Calls on the pub's landline were rare.

"Business, it seems. Some muckety-muck from a company I'd never heard of asked to speak to the owner. I said yeh were out, but yeh'd call them back later."

"Am I supposed to call tonight?"

"I'm guessing the mornin' will do well enough."

"And that's all they said?" Those few times the pub's landline rang, rarely was it a call for her. "They didn't tell you why they wanted to talk to me?"

"That they did not. Don't worry yerself about it, Maura. They probably want to sell you something."

"Then it'll be easy to say no, since we haven't enough money to buy much of anything."

The next time Maura looked up, Garda Sean Murphy was coming in, followed by another garda she'd never seen before. Trouble? Sean didn't look anxious, so it couldn't be too bad. When he was close enough to be heard, he said in an oddly formal way, "Maura, I'd like you to meet Sergeant Conor Ryan. He'll be joinin' us at the Skibbereen station, and I'm showin' him around, like." He turned to his companion. "Sergeant, this is Maura Donovan — she's the owner of this fine place fer the last year. But her family's from up toward Drinagh."

The new sergeant extended his hand. "Good to meet yeh, Miss Donovan." His handshake was firm and no-nonsense.

"Welcome," Maura said. "It'll be nice to know someone who's newer around here than I am. Can I get you anything? Coffee? Tea?"

Sean looked at the sergeant for guidance. Conor Ryan gave a small nod, then sat, and Sean happily took a seat next to him. Maura put two and two together and realized that the new garda was senior to Sean, although Sean had been at the Skibbereen station for more than a year. Maura nodded at Rose to start two coffees, then turned back to the men. "Are you from around here, Sergeant?"

"I've just been transferred from the big station in Limerick."

"I've never been there. The pub here keeps me busy, so I don't do a lot of sightseeing. Are you enjoying Skibbereen?"

"I can't say as I know it well yet. Yeh're American, are yeh not?"

"I am, from Boston. But my father was born here."

"Yeh're young to be running a place like this."

Rose handed Maura two cups of coffee, and she slid them across the bar to the men before answering.

"I inherited it from a relative of my grandmother's. Luckily, I had some experience with bars back in the States, and I've had help learning how things work here." She realized with some surprise that the man hadn't smiled yet. She had a feeling

24

that if she'd committed a crime, she'd be feeling pretty guilty right now, which was ridiculous. He was, well, kind of scary. She wondered why he had left Limerick — had it been his decision or someone else's? "Well, I hope you like Skibbereen." Should she compliment Sean on his policing skills, or would that open up a whole can of worms? She didn't feel like explaining how it had come about that she knew the Skibbereen gardaí so well.

She was relieved when Sergeant Ryan cut off the conversation and he turned to Sean. "Murphy, we have other stops to make, do we not?"

"Of course." They both drained the half-finished coffees, and Sean slid some coins across the bar. "Ta, Maura," he said.

"Good night, Sean. Nice to meet you, Sergeant." He didn't respond. Not exactly a warm and friendly guy.

She watched as the two men left. From the rear, they looked oddly mismatched: Sean was not particularly tall, fairly slender, and plainly the younger of the two. This sergeant person was taller, definitely broader, and seemed to be made of granite. His back was arrow straight, and he looked as though he was absorbing every detail of her pub without even moving his head. And he definitely made her uncomfortable.

Mick came up behind her at the bar. "What was that about?" he asked quietly.

"New guy at the Skibbereen gardaí, it seems. I'll have to find out more from Sean. Did we need more gardaí around here? I thought crime was pretty low," Maura commented.

"Maybe it wasn't his choice. Where'd he say he's from?"

"Limerick."

"Ah," Mick said. "Rough place, that. He'll probably be bored here in a week. But maybe someone wanted him here or wanted him out of his former station. I wouldn't want to cross him."

"I know what you mean," Maura told him.

The evening flowed on at its usual pace. Rose came back with her supper; Mick went out to find some of his own. In between pulling pints, Maura reviewed her own to-do list. She had survived winter in her cottage thanks to Mick, who had shown her how the heating system worked. The pub was generally cleaner than it had been when she arrived. She was still learning how to attract musical groups to play. So far they'd sort of invited themselves once they'd heard that Sullivan's was having music again, but that wasn't a long-term solution. From what

Maura had heard from other people her age, mostly back in Boston, you had to promote on social media to bring in customers, and she'd never had the time or seen the need to mess around with that. Did it make sense to learn now?

Jimmy came in around seven, looking peeved, but that was Jimmy's usual expression. Nothing ever seemed to make him happy, and that included his job and now his lady friend. Well, Jimmy's happiness was not her problem, Maura reminded herself. All she needed from him was that he show up more or less on time for his shift and do what he was supposed to do. Maura had a sneaking suspicion that Rose was preparing herself to make a move in a new direction — maybe that was what she had hinted at earlier? — and once she did, Maura wouldn't feel obligated to keep Jimmy on board. Heck, if business kept getting better now that there was the music, she might find more people wanted to work at Sullivan's.

Would it be worth the effort to serve food at Sullivan's? Full meals? Lunches only? What kind of staff would that take? Would she have to upgrade the equipment? What permits would she need?

Now she remembered again why she kept

shoving the whole idea on a shelf and ignoring it. She would talk to Rose about it — later.

THREE

It was always late and usually dark when Maura arrived home, and most nights she dropped immediately into bed. Morning was a different question. It was the only time she had to herself to potter around her small cottage, enjoy a cup of coffee or tea (making anything more than toast exhausted her cooking skills), and map out her day, week, or month without interruption.

But this morning, she felt unsettled, and she wasn't sure why. The pub was running smoothly. All licenses had been renewed, the taxes had been paid, and the income kept inching up. She knew her patrons fairly well now and was comfortable bantering with them over a pint. She was content with her progress that year. So what was bothering her?

Probably Gillian's home situation. Here Maura was trying to give her good advice when she had no idea what it was like being in love, having a baby, and setting up a home and making choices about where it should be and what it should look like. Even the house she now owned had been dumped in her lap, thanks to Old Mick, and she hadn't added anything to it. Not that she was complaining.

Back in Boston, she and Gran had lived in whatever place they could afford between them. They hadn't paid much attention to making it pretty or homey, more concerned that all the appliances and the heat worked. Of course they'd kept it clean, but with both of them working — or in school, in Maura's case — there wasn't even much time for that. It was a place with beds and plumbing and a stove to cook on.

Maura sipped her coffee and leaned back in her chair to study the main room. Two rooms on the first floor — no, *ground* floor in Ireland. One was fancier and would probably be called a parlor, but she rarely used that for anything. The bigger room was the "everything else" room. It still had a massive century-old fireplace, but there was also a sink, a working stove, and a table plunked down in the middle. The main door and two small windows were on the side facing the lane, whose main traffic was the herd of cows that belonged to a neighbor. The staircase to the upper floor was attached to the back wall, and under it a door led to the bathroom, which clearly was not original to the house. Upstairs there were two bedrooms and a small sitting area with a window looking over the lane.

And that was it. It was as much as she needed. More, in fact: she could have done without the parlor with the fancy mantelpiece and the second bedroom. Gillian had used that room, staying with her for a short while when she and Harry were working things out between them, but Maura really did like her privacy, especially after a long day at Sullivan's dealing with other people. She'd always been kind of a loner. The fact that she'd left few friends behind in Boston should have tipped her off. Now she had to save her sociable impulses for chatting up the guys at the pub.

But she had Mick's grandmother, Bridget Nolan, down the lane — and now Gillian over the hill — if she wanted company. Mick looked after Bridget, although Maura knew Bridget had other family around. How had that happened? He was a decent-looking man in his thirties, and not for the first time, she wondered why he was unattached. Easy to look at, competent, kind to his elders. What was the problem? When she'd arrived a year earlier, she hadn't planned to stay. When she had decided she was staying, she hadn't planned on getting into a relationship with anyone, and she needed Mick more as an experienced employee than anything else. Still, they'd shared two kisses — that they'd never talked about.

If she was looking for a relationship, Sean Murphy would be a more logical choice. She enjoyed his company, and she was grateful to have a garda in her back pocket because she kept running into the oddest assortment of problems that needed the attention of the police. But she hadn't detected any kind of spark between them — at least, not on her side. In a way, she wished she could because he was a really good guy. But she still wasn't looking for a relationship. Why bother? Her grandmother's husband had died, and Gran had never remarried or even looked at another man seriously. Her father had been killed in a work accident, and her mother had bailed out as fast as she could after that. Maura didn't have anything like a model for a good relationship. Now she was a home and business owner and self-sufficient. Why would she need a partner at all?

She realized her coffee cup was empty and thought about getting another cup. No, she decided: since she had some spare time, she should go see Bridget. She hadn't visited for a few days.

She showered and dressed quickly, then opened the front door and inhaled. Yes, there was a hint of spring in the air. Last year, she'd been too overwhelmed to pay any attention to it, but now she could take the time to enjoy it. Slow down, live in the moment. This was her life now. She snorted, though there was no one to hear her. *You've gone soft, Maura!*

Leaving her front door open, she ambled to the end of her lane and down the hill a hundred feet or so to Bridget's tiny cottage, one that was much older than her own. As she approached, she could see Bridget leaning over some large flowerpots next to her front door.

"Good morning, Bridget," she called out so she wouldn't startle the older woman.

Bridget straightened slowly, then turned to Maura with a smile. "And good morning to yeh as well, Maura Donovan. It's a fine day, is it not?"

"It is. How're you doing?"

"These old bones are always glad when spring arrives. Come, sit with me fer a bit." Bridget waved at the two chairs set up in the small area in front of her door. The land

33

rose up across from the house and kept the wind off, and the enclosed area held the sun, so even though it was still early in the day, it was comfortably warm. Maura moved to one of the chairs and waited for Bridget to settle herself before sitting.

"All's well at Sullivan's?" Bridget said.

"It is. You'll have to ask Mick to bring you by some day — maybe after church on a Sunday?"

"I don't do well with crowds at my age. How's Billy?"

"He's grand. But he doesn't have as far to go to get to the pub." Bridget and Billy were about the same age and had known each other forever. Maura wasn't sure whether to call them friends. There should be another term for a relationship that spanned decades without becoming any closer but without fading. That happened a lot in Ireland, Maura had found.

"Is my grandson behavin' himself?"

"Has he ever not?" Maura countered.

"He's a good man and takes good care of me. I do wish . . ." Bridget began, then stopped.

Maura chose her response carefully. "I don't mean to poke my nose into your business, or his, but I'm guessing you wish he had more of a life of his own?" Mick was

34

still an enigma to her even though they'd been working together for a year.

Bridget smiled, if sadly. "You see more than most give yeh credit for. And yer right. He shouldn't be wastin' these years looking after me."

"But he wants to. That's what families do for each other, isn't it?" Not that she knew much about families. It had always been just her and Gran. Gran had loved her, no question, and had done the best she could to make a decent life for Maura. But Maura had no clue what it would be like to have brothers and sisters and aunts and uncles and cousins. She'd found more family here in Ireland than she'd ever known before.

"Mick's too young to spend his free time with an old lady like me."

"You want to marry him off to someone?" Maura said, smiling.

Bridget looked away. "It's not my place to say."

Bridget's comment struck an odd note, Maura thought. Bridget wasn't one to back off, especially when family was involved. But even though she'd known Bridget for a year now, Maura was reluctant to press on personal issues — like Mick's love life, or lack of one.

Maura looked up to see Bridget watching

her face, her expression hard to read. "He'll tell you when he's ready," Bridget said softly.

Great, now Bridget had just made things even more confusing. Maybe that was just the way the Irish did things: they danced around and sneaked up on saying anything personal or serious. Well, she wasn't about to dash off and ask Mick what deep dark secrets he was hiding. She had no claim on him, and if he wanted privacy, she'd give it to him.

She stood up and dusted off her jeans. "I'd better be heading to the pub. Do you need anything?"

"I'm set, Maura. You go on now. I'll just finish cleaning up me pots here so I can plant me flowers, and then I'll go in fer a nice cuppa tea."

"I'll see you soon, then," Maura said. She helped Bridget out of her chair, then headed back to her own cottage, where she collected a sweater and her keys and then drove down the lane.

Was that a hint of green dusting the bog at the bottom of the hill? What the heck did bloom around here in spring? She should ask somebody. Maybe Gillian would know. Which reminded her: she needed to put together the plan for Gillian and Harry's place, sooner rather than later. Maybe Rose and Judith had come up with something. Or maybe Mick would have some ideas. All she knew for sure was that she needed to do something.

The drive to the pub was short, as usual. She almost had to laugh at the insane traffic back in Boston. Here in this part of Ireland, she rarely passed more than one car on her way to and from her cottage. She'd never pictured herself as a country girl, but here she was living in a pretty postcard place with bogs and cows. Life was odd that way.

There were no patrons in the pub yet, but it was barely ten o'clock. Mick was already in, swabbing off the top of the bar. No sign of Jimmy or Rose yet — or Old Billy either, but he was seldom in this early in the day.

"Morning," she said to Mick as she hung her jacket on a hook near the loos. "I stopped by to see Bridget this morning."

"Good of you. Was she out already?"

"She was. She's getting her pots ready for flowers. It was nice and warm in the sun, anyway. We have anyone booked for the weekend?"

Mick shook his head. "Yeh'll have to check the book. Yeh really need to learn to use the computer — yeh could be bringin' in a lot more bands and more people to hear them if yeh posted online."

"I hear what you're saying, but I don't know what to do about it. I don't own a computer, and I don't want to spend the money on one right now. And when would I have time to learn how to use programs to book bands and advertise? We're not even connected to the Internet here, are we?"

"It's easy enough. It's the same provider as fer the phone — give them a call. There's folk all up and down the street here that have done it."

"I don't have a computer," she said stubbornly.

Mick stopped wiping the counter, leaned back, and crossed his arms. "And how hard can it be to find yerself one? They sell them in shops, yeh know. And you don't need anythin' fancy or complicated. They don't cost much, and it's fer the business, not just a toy fer yeh to play with."

"I'll think about it," Maura said, eager to end the conversation. If she was honest with herself, she really didn't know why she was so anticomputer. Probably because she'd never had one back in Boston, mainly because she couldn't afford one. She'd used computers at school or the library, but she'd never had the time to explore what programs were available. She'd seen her classmates leapfrog over her with their computer skills, doing things she couldn't imagine on their cell phones. She'd been left behind, and it was embarrassing. "Maybe Rose has a friend who could show me what I need."

"And there yeh go!" Mick said. "Have yeh returned that call from yesterday?"

"Oh, no, I forgot. I've got the number here somewhere. Might as well call now before people start coming in." She fished the slip of paper out of her pocket, then retrieved her cell phone from another pocket and stepped into the back room to make the call. It took her only three minutes.

When she returned to the main room, Mick, who was moving chairs and tables around, looked at her and quirked an eyebrow. "What? Bad news?"

"No. Or at least I don't think so. Do you know a Crann Mor estate?"

"Of course. Grand old place out past Skibbereen. That was the place that called?"

"It was. The person I talked to, one of the managers or something, said the place had changed hands last year, and they were looking at the idea of reaching out to the community to provide a — let me get this right — 'more diversified experience for their clientele.' " Maura made air quotes. "They'd heard we were doing music and that this place had been around for a long time, and they want to 'check us out.' What the heck does that mean?"

"Could be nothin', or could be a nice bit of coin in yer pocket. They want the grand tour of the old place?"

Simultaneously, they surveyed the pub in all its glory and burst out laughing. "Well, we'd better polish . . . something," Maura said. "They'll be here in a couple of hours. Oh, and they said they were looking for, uh, 'ambience and authenticity.' Do we have any of those on hand?"

"I think we keep the ambience in the back room," Mick said, grinning. "The authenticity is a lot easier to find. Bring 'em on!"

FOUR

Rose arrived not long after, and Maura explained quickly about the guests arriving soon and set her to polishing tabletops and cleaning the large front windows. She still wasn't sure what these people wanted with her, and she wasn't sure she wanted to get in bed with them. She'd known from the start that she didn't want a cute Ould Irishe Pub, and based on her limited experience as an owner, going that route was not going to benefit Sullivan's. Her customers liked things the way they were, and so did she. It was a workingman's pub, not a tourist attraction. But she should hear the people out — maybe it would give her some ideas for the future.

"Do yeh want me to sit in on this meeting?" Mick volunteered.

"No, thanks. Don't take this the wrong way, but I'd worry that whoever shows up will look at you and decide you're in charge and pretend I'm not even there."

Maura was a little disappointed that he didn't contradict her. Instead he said, "You want me to leave altogether? Or hide in the back?"

"Well, no, not exactly. I'm not sure what they'll want to talk about, and it would help if you could listen in without butting in and translate for me after they're gone."

"Got it. I'll pretend to be 'just a bartender' and keep me gob shut. Will that suit? What do yeh want to do about Old Billy?"

"Well, I'm sure not going to throw him out just to pretty up the place. It wouldn't be fair to him. He's part of the ambience, right?"

"So he is. And here he is now."

Maura turned to see Billy making his slow way along the sidewalk toward the front door. She went over to open it for him. "Good morning, Billy. You're early today."

"Ah, Maura, the spring is easier on me joints, and I couldn't stay inside with the sun shinin'. Yeh want me to go and come back again?"

She smiled at him. "Of course not. You know you're welcome here any time. But I should warn you — we have some guests coming. Although I'm not sure 'guests' is the right term."

"Give me a pint, and you can explain it to me."

Maura glanced at Mick, still behind the bar, and he nodded. "Get yourself settled, and I'll tell you all about it. You want a fire today?"

"Mebbe a small one — takes a bit of time for the old stone walls here to heat up when the spring comes."

"Then I'll start on that." A nice little fire would probably add to the ambiance. Maura wondered if there was a checklist or test for measuring it. Were there points given for cleanliness? Fast delivery of drinks? She knelt by the fireplace and began stacking kindling. "Billy, you know what Crann Mor is?" she asked over her shoulder.

"Sure and I do. It's older than I am, though it wasn't always a hotel. Real nice, I'm told, though I've never seen the inside of the place. I've heard that the last owner sold it a year or more ago and the new one has big plans. Why are yeh askin'? Not planning to dip your toe in the high life, are yeh?"

Maura put a match to the kindling and watched until she was sure the fire had caught. Then she sat back on the floor and said, "Hardly, Billy. I don't even want to guess what it would cost to spend the night at a place like that, and I'm pretty sure I don't have that kind of money. But I got a call from somebody there who says they want to come over and check out Sullivan's to see if we're worthy of sending their precious patrons to if they're looking for a real Irish experience."

"And yer not happy with the idea?" Billy asked.

Billy was a shrewd observer, Maura noted, not for the first time. "I guess not. I don't consider myself entertainment for rich people, and I don't do quaint. Heck, I'm not even Irish — or I don't sound like it, at least. I can't imagine they'd be interested in this place. Aren't there bigger and better pubs in Skib?"

"Mebbe. Don't fret yerself, Maura. The new folk are just lookin' to see what's around. It may come to nothing. Just be who you are, and don't worry about this visit of theirs. Do yeh want me to do anything?"

"Like what, sing? You have a tin whistle in your pocket?" Then a sudden thought struck her. "You might be able to fill them in about the history of this building, though — I don't know all the details."

"I'd be happy to tell them."

Mick arrived with Billy's first pint of the

day, and Maura seized the moment to retreat and take a hard look at her pub. Small — no changing that. Kind of a clunky layout, but that too was dictated by the age of the building. Dark, but that was sort of deliberate to hide the less-than-perfect cleaning. The assortment of vintage posters and publicity items plastered over the walls (and occasionally the ceiling) was interesting and kind of unusual, but it looked chaotic, not that she would think of changing it — it was a minihistory of music in this part of Ireland and maybe even beyond. It reflected the long music history of Sullivan's, but Maura had serious doubts that the selection of performers she was attracting now would appeal to classy patrons. Most of the bands were small, funky contemporary groups. Would the Crann Mor clientele prefer traditional Irish? Even Maura thought that was kind of over. Besides, she could name at least two pubs in Skibbereen that held *seisúns* for tourists, and the snooty folk would probably be more comfortable there if they wanted a dose of local flavor.

Just get through this silly meeting and they'll go away, she told herself.

Shortly after eleven, Maura watched as a gleaming dark van pulled up in front of Sul-

45

livan's. She glanced at Mick, who gave her a nod but said nothing. Then she walked to the front door and, opening it, plastered on a smile and stood like a sentinel by the entrance, inventorying the people who emerged from the van.

A driver hurried out first and raced around the van to open doors for the four people who climbed out: two men and two women. Then the driver discreetly retreated to the van. Maura made a quick judgment of the group. The older guy, the one with the dash of gray in his hair, was clearly the boss, and the younger man looked like his lapdog. Both were wearing nice tailored clothes but not suits, and they'd left their neckties at home. The two women were a similar pair. The older looked to be in her late forties but obviously took care of herself, and the younger one was her assistant, although she was nowhere near as fawning as her male counterpart. The women wore nicely tailored pantsuits in muted colors, and the older women had added a colorful scarf.

Finally, everyone was lined up on the sidewalk, and Maura approached them. "Welcome to Sullivan's. I'm Maura Donovan, the owner. Please, come in."

The older man spoke first — the head bull, as Maura had guessed. "Good morn-

46

ing, Miss Donovan. May I call you Maura? I'm John Byrne, one of Crann Mor's new owners. I'm the head of the JB Management, usually called JBCo, the investment consortium that purchased the property. Our home office is in Chicago." He extended his hand, and Maura took it to shake. His handshake was carefully calculated, not too weak and not too strong. She couldn't quite place his accent. It sounded like newscaster American but not quite natural. "I'm sorry to descend on you on such short notice, but we've been impressed by what we've been hearing about this place, and we felt we needed to see it ourselves to determine if perhaps we could work together. I take it you're a newcomer to this area?"

Maura nodded. "I've been here almost a year now, but I had family from here. I'm glad to hear that our publicity has been working, but I guess I'm surprised to see your whole team here. If I'd known you wanted to see the place in action, I'd have invited you for one of the nights we have music."

"Again, I apologize for our lack of planning, but we've only just arrived in this area. Let me introduce the rest of the team. Andrew Whitaker is my indispensable assistant, Helen Jenkins here handles the infrastructure side of things, and Tiffany Martin is her assistant." Everybody nodded cordially, but no one else stepped forward to shake hands with Maura. Helen seemed to be studying her, although she didn't say anything. What, she'd never seen a female pub owner before?

"I'm sorry," Maura said, "but I don't know the hotel. I've heard about it, but I've never been there. You said you're one of the new owners?"

"Yes," John replied, "in a sense. As I said, I'm the CEO of JBCo, which is a consortium that specializes in acquiring and managing hotels and resorts in the US and a few other countries. This particular property in Skibbereen came on the market at a propitious time for us, and we moved quickly to secure it. You must come see the place — the gardens are spectacular. In any event, we took possession about six months ago, and this is our team's first site visit. We've been planning some necessary remodeling and renovation and getting acquainted with the area and what it has to offer."

Maura couldn't see where she fit, but she might as well be polite. "Well, I'm delighted to show you Sullivan's. Come on in." She held the door, standing aside to let everyone pass. She watched them once they got inside, looking like a flock of curious chickens, strutting around and poking into corners. "Can I get you something to drink? Coffee?"

The younger woman had noticed the gleaming coffeemaker behind the bar, and she nudged the other woman. The latter said quickly, "Coffee would be great. Thank you."

Maura turned to the bar. "Mick, can you take care of that, please?"

"Sure. Won't be but a minute." His tone was properly deferential, and Maura had to squash a smile.

"This is Mick Nolan," she said, turning back to the group, "my main bartender. He's worked here a lot longer than I have, and you might want to talk to him. And by the fire there is Billy Sheahan. He was a friend of the prior owner, who's been gone a year now. If there's anything you want to know about this place or the village, he's the man to ask." The Crann Mor people dutifully turned to look at Billy, who gave them a brief salute, beaming cheerfully, but the visitors dismissed him quickly as not worth their attention. That annoyed Maura

— it seemed rude. "Why don't we sit down?"

The group distributed themselves around the two tables that Mick had crammed together in anticipation of the meeting, and Mick delivered the coffees to the women and retreated again.

When they were all settled, Maura said, "So, what do you want to know from me?"

John took the lead. "While the Crann Mor property is impressive, we know that our guests like to see something of the local area — the countryside, the institutions, the historical sites. I've been informed that your place here has played an important role in the regional music culture for years, and we were pleased to see that you've revived it now. How's that working for you?"

So he'd been doing his homework, Maura noted. "Frankly, I've had little experience with that kind of management" — or any other, for that matter, but she didn't need to add that — "and I and my staff have been feeling our way along. Word of mouth plays a big part of bringing in groups, and we're pleased that bands have begun coming to us, rather than us chasing them down. Why is it you think your guests would be interested in small bands in a small pub like this?"

"We'd like to think we serve a fairly sophisticated clientele. As you might guess, they're not looking for the traditional fiddle-and-penny-whistle style, although there is some charm to that."

Yeah, for the clueless tourists who think they're getting the real thing, Maura thought. "So you think Sullivan's offers something more, I don't know — authentic? Real?"

"Exactly. We wanted to see your venue to get a sense what might be possible."

"This place doesn't hold many people," Maura said. "How many are you thinking about?"

"Your size could be a plus. We're not talking about sending busloads of guests over, just a few with more discriminating tastes, who would appreciate both the music and the chance to mingle with local people. An authentic music experience, as you suggested. Of course, some changes might be desirable."

Maura tried not to bristle. "Like what?"

"How do you handle parking, for example?"

Maura managed not to laugh. "We don't. People have to work that out for themselves. And as you can see, there's nowhere to add a parking lot."

"Ah. And you might want to improve your

seating and furniture."

This isn't a cocktail lounge, pal — this is a small Irish pub in a small village, Maura fumed silently. "My patrons like it the way it is."

"We might be able to help you out if it's the financial considerations that worry you."

Maura wasn't sure if she wanted to hand over control of her furnishings to the guy or his crew. She tried to picture the room they were in filled with matchy-matchy modern blond furniture and almost laughed. "I'd be interested in hearing your ideas," she said carefully.

"Excellent!" John clapped his hands together. "Oh, and if you have a music session scheduled, perhaps we might sit in?"

"Of course. Mick, who is it we have booked for Saturday night? Screaming Badgers?"

"No, that's next weekend. This week it's Roadkill."

Maura turned back to the group. "So we'd be happy to see you here on Saturday to hear Roadkill. Things usually warm up about ten o'clock. You can get a real feeling for the ambience."

John stood up. "That's great, Maura. We'll see if we can make it. Anybody else have any questions?" The rest of the group remained silent, as they had through most of the meeting. John turned back to Maura. "Thanks so much for making the time to see us on such short notice." He offered his hand, and Maura shook it. The others didn't offer, so Maura escorted them to the door.

Helen hung back for a moment until the others were getting into the van. Then she said in a low voice, "Maura, I know John comes on strong, but at least think about the idea. Will you?"

"Sure, I guess. But you have to know that we like things the way they are."

"I understand. It was great to meet you, and I hope we can make it for the music." She offered her hand this time, and Maura shook it. She was surprised when Helen didn't seem to be in any hurry to let go.

After Helen had left, Maura shut the door, then leaned against it. She and Mick exchanged a glance, then both burst out laughing.

"I'm sure they'll love it," Mick said.

"Sure," Maura replied. "Especially after they've had a tour of the loos."

FIVE

Maura waited until the van had pulled away before saying to Mick, "Seriously, what a pompous bunch of stiffs. Mr. Smarmy in his custom-made suit and all the little smarmies following him around like a bunch of baby ducks."

"Do I take it yeh're not impressed by our guests?"

"Go right ahead. Please. Billy, what did you think?" Maura called out to him.

"Sure, and we haven't seen the likes of them in this place before," Billy said with a gleam in his eye.

"You think they're going to want to do business with us? Or have I scared them off?"

"Is that what you were after doin'?"

"Well, it's my place, so they're supposed to be wooing me, if that's the right word. Can you really see a van full of rich tourists pulling out of this posh hotel and coming to

Sullivan's to hear Joe Snot and the Sneezes play? And then they'd go home and tell their friends what an authentic experience they'd had in this nowhere town in Ireland."

"Yeh sound angry, Maura," Mick said quietly.

"Maybe I am. They come in and look down their noses and decide whether this place meets their standards. Which I doubt it does. They're judging the place, and us, and me. You know, they might have done better to slip in on a night when there was music and just look and listen. They'd have learned more about who we really are."

"That's a good point, Maura, but from what I hear, it's not how big companies operate. They like doin' things by committee."

"And yet some of them barely opened their mouths." At least at the end, this Helen person had tried to soften the impression John Byrne had made. But thinking of John Byrne made her mad again. "And they want to 'improve' our furniture? Seriously? We wouldn't be who we are if everything matched. We've earned every nick and scratch."

"So it's a no I'm hearin'," Billy said.

"Yeah, I'd say so. Let them find a nice place in Skibbereen that'd be glad to have their business."

"Don't be so quick to brush them off, Maura," Mick cautioned. "Could be there'd be money involved, apart from the money yeh'd make off the drinks. Yeh never got around to discussing that side of the question."

"Hey, Mick, even I know you don't talk money at the first meeting. They came, they looked, they left. If they hated the place, we won't hear from them again. If they're interested, they'll get back to us. End of story."

"It's your place," Mick said neutrally and went back to polishing glassware. "But a few more euros wouldn't hurt."

"You're saying we aren't earning enough?"

"I'm not tellin' yeh that, but yeh're cutting it pretty close. All I'm sayin' is keep yer mind open, listen to what they have to say."

"Well, I'm not going to lose any sleep over it," Maura grumbled — and wondered why she was so ticked off at the group. Maybe it was the suits. She didn't see many of them in West Cork. Maybe it was the way that older woman had kept starting at her like she was judging her. Or maybe it was because they all seemed so out of place, no matter where it was they came from. Anyway, if some kind of deal happened, it would happen, and she wasn't about to chase after it now.

Business was slow early in the day, so Maura sat on a barstool and grabbed a few minutes to talk to Rose. "What do you know about this Crann Mor place?"

"I've never set foot in the hotel, although I've heard others talk of it. A bit rich for the likes of us, I'm guessin'."

"What exactly is it? A hotel? Another place like Mycroft House that used to be a manor except now it's turned into a business?"

Rose perched on a stool next to Maura. "Back a few years, before my time, it might've been a house, but far grander than Mycroft House ever was. I'm told the gardens are something special, and folks like us can walk through them. It's been a hotel for a while, I guess, but then those new buyers came in. Folks are worried they may turn things upside down."

"How do you mean?"

"Take a look around yeh, Maura. This part of the country is doin' well these days. It's one of those places the travel people like to call 'unspoiled' and 'scenic.' And the Cork Airport makes it easy to reach. The business folk see an opportunity here."

Maura sat back on her stool and looked at the girl. "Rose, how come you know so much more about this than I do?"

"Yeh've been here no more than a year, Maura. I've lived here all me life. And yeh've come from a big city where things change all the time. Things move more slowly here, and changes stand out more."

"Would you play ball with this crowd?"

Rose looked bewildered for a moment, then said, "Are yeh askin' would I play their games and shine this place up? That's not fer me to say, but I think it would be like puttin' a dress on a pig."

Maura laughed. "So you're calling this place a pig?" When Rose started to protest, Maura held up a hand. "No, I know what you mean. My gut says it just wouldn't work. But I'm still the new kid here, and I'd want to hear some other opinions."

"From what I heard, there's no choice to be made yet. And Maura? Thanks fer askin' me what I think."

"You're a smart kid, Rose. I should be listening to you."

Things picked up over the course of the day, and Maura didn't give any more thought to the Crann Mor visitors. She really wasn't interested in becoming part of some corporate scheme, and she hoped she felt that way because she knew the limitations of her business rather than out of fear of change or trying new things. The music side was still growing, and she was curious to see where it went over time. Still, that was reviving an old tradition, not creating a new one. But that was how she saw Ireland: a lot of old things survived, if maybe polished up and pushed forward again. She wasn't about to tell her patrons that they should move with the times. The old times seemed to suit them fine.

It was past five when Maura noticed a woman who'd come in alone and recognized her as Helen Jenkins. Why was she back? She'd changed out of her serious business clothes and looked almost . . . ordinary. The woman looked around hesitantly, then took a table near the bar. Rose looked at her, then at Maura. "You want me to . . . ?"

"No, I'll do it, thanks." Maura came out from behind the bar and walked over to the table, wondering why the woman looked so nervous. "Hi," Maura greeted her. "You're Helen, right? Can I get you something?"

"A coffee, please. Do you have time to talk?"

"Sure." Maura signaled to Rose to start a cup of coffee, then sat down at the table across from the woman. "You were here earlier, with the Crann Mor people. Are you still trying to sell me on your ideas?"

"Well, no, not exactly. I . . . kind of wanted to apologize for them."

"Why? You already did. Why do you think it matters?"

"Well, John — he's the CEO — is a smart businessman, but I'm not sure he quite gets the way things work around here — in Ireland, I mean. Or this part of the country. He's more of a city person."

"And how do you think things work around here?" Maura had to wonder how much this city woman could know about West Cork.

"Quieter. Slower. Smaller. JBCo has a hotel in Dublin, but of course that's different. But I think I'm not making myself very clear. I think what I'm apologizing for is making you uncomfortable in your own place. For telling you that we like this place for what it is, but we want it to be different. We have no right to come marching in here and asking you to change if you're happy with what you've got. And I don't want you to make a decision that doesn't work for you just for the money."

Rose arrived with Helen's coffee, set it down, and winked at Maura before returning to the bar.

Helen watched her go. "Is she old enough

to be working here?"

"Barely. It's complicated. But she's been working here longer than I have."

"Which is how long?"

"Just about a year."

"And before that? You're American, right?"

"Boston born and raised. I inherited this place."

"There must be an interesting story behind that."

Maura shrugged. She wasn't in the habit of sharing her recent life history with strangers off the street. "About what you said, we get by and we're growing. Did your boss send you here to talk to me? Maybe soften me up?"

Helen shook her head. "No, I came on my own."

"Why?"

"This is a fact-finding trip. The consortium owns the hotel property, but how it's going to be managed and what clientele we want to attract are still under discussion. I know he throws his weight around, but I can tell you he's very good at what he does."

"You'd know better than me. Why do you work for him? Because he's smart and successful? Is the money really good?" Maura saw the woman studying her again, the way she had earlier in the day.

Finally Helen answered. "No, or not primarily. As I said, he's smart, and he makes good decisions, at least about the business and investments. He's the guy who charms the high-end investors. I run the numbers and make the deals work." She hesitated briefly before adding, "Can I ask you a question?"

"Sure. I've been asking you questions."

"You seem young to be managing a pub — or any business, for that matter — especially in a country that's not your own. How's that working for you?"

For a moment, Maura thought that Helen was trying to pry into her private life, but she looked sincerely interested. "I won't give you the whole story, but the package — pub and house — kind of got dumped on me all at once when I first got here. My choice was either to throw it all away and go back to Boston or to stay here and see if I could make it work. I had no real reason to go back to Boston, so here I am, a year later."

Helen smiled a little wistfully. "You look like you're enjoying it. You certainly defended it earlier."

Maura considered. "I guess I am enjoying it. I never expected to own or run anything. Some days I wake up and look at myself in the mirror and wonder how the heck I got here."

Helen nodded once, more to herself than to Maura, and then she straightened in her chair. "I don't want to take up any more of your time, Maura. Maybe we made a poor first impression, but I hope you can see past that. Listen, why don't you come see Crann Mor? Even if nothing comes of our talks, it's still a beautiful site, and I think you'd enjoy it."

"Not exactly my style, you know," Maura said dryly. "I don't think I have anything I could wear — anybody who saw me would figure I was hired help. Look, I haven't been in the business long, and I haven't been in Ireland long either. I'm still finding my way. But I'm pretty sure I'm not ready to make any changes now. Bringing the music back was a big thing for me, and we're still working out some of the details. I don't want to move too fast. So I'm not exactly going to jump in a different direction just because you guys want me to."

"I understand that, Maura, and nobody's pressuring you. There are some nice places in Skibbereen or Schull that would be happy to partner with us. All I'm saying is, check out what we're doing and think about it. Will you do that?"

Maura wondered why Helen was working so hard to enlist her, but she was in fact curious. "How about this? You take me to lunch or tea or whatever at your hotel, but in return you have to come back here Saturday night and see this place with music going on. You may decide it's not right for what you want."

"Just me, not our professional management team?" Helen smiled.

"Yeah, just you. Bring the team of suits along, and the whole mood will go flat. Did you bring a pair of jeans along?"

"I think so."

"Just come and watch and listen. Deal?"

"That sounds good. When do you want to have lunch? Or would you rather have high tea?"

"Lunch is fine. As long as I don't have to dress up."

"Does tomorrow at noon work for you?"

"Sure. I'll meet you there, okay?"

"Great." Helen drained her coffee, slipped a few euro coins beside her cup, and stood up. "Thank you, Maura. I'll see you tomorrow. Oh, let me give you my card with my mobile number in case something comes up." She pulled a card from her bag and scribbled a number on the back before handing it to Maura. "Bye for now."

Maura stood and watched her leave, then went back to the bar. "So?" Rose said. "Have yeh sold out already?"

"Not exactly. I said I'd have lunch with her tomorrow at her fancy place, but only if she'd come to hear the music on Saturday night. In disguise as a normal person."

"Grand. At least yeh'll get a good meal out of it. Take notes fer me, will yeh?"

"What, no doggy bag?"

"Yeh mean leftovers? If yeh can manage it, sure."

Six

For all her reluctance to suck up to the Crann Mor people, Maura found that she was nervous the next morning as she got ready for her lunch. She was out of her comfort zone in classy places. In Boston, she'd walked by the Ritz-Carlton and the Parker House and peered in the windows, but she'd always been afraid that if she walked in the door, a gang of bouncers wearing fancy uniforms with gold braid would grab her and escort her out again. She just didn't belong.

She stared at her one pair of black pants, bought at a thrift shop in Skibbereen. With a decent sweater over it, they would have to do. And why was she even worrying? Crann Mor was nothing to do with her. Besides, she wasn't planning to hang out there long — she had to get back to Sullivan's. She had a business to run.

When she arrived at the hotel, she parked

and turned off the car engine, then studied the place. It wasn't exactly what she had expected. For one thing, it didn't look like a hotel. Instead, it looked like the manor house it had once been. There was a wide graveled parking area and a two-story stucco house with three chimneys facing it — big, but not exactly a castle. A chunky covered porch sat at one end, and in the middle was a large arched window over an equally wide round window at ground level. No tacky signs, of course. No "Enter Here" or "This Way to Registration." Maura couldn't see anything except the hotel's buildings from where she stood, although the place wasn't far from Skibbereen. The driveway had to be half a mile long. How much property did the owners have here? And which fat-cat Englishman had owned it before it became a hotel?

Helen was waiting for her under the porch thingy — *portico!* That was the word she'd been looking for — and stepped forward, smiling. "Maura! I'm so glad you came!"

"I said I'd be here." She had to admit that she still wasn't sure what she was doing here. She could have said no and ended the whole thing before it even started, but no doubt Mick would have been disappointed, which seemed to matter to her.

"Well, please come in. Would you like a tour now, or would you rather go ahead and eat?"

"I can't take too much time off from the pub. Maybe we should take a quick look around, then eat. If that's okay."

"Of course. Why don't we go around the side?" Helen led the way around the end of the building. "I think I mentioned that this place has a long history. The property belonged to the O'Donovan family for a long time, although this house wasn't built until the 1850s. You probably know something about the local O'Donovans, since you bear their name, although I must say, who is descended from whom is a murky mess that genealogists are still fighting over. But they go way back. This was kind of their last fling around here. Once they sold this place, it had English and American and even Swiss owners. It's been a hotel on and off, but also a site for rock concerts, food and art festivals, and more recently weddings and public events."

"And it's a hotel now? Or again?"

"Yes, that's right. It's got twenty-five rooms in two main buildings, plus the lodge, and our restaurant features locally sourced food, much of it grown on-site behind that row of buildings there." Helen waved vaguely at a long single-story building off to the right. "For those guests who are interested in fishing, there's a fifty-acre lake down the hill there" — Helen pivoted and pointed past the main building — "and also some limited boating. And, of course, there are some wonderful walks, although it's hard to appreciate them so early in the year. By summer they should be glorious."

Sullivan's was in no way in the same class as this mellow, gracious place, which clearly catered to people with money. Sullivan's most definitely did not. "You sound really into the place," Maura said. "Are you going to be based here permanently?"

"Oh, no, my home's in Chicago — that's where the company is located, although we all travel a lot. But I believe in doing my homework and in being thorough. There are so many wonderful options, both here on the estate and in the surrounding area, and I need to explore them all to know what we can offer our guests. Would you like to go in now?"

"Sure, fine," Maura said.

She followed Helen through the main entrance, trying to maintain a neutral expression at the sight of soaring ceilings, elegant groupings of upholstered furniture, and a reception desk discreetly tucked into a corner. Helen kept going toward the back, then stepped through some multipaned glass doors into the restaurant, a large room with a bank of windows on the far side overlooking what were probably the gorgeous and famous gardens. It was barely noon, so there were few people in the room, and Helen guided her to a table for two near a window, apart from the other diners.

A waiter appeared as soon as their backsides hit the chairs, Maura noted, and handed them each menus printed on heavy paper stock, then retreated silently. "Would you like something to drink before we eat, Maura?" Helen offered.

"Coffee's okay," Maura told her. "Friday's usually a busy day at the pub, and I'll have to get back."

Helen must have raised an invisible finger because the waiter reappeared in seconds. "Two coffees, please." The waiter disappeared again, as though he was running on wheels.

"What do you like to eat?" Helen returned her attention to Maura. "The chef here is outstanding, and everything I've had is good."

"I'm not picky. Why don't you decide?" Maura watched Helen scan the menu. "Is this your first trip here?"

"Actually, yes. I wasn't part of the initial discussions when we learned the site was available. But once we'd acquired it, I was promoted and joined the team."

"You've run hotels before?"

"Oh, I don't run them. I plan them. I coordinate the departments — hospitality, food service, promotion, event planning, and the like — and I keep a close eye on budgeting for each. At the risk of sounding crass, while we want to offer our guests a memorable experience in a small hotel, we also want to make money doing it. After all, we have investors to think of."

The waiter reappeared, and Helen delivered their orders after a brief conversation. Maura waited until he had retreated to what she assumed was the kitchen. "It really is nice, and I could see why people would enjoy staying here, but what's it got to do with Sullivan's? We might as well be in a different universe."

Helen studied her for a moment. "You grew up around Boston, right? So you know what a city is like. Our investor group does have city properties in the places you'd expect, including Dublin, but we know that isn't what all people want. There are those groups who want to get their business done in a more relaxed setting, someplace removed from the usual busy corporate life. We've found that in many cases, that makes group meetings more efficient and productive. So here, we want to bring people to a reasonably luxurious place, which is what they're accustomed to — but also to offer them a diversity of experiences. Like visiting prehistoric ruins or touring a distillery or whale watching. Or, as in your case, hearing contemporary music. We've done our research, and Sullivan's is famous in its own way. Haven't you had people coming in who talk about the good old days? And then stay to listen?"

"I guess. But most of the groups who come in are pretty young — more my age than yours."

"Still, the tradition of music at Sullivan's lives on, doesn't it?" The food appeared, and the waiter distributed it carefully — no clanking of plates, all the silverware neatly lined up, water glasses topped off. Maura felt an urge to grab her napkin in case the guy took it into his head to tuck it into her lap for her.

"What about you, Maura? How did you end up here? If you don't mind my asking."

Maura didn't like to talk about herself, but she thought it would be rude to just brush off Helen's question. "Most people are pretty curious about that. 'What's a young American woman doing running a pub in West Cork?' The basic story is that I was raised by my grandmother, who kept in touch with family and friends around here. Mick Sullivan, who owned the place, was some kind of cousin or something. He didn't have any children or other close family, so he and my gran cooked up the idea to leave it to me. Gran told me that when she died, I should come over and say her farewells, and when I got here, some lawyer dumped the pub and Mick's house into my lap, free and clear. End of story."

Helen smiled. "Not exactly. You're still here. You could have sold the whole lot and gone back to Boston."

Maura shrugged. "I didn't have any reason to go back, really. No family, no place to go back to, no job."

"Did you have any business experience before you arrived here?"

"I had plenty of dead-end jobs, like waitressing, and a couple of night-school courses under my belt. Did I ever run anything? No way."

"And now you've got a business and a staff. How many?"

Maura had a hard time thinking of her employees as a staff. "Well, Mick. And

Jimmy and his daughter. They all came with the place, and they stayed on. And me. That's about it."

"Do you have a business plan?" Helen asked.

Maura snorted. "Yeah, staying alive. Paying the bills. Keeping the customers I've got."

"But you added the music back, didn't you?"

"Yeah," Maura admitted reluctantly. "But it just sort of happened when this guy who used to be kind of famous showed up one day and said he'd play, and that attracted some of his old music buddies, and then people started showing up to hear them. I can't take the credit for it."

"But you went with it. I may sound like a corporate wonk, but that's the kind of real experience I want our guests to have. Call it luck, serendipity, or magic. Anybody can call up a bunch of players who know all the old songs and sit them down together, and they'd probably produce a respectable evening of music. But what's happening in your place is different. Can you see that?"

Maura took a moment to taste her lunch — and avoid Helen's eyes. *Damn, the food was good.* She didn't want to get used to it, because she knew she could never make anything like it. She wasn't even sure what it was. Maura wondered if there was a way to get Rose into the dining room here to try this stuff. She could probably figure it out.

"Maura?" Helen interrupted her thoughts.

"Oh, right. Look, I'm the new kid here. We've made it through my first year, and even in that time, things have changed. I've learned a lot, but I'm still learning. Now you walk in and tell me you want to change things according to your own plan, and I'm just not ready for that. I kinda like things the way they are, and so do the people who come in to drink and talk. They don't want fancy; they want comfortable."

Helen nodded. "Maura, I understand. Really. Look, on our end, we're still in the early stages here. We're looking at all the possibilities. We don't want to impose our changes on you, believe me. All I'm asking is that you think about it. If you don't want to move forward, so be it. It won't be the first time we've heard no."

Mick's comment rose up in her memory. "Say we did go ahead. How would I benefit — apart from a few more people buying drinks?"

"You mean, is there money attached? Possibly. For instance, we could ask that you guarantee two or three performances a month, maybe coordinated with events we might be planning, and in return, we guarantee to cover certain expenses — maybe a fixed stipend, or maybe we'd pay some or all of the bands' fees up front. You wouldn't lose, I promise, and we'd have to work out the details. But will you at least think about it?"

"I'll run it by my staff," Maura said, her mouth quirking in a half smile. "What's your time frame with Crann Mor?"

"Maybe a soft opening in summer if everything works out."

"Soft?" Maura asked, confused.

"Yes — we'd open the place to guests, but without a lot of fanfare. The grand opening could come later, after we've worked out any glitches."

"If you and your guys are based in the US, who's going to be running the show here?"

"Probably a mix of local managers and some of our own. Let me tell you, our people are eager to relocate, at least for a year or two. West Cork has a great reputation."

"Well, then, I'll think about it all. Look, I'd better get back to work. The food is really great here. Is there a separate bar?"

"Of course. We can walk out that way.

Checking out the competition?"

Maura gave a brief laugh. "I don't think I have to worry."

SEVEN

Maura arrived back at Sullivan's shortly after two. When she walked in, all the patrons turned to stare at her — all three of them, not counting Old Billy, who was more part of the building than a customer. It seemed she hadn't missed much. On the other hand, the regular patrons had probably never seen her in anything but jeans, so they were thrilled to have something new to talk about.

Jimmy looked up from his conversation with one man in the corner, then looked away, signaling his lack of interest. Mick cocked his head at her. "So?"

Maura shucked off her jacket and stalked behind the bar. "So, not much. It's a nice place. Great dining room — big, with lots of white tablecloths. Acres and acres of trees and stuff."

Rose came out from the kitchen at the back. "I thought I heard yeh, Maura. How was it?"

"We didn't have time for the grand tour of the designer gardens, and I only saw the first floor of the main building. There are apparently other buildings scattered around in case you want to be really, really private. There's a lake, but I didn't see it. Mainly we had lunch."

Rose perched on a stool in front of the bar. "How was the food?"

"Very good, from what I could tell. I have no idea what it was. If we end up working together, maybe you and I can go have lunch there together. Anyway, Helen told me they grow a lot of their own stuff out back somewhere, and they source the rest locally, which I guess is trendy."

"Ah, Maura, you really should get out more!" Rose chided her. "Local food is popular because it tastes better and it's good for yeh. None of that artificial stuff in it. Maybe sometime I'll do a blind tasting for yeh, and yeh'll find out what a difference it can make." Rose let out a longing sigh. "I hear they're doin' afternoon teas."

"And I'm sure they're lovely," Maura said tartly, "but that's not our style."

"What did the woman want with yeh?" Mick asked.

"Mostly to impress me, this time around, and I think she still feels they were kind of rude on their first visit. Or maybe she was just curious about the pub . . . and me."

"And Sullivan's? Where's that fit?" Mick pressed.

Maura turned to face him. "Why do you care so much, Mick? I mean, things are going well, especially now that we've added the music. Why do you think this bunch of business guys can do anything for us? And why should we be interested?"

"Maura, yeh're still new to this business," Mick began.

Maura didn't want a lecture. "Yeah, I know that. So?"

"Yeh've brought in a lot of folk since yeh took over. But part of that was curiosity — who were yeh and what were yeh doin' here? And then the music — plenty around here remember the old days under Mick Sullivan and stopped in to see what was goin' on. But that doesn't mean they're comin' back, now that they've checked us out. And I don't know if yeh've noticed, but even Skib has stepped up its game — the Eldon's redone itself, the West Cork Inn has a good chef, and that café at the Arts Center pulls in a good crowd at midday. Mebbe Sullivan's and its kind are beginnin' to feel old-fashioned. Or more like out of step. Yeh've got competition, and if yeh lose customers, the business could go under."

Maura stared at him for a moment, wondering where that outburst had come from. Wondering why he had been thinking about it at all and for how long. "Gee, thanks for cheering me up. You'll be happy to know that I didn't say no to anything Helen said. This was just round one, right? But there's no offer on the table yet. And I still draw the line at fancying up the place."

Mick raised his hands in surrender. "It's yer place, Maura. I'm just after givin' you my opinion."

"And I appreciate it, Mick. But there's nothing to decide about yet. Can't we just take a day or two and think about it? Think about what we want from this place? Maybe have a meeting with all of us together and share ideas?" When nobody protested, Maura went on, "How about Sunday? We don't open 'til after noon that day, so there'd be more time."

"Done. Hear that, Jimmy?" Mick called out.

"Yeah, yeah, ten o'clock, Sunday," he muttered just loudly enough to be heard.

Jimmy's lack of enthusiasm was clear, and Maura wondered, not for the first time, how long he'd stick around at Sullivan's. Or how long any of her staff would. Jimmy was probably getting married soon, and his intended, Judith, who was clearly a strong-willed woman, probably had plans for him on her dairy farm. Rose should've been out somewhere getting herself an education, or at least some useful training, not just serving up pints in a small village.

And Mick? Mick was still an unknown quantity to her, even after working with him for a year. What was he doing here? He had some experience outside of Leap, so why was he content to stay in this little hole in the wall? Couldn't he be doing more with his life? So far he'd hidden behind the excuse that he was taking care of his granny Bridget, but he could still do that with a better job, couldn't he?

If she was a pessimist, Maura could say that most of her staff had no particular loyalty to the pub or her and could walk away at any time. They were here only because they didn't have the energy to go somewhere else. How on earth would she manage to hire anyone new? She had little to offer anyone, just long hours and low pay. Great — now she *was* depressing herself.

Shortly after three, Maura looked up to see Gillian come in. Late in her pregnancy, Gillian had a tendency to waddle, a gait very unlike her usual confident stride. Gillian had always dressed well, looking like the Dublin artist that she was, at least part of the time, but none of her city clothes would fit anymore. At least she looked comfortable in a long flowing skirt with a loose tunic top over it, both in bright colors.

"Hey, Gillian. Make yourself comfortable."

"As if I could." Gillian sighed and headed for the seat by the fire hastily vacated by one of the regulars. "Could you do me an herbal tea, please?"

"Of course."

"I'll take care of it," Rose told her, grabbing up a mug. "Yeh'll want to be tellin' her about yer fancy lunch, I'm guessing."

"Thanks, Rose." Maura collected a chair as she made her way toward Gillian. "What's up?"

"Since the O'Briens left, Harry and I have been trying to do everything at once." She gestured at her pregnant belly. "You can guess how much use I am these days."

"You couldn't get them to stay on a bit longer?"

Gillian shook her head. "They stayed on only until Harry figured out what kind of financial settlement he could make for them after all their years of service to Eveline. It was probably smaller than they hoped. But

I think the real sticking point was that Florence had never had a child and she was terrified that I might pop this one out on a moment's notice. So they packed up and went to Bandon to live with her sister."

"And Harry?"

"He's talking to the computer boys in Skibbereen about that new tech center."

"The what?"

"The new hub." When Maura still looked blankly at her, Gillian sighed. "I'm talking about the place behind Fields where they've got business space with digital connections. You know Harry's going to try to give it a go working from home, but he needs a place to meet with clients and a way to videoconference now and then. That kind of thing."

"So this place has all of that?"

"It does, or so they say. That's why he's talking to them now."

Maura made a mental note to check out the place sometime — maybe she could learn something about computers there if she ever had any free time. "And he left you all by your lonesome?"

"No, Harry dropped me off here before heading to Skib. He figured you'd entertain me. I can't fit behind the wheel of my car anymore."

"At least it won't be forever. And of course

you're welcome here any time."

"It won't be the same when I'm out at Ballinlough," Gillian said a bit wistfully.

"It's not far. Mick goes out there all the time to see Bridget, and I live there, remember? And you'll have plenty of time to paint. Any luck finding a childminder?"

Gillian shook her head. "We really haven't had time to look, what with closing on the house and studio and trying to get them ready to live in, doing the inventory on Mycroft House for the National Trust, and Harry trying to get a business going. And we don't want to start paying someone until the child actually appears."

"When's that going to be?"

"Whenever he or she decides. When I last saw the midwife, she thought maybe two or three more weeks. First children often arrive late."

"And you're still going to the hospital to have the baby, right?"

"That's what the midwife recommends. Harry's going to hold my hand and look the other direction and hope he doesn't throw up. The whole thing's ridiculous, isn't it?"

"Pushing out a baby? Well, it seems to work since the human race has survived this long. You'll do fine."

"So what's this lunch Rose was talking about?" Gillian tried to find a more comfortable position in the battered armchair, which creaked under her weight.

"Oh, right, you missed the start of that," Maura said and proceeded to outline the phone call, the arrival of the Crann Mor gang the day before, and her lunch with Helen. As she wrapped up her summary, she said, "I really don't know what to think."

"Do they want a decision soon?" Gillian asked.

"There's nothing to decide yet, just a vague idea."

"And you're resisting it," Gillian guessed shrewdly.

"That's what Billy asked too. Is it that obvious? Yeah, it kind of feels like a bad idea to me, or at least a bad fit."

"Check with Harry if ever you get to any outline of a deal, and he can look at the numbers. What is it that troubles you about what you're hearing?"

"That I, or the pub, don't belong with these people." Maura sighed. "I don't seem to get out much, not to see other pubs or hear what kind of music they're doing, and certainly not to visit fancy hotels. I mean, I could see that the hotel is really, really nice, but I don't feel like I belong there. And wouldn't the guests feel the same way coming here, only in reverse?"

"You don't have to be anything you aren't, you know. Do you need the money?"

"We're getting by. But I don't know if that's enough, and Mick says we're cutting it close. Remember, I never ran a business in my life, and now I'm supposed to be negotiating with a multinational consortium? It's crazy."

"Ah, enjoy the ride, me dear," Old Billy chimed in. He'd been dozing on the other side of the fireplace, but now he seemed ready to jump in to the conversation. "If it comes to nothin', yeh've lost nothin."

"I guess. Do you think it's a good idea, Billy? You've probably got the longest memory of this place as anyone."

"That's fair to say. I knew Mick Sullivan from the cradle, near enough. I was a young man when he took on this place. I remember when he brought the music in, fer that was his real love, and I remember when he started to let it fade away. He never went bust, else yeh wouldn't be sittin' here now. But he never got rich. What is it yeh're wantin' from the place, Maura Donovan?"

"That's the problem, Billy — I don't know. And I don't want to feel rushed into deciding. Either it's a terrific idea to cut a deal with these people, or it'll trash what we've got now. I just don't know which will happen."

"Hear them out, Maura. Yeh don't have to decide right away. This is Ireland — things take time here. Those folk need to learn that themselves. They may know the hotel business, but things don't always go like clockwork here, no matter how well yeh plan."

"Maybe they should hire you to sit by the fire in their giant, shiny lobby and hand out wisdom to the guests. Would you like a sign? 'Sage advice from our very own old codger'?"

"And they'd pay me fer it?" Billy asked with a twinkle in his eye. "Whaddaya think I'm worth?"

"Billy, you're priceless. And we need you here."

"And I'll be happy if yeh pay me in pints."

"If that's a hint, I'll take care of it. You can entertain Gillian here."

"The pleasure's mine," Billy said, beaming.

EIGHT

Maura woke up early on Saturday morning. She didn't need to get to the pub until ten or so, so she wandered out her front door and took a deep breath. Spring was definitely happening, apparently scented with manure. It was, after all, a dairy region, so there were cows. Cows had never figured in Maura's day-to-day experience until she had landed in Cork, and she was still kind of wary of them. They were big and, to her mind, unpredictable, even if they had rather small brains. And they all produced large amounts of manure — Maura had learned quickly not to wander through a pretty meadow without watching where she put her feet.

She strolled down to the end of the lane that led to her cottage and looked in all directions at the crossroads. She could see a lone car passing along the bog road at the bottom of the hill, and there were a few clusters of cows grazing here and there. Small flowers bloomed in the hedges, and scattered clumps of daffodils made cheerful splashes of color as they bobbed in the wind.

Maura spied Bridget in her small front yard, poking yet again at her large pots with what must be a trowel, and decided to head down the hill to say hello. When she neared, she called out, "Are you trying to grow something?"

"And good mornin' to yeh, Maura. Yes, every year I have high hopes fer just a bit of color outside my front door, and every year the weeds do me in. But I keep hopin'. Are yeh a gardener at all?"

"Me? No way. I could never even keep an African violet alive on a windowsill."

"Would yeh be wantin' to start now? It's Ireland — nature will take care of the waterin' for yeh."

"What should I be planting? Not potatoes, I hope."

"Plant somethin' that gives yeh pleasure to watch as it grows. If yeh can, stop by the farmers' market — they have plants there, and they'll be happy to tell yeh what to do with them."

"I don't get over to Skib much on a Saturday — I'm always working." Although plenty of people had told her great things about the once-a-week market. Maybe she should check it out.

"Sure and yeh can take a break for lunch, can't you? And it's a grand place to talk with people and see what's what. Mick can tell yeh. He takes me over when I feel up to it, nearer to summer." Bridget gave one last exasperated poke at the dirt in a pot, then said, "Sit down fer a bit, unless yer running off already?"

"Happy to. Has Mick told you about the Crann Mor people who came to call?"

Bridget perked up noticeably. "That he has not! That's the big hotel now, isn't it? It was an O'Donovan estate, years past, but that line is gone now. What are they wantin' with yeh?"

Maura explained quickly what the group had proposed, or at least suggested, and finished up with her own hesitations. Bridget took her time in answering. "Yeh sound like yeh don't want to do it," she said.

One more person who seemed to be reading her mind. "I know. The problem is, I don't know what I feel. Part of me says no, but I wonder if that's for the right reasons. Another part of me says it's the smart thing to do, but what do I know? Those people are important and rich and they know what they're doing. It doesn't matter to them if they drive my pub into the ground or change it to match what their idea of what a cute Irish pub should be. But I don't want to blow the chance if it could do some good."

"And what's my grandson got to say about it?"

"Well, he hasn't exactly talked to them — mostly he listened when they came by the pub. If I had to guess, I'd say he's kind of leaning toward saying yes. Bridget, can I ask you something? I mean, something personal about Mick? You can tell me to mind my own business if you want, but you've kind of hinted about . . . Well, is there something I need to know?"

Bridget cocked her head at Maura, curious. "If yeh've a question, ask away."

"Why does Mick stick around, working in a small place that's seen better days? It's not like there are a lot of prospects in Leap or even Skibbereen. Couldn't he do better for himself in a bigger place like Cork?"

"Ah, Maura, there are times I've wondered if it's me that's holdin' him back. He looks after me. His sister's too busy with her own children and her job, so it falls to Mick. But there's more to it than that . . ." Bridget's voice trailed off.

Maura didn't want to interrupt her.

Bridget kept dropping hints about something in Mick's life that he hadn't shared with her. How big was this something that might or might not be keeping him stuck at Sullivan's? Did she have a right to know? She wanted to keep the pub staffed up, especially as summer was approaching. But Mick clearly could be doing other things. Should she ask him?

Finally Bridget said, "Maura, leave it be fer now. It's his story to tell. If these hotel people make yeh an offer, things might change. But I wouldn't go lookin' to hurry things up."

In spite of herself, Maura smiled. "That's pretty much what Billy said. I've been a city girl all my life, and I'm used to things moving faster. But that's not the ways things are here, is it?"

"In this corner of the world, things most often work themselves out. Listen to what these hotel people have to say, will yeh? I don't hold with changin' things just for the sake of change, but yeh need to think of what's best fer yer business."

"Don't worry, Bridget — I will. I guess I should feel good that they might want me — I must be doing something right with the pub." Maura stood up. "I'm going to the village. I'll say hi to Mick for you, okay?"

"You do that, but tell him I don't need anythin' right now. He'll come by to see me to church in the mornin', I expect."

"I'll let him know. You know, you should come by and hear the music at the pub sometime. Maybe we could do a session after church on a Sunday afternoon and bring in a different crowd, and you could come to that. If it doesn't get in the way of everyone's Sunday dinner."

"It's worth thinkin' about, I'd guess. Ta, then, Maura."

Maura went back up the hill to retrieve her car, still wondering what Mick was hiding. Or maybe it was nothing. Maybe he was happy passing his days in Sullivan's and visiting his grandmother. There were worse ways to live. She still had to learn to stop applying Boston standards to rural Ireland. The sun was shining; the flowers were blooming. *Chill out, Maura!*

She was first to arrive at the pub and left the front door open wide to get some fresh air into the place. She went to the back room to open a door there as well, hoping the air would flow through. When she returned to the front, she was surprised to see Garda Sean Murphy standing hesitantly on the threshold.

"Good morning, Sean!" Maura said. "Can

I get you a coffee?"

Sean took a hesitant step into the room but didn't smile. "Sorry, Maura, but this is official business, yeh might say. There's been a death at Crann Mor. Do yeh know the place?"

A death? It couldn't be something as simple as a heart attack, not when Sean looked so serious. But what could it have to do with her? "I saw it for the first time yesterday — I was invited to lunch there. What happened?"

Sean nodded as if to confirm to himself that what she had told him matched what he knew. "Did you meet John Byrne?"

"Not yesterday. My lunch was with one of his coworkers, Helen Jenkins. But I did meet John on Thursday. He and his whole crew came here to Sullivan's to look it over. What's this about?"

"John Byrne was found dead on the grounds early this morning by one of the groundskeepers."

So now most likely I won't have to make the decision that's been worrying me, Maura thought and immediately felt ashamed. "Why are you telling me, Sean?"

"Of course we're talkin' to the folk that were travelin' with him as well as the staff at the hotel. But Mrs. Jenkins asked to speak

95

with you before she told us her story, and I've come to take you over to the station if yer willin'."

That was odd. Did Helen need an alibi? Maura could account for her activities only between noon and two. "I don't know why she'd need to talk to me — I left there about two yesterday after lunch. When did John die?"

"Late yesterday, it seems. After he'd had his supper."

So she had nothing that would help Helen. "If you think it will help, I'll be happy to come with you. Just let me leave a note so people will know where I am."

"That's fine, Maura." Sean looked oddly relieved that she hadn't argued.

What had he expected? Maura wondered. And why would Helen want to talk with her first? Maura went around to the back of the bar and scrounged up a pad and a pencil, and she wrote a brief note. She was sure Mick and Jimmy could cover, and she couldn't possibly need to stay long at the Skibbereen station, could she? John's death had nothing to do with her.

"Ready," she announced, weighting the note down on the bar with an empty glass so it wouldn't get lost. Sean led the way out the front, and Maura locked the door

96

behind her — she decided not to worry about the back door; Mick would be in soon enough. Once in the car, an awkward silence fell. Maura wasn't sure what questions she could ask about John or what Sean could tell her. The weather was the only safe topic she could think of, and that seemed like a stupid thing to discuss on the way to a police station to talk about a death.

"How's your new sergeant settling in?" she finally ventured.

"He's not a local man," Sean said, tight-lipped, as if that explained anything. Which, Maura realized, it did — so much of the local police work she'd seen had been based on knowing who was who and how they were related.

The drive took no more than ten minutes, and Sean lapsed into silence for the rest of the trip, which was unlike him. If she hadn't known she was innocent of anything remotely like wrongdoing, Maura might have been nervous. Still, she counted Sean as a friend, and his silence unsettled her. Of course the gardaí took any death seriously, and from Sean's attitude, she was willing to bet that it was possible that this death was not natural. But where the heck did she fit? She'd met the dead man exactly once.

Sean parked alongside the station building. Maura climbed out of the car, but Sean moved quickly to accompany her as she started for the door. She knew the way all too well, and she was surprised that he thought he needed to escort her. But this was his party, so she followed his lead. Sean nodded to the young garda behind the desk in the tiny vestibule, and Maura smiled at him, recognizing him from past visits, but Sean just kept going toward the conference room on the other side of the building. He opened the door for her, and she found herself facing Detective Inspector Patrick Hurley, or officially detective superintendent, head of the gardaí in Skibbereen. There was no one else in the room.

"Thank you, Sean," the detective said, dismissing him. Sean left, shutting the door quietly behind him. Detective Hurley waited until he was gone before speaking. "Maura, you must be wondering what's going on, and I can't blame you for it. Let me explain."

"Okay," Maura said cautiously. "Sean said John Byrne was found dead at Crann Mor?"

"Yes. We've only begun looking into the circumstances, but there are elements that don't make a lot of sense to us. I understand you met with him the day before yesterday?"

"Yes. He came to the pub with his team, I

guess to check it out. He was thinking about some sort of business arrangement with Sullivan's, although we never got to details."

"And you visited the hotel yesterday?"

"Yes. I was invited by Helen Jenkins, who worked with him. I'd never seen the place before. We had lunch, she showed me around a little, and I went back to the pub. When did he die?"

"We haven't narrowed it down yet, but well past the time you were there. Don't worry — we don't suspect you of anything."

Even though she'd expected that, it was still good to hear him say it. "So why am I here?"

"Whenever there is an unexplained death — in this case, when a body is found — the gardaí must contact the regional coroner. This does not mean there is a crime involved, only that the cause of death is unknown. It is the gardaí's responsibility to gather any relevant information to pass on to the coroner. Naturally, we started our investigation by speaking to the man's colleagues at the hotel. Helen Jenkins is apparently one of his senior associates and is closely involved in the Crann Mor project."

"And?"

"Once she learned of his death, she asked to speak to you before she answered any of our questions."

That made no sense to Maura. "Sean told me that. Why does she want to talk to me?"

"She declined to say, but she was very clear about it. So I sent Sean over to collect you, and we met with the other members of Byrne's group in the interim."

That was only the two assistants, Maura recalled. "Is Helen a suspect?"

"The man's body was found only a couple of hours ago, at first light, and we can't be sure as to the cause of death yet, much less who might have wanted to do him harm. That is not the responsibility of the gardaí, although we may form our own opinions. Do you have any objection to meeting with Mrs. Jenkins?"

"No, of course not. Will you be there?"

"She asked to speak privately with you first but promised to tell us what she knows after that."

Maura shook her head, hoping to clear it. "Look, Detective, I have no idea what any of this is about, but I'll be happy to talk to her if it helps."

"Excellent. I'll bring her in. And if she happens to be suspicious, you can tell her that we're not recording anything you may say to each other. Currently we are only collecting information, and we'll respect your privacy."

"Good to know," Maura said, feeling like she'd wandered through the looking glass. "Are we doing this now?"

"If you don't mind. I'll bring her to you."

NINE

Maura sat alone for a minute or two more, and then Helen Jenkins quietly let herself into the conference room and closed the door carefully behind her. She leaned against it, studying Maura's face, and Maura couldn't read her expression.

"I didn't mean for this to happen quite like this, Maura," she began tentatively.

"What? Why do you need to talk to me before the gardaí?" Maura's words came out more sharply than she intended.

Helen took a seat across from Maura, so she could see her face. "Maura, this is difficult for me to say, and it may be hard for you to hear. But please let me say my piece. I'm sure you'll have questions when I'm done."

"All right."

Helen nodded once. "There's no easy way to say this. I'm your mother."

Maura felt her whole body go still. *Well, I*

102

didn't see that one coming, she thought ir-reverently before her thoughts exploded into chaos. *No. No way.* Her mother had vanished from her life over twenty years earlier. She had no memory of her. She'd never known where she'd gone, and she'd never looked for her. Her gran had been mostly silent about her: she hadn't criticized or com-plained, but she'd more or less erased her daughter-in-law Helen Lafferty from her life. And Maura had accepted that.

To the best of her knowledge, Helen had never made an effort to contact her, even though Gran had stayed in the same neigh-borhood for those past decades and she could have found her easily enough. If Helen had written to her, Gran hadn't kept the letters or shared them with her, and Maura hadn't found any in what Gran had left. Certainly Helen hadn't sent any money. For all practical purposes, she was dead to Maura.

And now here she was, sitting in a small town in Ireland, in a police station of all places. How many things were wrong with this picture?

Helen had wisely remained silent while Maura worked through this jumble of thoughts, although she was watching anx-iously. She was clearly expecting some kind of response, but Maura didn't know where to start. She was surprised — hell, yes. And angry, too. Why did this woman have the right to walk into her life now? She was definitely confused, and she had no idea what the gardaí might be thinking.

Well, she was a grown-up now. If she'd been hurt and angry as a child that her mother had abandoned her, she'd have time enough to deal with that later. She was here to help the gardaí figure out what had happened to John Byrne — who just happened to be Helen's boss. She took a deep breath. "You're going to have to explain. A lot. Is Jenkins your name now?"

"Yes, it is. After I . . . left Boston, I went back to my maiden name, Lafferty. I pulled myself together and made a lot of changes in my life. And I got married again after a few years. You have a brother and a sister in Chicago. Well, half brother and half sister."

Maura shut her eyes for a moment. *This just keeps getting weirder. Now I've got even more relatives?* "Let's skip that for now. You left, you went on with your life, fine. How did you end up here? And why is your boss dead?"

"I can answer the first question. As for the second, I have no idea."

"Then start with the first one."

"I'm sorry you had to find out this way, Maura."

"Were you planning to tell me, or were you just going to disappear again?" Maura heard the bitterness in her own voice and tried to quash it.

Helen looked away. "I know it's awful of me, but I hadn't made up my mind. I wanted to know if you were happy, if you had a good life. I was going to decide after I'd spent some time with you. I know none of this makes me look good, and I'm sorry. For the past and for now. I never expected anything like this."

Inwardly, Maura was seething, but that wasn't much help right now. "Let's worry about that part some other time. Right now the gardaí are just asking questions. I don't know all the facts about investigating a death, but I've worked with them over the past year, and they're good guys. And not stupid country bumpkins, if that's what's worrying you."

"What is it you call them? Gardee?"

"Yes. The full name is Guardians of the Peace — *gardaí* is the Irish word."

"Thank you." Then Helen looked confused. "Wait — back up. You've worked with the local police?"

"Yes. Save that discussion for later too."

The list of "later" topics was growing fast. "For now, just answer their questions. They're already looking at you funny because you insisted on talking to me before you talked to them, but as far as I know, they're not even close to arresting anyone now because it's not even officially a crime. Just a body found where it shouldn't be, which I guess counts as suspicious circumstances. So they're investigating."

"I think I understand. I know it must have seemed odd, my asking to see you first, but I didn't want you to hear about who I really am from a stranger first. And I couldn't not tell them because it's part of the reason I'm here. I'm sorry. Again."

"Got it." Maura thought for a moment. "Clearly you and I have a lot to talk about, but that's personal stuff. The gardaí want an explanation for this death or at least to give the coroner something to work with. You haven't been here long enough to notice, but crime's pretty low in this part of Cork. Murder is rare, and murder of rich outsiders even rarer — if that's what it is. So they'll be looking hard at it, I'm guessing, and you're right in the middle. How about you talk with them now, and I'll sit in if they don't mind? It'll save you from repeating yourself."

Helen seemed surprised that Maura had taken charge of the conversation, but she didn't protest. "I assume they'll want the JBCo people to stay around here until this is cleared up, so I suppose you and I will have time to talk later. Fine, bring in the detective. I'll tell him everything I know."

"All right." Maura stood and walked over to the door, opened it, and signaled to Sean, who was back at his desk. He nodded and went to fetch his boss. When he arrived, he nodded to Maura and then gestured toward the conference room, and together they strode quickly across the room to the conference room — followed by the gazes of anybody else at their own desks. Was this an important case for them? They were joined a moment later by Sergeant Ryan, and Maura wondered whether he had been invited or had invited himself. But no one commented on his presence, any more than they had questioned hers, and the men spent a minute rearranging chairs to accommodate the group in the small room. Maura studied their expressions once they had finally sat: Sean looked intent, but Sergeant Ryan looked . . . ominous? Was he ticked off that she was there?

Detective Hurley spoke first. "Mrs. Jenkins, you've already met Garda Murphy, and this is Sergeant Ryan. Are you ready to give us your account of events for the past few days?"

Helen pulled her chair closer to the table and squared her shoulders. "I will be delighted, Detective. And perhaps I should start by explaining why I wanted to talk to Maura before I talked to you." She glanced at Maura, who gave a sharp shake of her head. "Or I'll let her explain it later, but it was a personal matter with no connection to John's death. Shall I start from the beginning?"

"If you don't mind, Garda Murphy will take notes."

"That's not a problem." Helen seemed more composed now, Maura thought. "Would you like me to tell this in my own words, or would you rather ask questions?"

"Why don't you proceed, and we can ask questions if we need to. This is not a formal interview — we merely want to know about the man and if you can shed any light about his activities last night. Could you start with your name and the like, please?"

"Of course. My name is Helen Jenkins. I'm marketing manager for JB Management and Investment Company, usually known as JBCo, named for John Byrne, its founder. We assemble investors for different entities in the hospitality industry, primarily hotels, and we provide management consulting services for them. We acquired a hotel in Dublin two years ago, and when Crann Mor came on the market, it seemed to present a good opportunity to take a different approach in this country. JBCo purchased the property last year, but it's only recently that we've taken a closer look at how it's been managed and what we would like to do with it going forward. Neither John nor I had been here before."

"How long have you worked for this group?" Detective Hurley asked.

"About five years."

"And your current position is pretty senior?"

"Yes, although my promotion to my current position is fairly recent. I worked my way up. I've participated in a couple of other projects with John. It was unusual for him to take part in a preliminary assessment like this, but I think he believed this would be a quick and easy trip, and I'm told there are some excellent golf courses in this area — he may have hoped to combine this with a few rounds."

"How did he get along with his employees?" the detective asked.

"The ones on this trip or in general?"

"Either."

Helen reflected for a moment. "He was successful at what he did. The company has grown quickly, and most employees have shared in that success. But at the same time, John was impatient, and he didn't suffer fools gladly. I'm sure there were a few people he rubbed the wrong way. Not those that came with him on this trip."

"How long has this project been under way?"

"Well over a year. The purchase of the property was quite public. I suppose the price tag was a bit too steep to attract much local interest here, but we never concealed our role in its purchase. Was there local resistance to our acquisition?"

"Not necessarily. The hotel has had multiple owners over time, as I'm sure you are aware. It's not as though a long-lost heir emerged and felt he was being cheated out of his birthright."

"We did our research on the title to the land, Detective. There were no red flags."

"Could you give me a timeline for the last time you saw John?"

Maura cleared her throat. "Excuse me — can I ask a question?" Sean didn't look up from his note-taking, but the sergeant looked startled at her interruption. When

Detective Hurley nodded, she said, "How did he die?"

"He was found in the gardens behind the hotel — or rather, one of those areas left wild between the more cultivated gardens — about halfway between the main house and the lake. It appears that he slipped and fell down a hill and fractured his skull in the fall. There may be other injuries, but we won't know until after the postmortem."

"You think that's suspicious?" Maura asked.

"The fall, you mean?" Detective Hurley asked. "Only in that he was not dressed for a stroll, particularly after dark. His injuries appear to be consistent with a fall. But at this time, we have called this an 'unexplained death.' The postmortem may take several days."

Since he seemed willing to answer her questions, Maura pressed on. "Was this last night or early this morning?"

"Most likely last night, late." The detective gave her a half smile. "If I may continue, Byrne was dressed in clothing inappropriate for a ramble amongst the gardens. Particularly his shoes, which were rather fine leather and had thin, slippery soles. Tell me, Mrs. Jenkins, was he meticulous in his dress?"

"I'd say yes. He enjoyed tailor-made suits and fine accessories."

"Was he particularly athletic?"

"You mean, did he exercise regularly? Go jogging?" When Detective Hurley nodded, she added, "No. He liked golf, but that was about all. Was he robbed?"

"He was wearing a Rolex watch, and his wallet was in his pocket with nothing obviously missing, although we have not yet found his mobile phone. Are you aware of any late or early appointments he might have made?"

"No. He didn't share his personal calendar with me. You can check with his assistant, Andrew. So there were no signs of violence?"

"As I said, none that could not be attributed to a fall. It was a rather steep hill, running some distance down to the lake. Any health issues that you might be aware of? Anything that might have caused a dizzy spell? Did he drink heavily?"

"If he had health problems, he didn't tell us. And he wasn't much of a drinker, although he did enjoy a good wine." Helen paused for a moment. "You know, as I'm saying all this, I realize what a private person he was. In a meeting, or even one-on-one, he was, well, larger than life, but he never said much about himself or his personal life."

"Was he married?"

"Yes, although I never met his wife — they live in a suburb outside of Chicago. I think they have two children. But he wasn't the type of man who kept pictures of them all on his desk. He kept his professional life and his private life quite separate."

Detective Hurley sat back in his chair and was silent for a few moments. "So from what you've told me and what we've learned, John Byrne was a healthy, successful man who enjoyed his work, who traveled to this corner of Ireland on business, and who ended up dead from a fall. The postmortem may provide some additional information, but as of this time, we can say no more than that his death may be suspicious. He could have slipped, or he may have been pushed. No one has come forward to say they heard or saw anything at the time, but we've only just begun collecting information and interviewing people at the hotel. Thus far no one has admitted meeting with him last night."

Helen spoke after a long silence. "Will you be asking the rest of our team to stay around for now?"

"For the next few days, at least. Please don't think we're dragging our feet, but there are procedures that must be followed. Let us hope it's no more than a couple of days. I've told the others in your group the same thing."

"It's not a problem," Helen was quick to say. "Is there any more information about the hotel or our acquisition that you'd like me to request from our main office? Staff lists? Financial statements? Or is that premature? How and when do you decide whether John was murdered?"

"Do you have any reason to believe that he was?" the detective asked. When Helen shook her head, Detective Hurley chose his words carefully. "I know that where you come from, investigations happen fairly quickly. The process is different here. I've seen my officers' reports, and they couldn't say whether there was anything suspicious about Byrne's death, nor is it their responsibility to make that determination. We are obligated to report this death to the coroner. Which doesn't exactly answer your question, Mrs. Jenkins, so let me put it this way: the lists and such that you mentioned could be of value if the postmortem points in a certain direction. If it's not easy for you to obtain those documents, you might request them now so they'll be on hand if they're called for."

"That's not a problem," Helen agreed quickly.

"I'm glad to hear that, and thank you for the excellent suggestion." The detective stood up. "You've been most forthcoming, and I appreciate your assistance. We will keep you apprised of any new determination, but I'd guess we won't have anything definitive until midweek." He opened the door and gestured for Helen to leave the room.

He was prepared to follow Helen when Maura interrupted. "Uh, Helen, I'll meet you in a minute. I have a question for the detective." Helen looked bewildered but went into the next room to wait.

"What do you need, Maura?" Detective Hurley asked. "Does it have to do with that closed-door meeting Mrs. Jenkins requested earlier?"

"No. Like she said, that's personal, and as far as I know, it has nothing to do with what happened at the hotel. If I learn anything different, I'll let you know. What I wanted to ask was, is there anything I can or can't say to my customers at the pub?" Maura asked. "What do I say if one of the regulars asks if it was a murder, which of course is the first thing those guys will think of?"

"You may tell them that our inquiries are

incomplete and the coroner has made no determination yet. Which is the truth. He's only just been informed, and it's up to him to locate a pathologist for the postmortem."

"Thanks, I guess. Although they probably won't buy that coming from me. They know I've got your ear and Sean's."

"Then just tell anyone who's interested that we haven't shared anything with you. Most likely they're aware of the procedure in any case, more than you might be."

Sergeant Ryan, who had been silent throughout the talk, now shoved his chair back into the wall and stood up. Sean stared up at him apprehensively. "Why aren't yeh callin' it a murder? Do people visitin' fine hotels in yer backyard often fall off a hill and smash their skulls?" His tone was angry.

Detective Hurley eyed him for a moment before answering. "Are you questioning my interrogation?"

Sergeant Ryan didn't back down. "Nah, I'm questioning whether yer afraid to call it what it is. And why yer not pushin' harder for answers."

Detective Hurley's voice was colder when he answered the sergeant now. "I see no reason to call this anything but an accidental death at this time. My men began interviewing people at the hotel as soon as the body was located and retrieved. The regional coroner was duly notified and has removed the body and will have to appoint someone to examine it. The procedure would be no different if the man had been found with an ax buried in his head. Please remember that you are not in Limerick anymore, and trust me to know my responsibilities."

Maura, holding her tongue, watched as the sergeant turned a darker shade of red. Unfortunately, Sergeant Ryan turned his attention to her since the detective had not risen to the bait. "And what's this one" — he waved a dismissive hand at Maura — "doin' in the room when yeh're interrogatin' a witness? She has no place here."

Maura watched apprehensively as Detective Hurley controlled his anger. "Maura Donovan is here at my discretion," he said in a calm voice. "You will not know this, but she has gathered important and timely information in more than one fatal event prior to this. She can be trusted."

The sergeant glared at her but didn't say anything more. Detective Hurley turned to her. "Let me see you and Mrs. Jenkins out."

Once outside the interrogation room, he moved to a discreet distance before saying, "I apologize for the sergeant. He's just joined us from Limerick, and he's not yet used to our ways here."

"That's kind of obvious. Limerick's pretty rough?"

"Perhaps the polar opposite of our corner of the country, even though it's not far away. I want to give him time to settle in."

"What if he does go charging around calling John Byrne's death a murder? Will it make a difference?"

"I will try to rein him in. I'd venture to guess interrogation techniques in Limerick are rather unlike ours. And perhaps he's too eager to prove himself right now."

"Thank you for explaining. And for the compliment — I'm always happy to help if I can. So we're free to go?"

"You are. Sean can take you back to Leap." He waved for Helen to come over. "Mrs. Jenkins, will you need a lift to the hotel?"

Helen glanced at Maura. "I will, yes."

Sean had emerged from the interrogation room and was waiting for further instructions. "Well, then, Sean, please take these ladies wherever they wish to go. And thank you both for your assistance."

Maura and Helen waited outside while Sean went to fetch a car. "Maura, I . . ." Helen began.

Maura stopped her. "No. Not now. I know we need to talk — or at least, you want to — but I need some time to process this."

"Maura, please . . . Look, I've got twenty years of apologies to make. Will you at least give me that chance?"

Maura waited until her emotions were almost under control, then said, "Yes. Not because I feel like I owe you anything, but because I want to be fair. How about we meet for breakfast tomorrow at the West Cork Hotel in Skibbereen? You know it?"

"Neutral ground? I'll find it. Say, nine o'clock?"

"Fine."

They didn't speak as Sean drove Helen back to Crann Mor, then took the back way to Leap. He pulled up in front of Sullivan's and stopped but left the engine idling. He looked like he was getting ready to speak, so Maura cut him off. "I don't want to talk about it. Not now. Not yet."

"I'll listen to yeh when yer ready, Maura."

"Thanks, Sean." She clambered out of the car and into the familiarity of the pub.

TEN

Maura had lost any sense of time and realized it was well past noon now. The pub was fairly well filled for a midday Saturday — maybe everyone wanted to get out after a winter cooped up inside their homes. Or they were avoiding the cows frisking in the fields and the work that went with them.

"Everything all right?" Mick asked when she came around the back of the bar and stashed her bag.

"Yes. No. I don't know. I'll have to explain later if I get anything figured out."

"What about the death?"

"How do you know about that?"

"One of the lads from Skibbereen was talking about it while you were out."

It kept surprising Maura how quickly news spread by word of mouth around here. "You know who it was?" When Mick nodded, she told him, "The gardaí have barely begun their investigation and didn't share any information."

"So yeh can't talk about it, even to this lot?" Mick said, clearly seeing through her careful words.

"Got it in one. Particularly with this lot. But they really are just beginning — they only found the body a few hours ago — so we'll have to wait and see." Maura was relieved when a newcomer came in and asked for a pint.

She found some kind of autopilot setting in her head. She couldn't think about what Helen had said and manage to fill a glass the right way and make small talk with her patrons, not all at once. She didn't have the luxury of going home and wallowing in . . . what? What did she really feel? Shocked? Sure. Angry? Well, maybe. Hurt that it had been so easy for Helen to walk away from her and that she'd had the nerve to go on and make a good life for herself while Maura and her grandmother barely scraped by in Boston? Definitely.

"Maura, those pints are settled," Mick said quietly in her ear.

"Oh, right. Sorry." She topped them off and slid them across to the waiting men, summoning up a smile from somewhere, and collected their coins.

"Do yeh need to take some time fer yerself?" Mick asked.

"That's the last thing I need. Then I'd have to think. Right now I don't want to think."

"Are yeh in any sort of trouble?"

"No, nothing like that. I'll explain later. Right now I just want to keep busy."

The day passed. Her face was getting stiff from smiling without meaning it. She said the right things, kept the orders straight, and avoided talking to her staff. Jimmy didn't notice, but Mick and Rose were keeping an anxious eye on her as she moved through her duties like a zombie.

There was a lull about four o'clock, and she dropped into the chair across from Billy's by the fire. "Somethin's not right wit' yeh," Billy said softly.

"You could say that, Billy." Maura leaned back and shut her eyes.

"Is it bad news?"

"I don't know. Not really, I guess. Just unexpected. Very unexpected. I don't know what to think."

"If there's anything I can do fer yeh . . ."

"Thanks, Billy. It's nice to know I've got friends here, friends like you, who want to help. I'll be okay. I just need to wrap my head around this. Are you ready for another pint?"

"I'd be glad to see one," he said, smiling.

By around nine, the early crowd had thinned, and the music followers were beginning to trickle in, so she gathered her staff around and said, "We'd talked about having a meeting tomorrow morning, but what with John Byrne's death, that's kind of off the table, at least for now. But I do want to get together sometime soon and go over how things are going here in general — what's working, what isn't, what we can do better. Just think about it, will you?"

"Yeh've had no further word about the dead man?" Jimmy asked predictably — he loved appearing like he had inside information.

"Who's been talking now? Maybe the gardaí would like to know," Maura said.

"A man come in, heard it from another man and wanted to share. You know how that goes," Jimmy said. "So there's no more news?"

"You'll be the first to know. But that's nothing to do with us, so don't worry about it."

"Maura, why don't yeh go home?" Mick asked. "Yeh've had a long day, and we can cover here."

Much as she hated to admit defeat, Maura was grateful that he had suggested it.

"Thanks, Mick. I'll be in for opening tomorrow. Enjoy the music."

She gathered up her things and went out into the dark to her car. But once she got in, she didn't know what to do. She couldn't stand any more making nice to customers at the pub, but the truth was that she wasn't sure she wanted to be alone in her cottage either. She wasn't the type to find another pub where nobody knew her and drink away her sorrows, and she didn't have anything to drink back home either. Not that getting drunk would solve anything, except to numb her. No way was she going to try to contact Helen, not until she'd had time to settle down in her own mind. Maybe she was just hungry — was there anything edible in her refrigerator? Leftovers? Bread and cheese, probably, and always butter. Great, she could go home and make herself a grilled cheese sandwich and a cup of tea. Which of course reminded her of Gran. She drove home with tears sliding down her cheeks.

Back at the cottage, she managed to keep busy with the sandwich: slice bread, slice cheese, get out the pan and let it heat. Boil some water for tea. Strong tea. Her gran's remedy for almost anything. She brushed away more tears angrily. This was stupid.

Nothing had changed. She'd always known she had a mother somewhere, one who didn't give a shit about her. She just hadn't been ready for that mother to show up in front of her without warning. After a few days, Helen would go back to wherever she'd come from, and that would be the end of it.

She was cleaning up her few dishes when there was a knock at her door. Odd — it was late for callers. But if it was someone who wanted to do her harm, he wouldn't knock, would he? And she hadn't told Helen where she lived, which was hard enough to find by day even if you knew where you were going. *Open the door, you idiot,* she told herself.

It was Mick.

"Hey, what're you doing here? Is Bridget all right? Did the pub catch fire or something?"

"Are yeh goin' to ask me in?"

"Sure, come on in. There's still some tea in the pot if you want it. If Bridget and the pub are okay, what are you doing here?"

He walked in and shut the door behind him. "I was worried about yeh." He prowled around the room like a cat, then pointed to the teapot.

"Mugs are on the shelf there," Maura told

him. "I'm fine."

"Are yeh? You looked like you couldn't remember yer own name after yeh got back from Skib."

"Well, all right. I learned something I didn't expect, and I guess I didn't react well to it."

"And you don't think yeh can tell us?"

"It's personal. It's not about the pub."

Mick concentrated on pouring tea into the mug he'd found, then adding sugar. As he stirred, eyes on the mug, he said carefully, "And where do yeh draw the line between the two? We work together every day, all of us. It's like family, is it not?"

"I wouldn't know. I've never had a family apart from Gran." Until now, today, when a missing piece from her past had walked in and upended her world. She turned her back on Mick, fighting tears. Damn, she never cried. Not alone, and certainly not in front of anyone else.

And then he was behind her, his arms around her shoulders. Just holding. Just warm human contact, something she didn't get very much of. Not since Gran had died. Not since she'd gotten to Ireland and had to string together an entirely new life. She'd thought she was doing a pretty good job — until Helen showed up and the whole thing had crumbled.

Mick felt . . . something for her, but he hadn't pushed it. And she hadn't followed up. Well, the hell with that. She pivoted in the circle of his arms until she was facing him. Body to body. Warm. Real. "If you really want to know, I'm upset because Helen Jenkins turns out to be my mother."

When he tried to draw back in surprise, Maura wouldn't let him. "You said she was dead," Mick protested.

"She might as well have been. She left before I was old enough to remember her. Gran and I never heard a word from her after that. She was just . . . gone. But we survived. Then Gran died." Maura found she couldn't talk because of the lump in her throat. She didn't talk about things like this with anyone.

"Maura," Mick whispered in her ear, "yeh've every right to feel . . . whatever it is yeh're feelin' right now. She was wrong to do what she did back then, whatever her reasons. Yeh don't just walk away from yer family. Yeh don't give up on them. And it wasn't yer fault."

"It sure as hell felt like it," she said into his shirt. "I was the kid with the dead dad and the missing mother. But I didn't want anybody's pity. I worked hard; I didn't get

127

into drugs or drop out. Like I was trying to impress somebody who wasn't even there — see what a good kid I am? But it didn't matter. She never came back. Until now. She has no right . . ." She couldn't go on.

Mick spoke in a low voice over her head. "But, Maura, look at what yeh've made of yerself. Yeh're a strong, smart woman. Yeh've done it by yerself, for yerself. Don't waste yer time being angry at her."

Now she pulled back. "What, I can't be angry?"

"Of course you can, but don't let it shape yer life any more than it already has. Yeh're yer own woman. Invite her into yer life, or show her the door. Yer choice."

"You know, for a bartender, you're pretty smart, Mick Nolan."

She grabbed his head and pulled him closer, and this time he didn't hold back. Neither did she. Hell, everything was already ass-backward in her world now — why not throw Mick into the mix? There'd been an attraction flickering between them for a while; what was she waiting for?

"Upstairs," she said.

He hesitated only a moment. "Yeh're sure?"

She grinned through the leftover tears. "I

am. Besides, if it's lousy, I can always fire you."

Sunlight drifted through the window that she hadn't bothered to get a curtain for. There were thoughts working their way to the surface, and she supposed she couldn't just shove them back down. Let's see: first, there was Mick beside her, snoring lightly. Last night had definitely not been lousy, at least based on her limited experience. Much better than lousy. But more important was the fact that he'd been there for her. He'd known she was hurting, and he'd cared enough to check on her. She couldn't remember anybody doing that for her apart from Gran. Maybe that was her fault. Maybe she'd been so busy trying to act tough that she hadn't let anybody in. But that had stopped working yesterday when Helen had made her big announcement.

Couldn't Helen have done it a bit sooner? Like, maybe ten or fifteen years sooner? But that was the past. What was she supposed to do now? She had a mother — a living, breathing one — who had mysteriously shown up in this corner of Ireland. Co-incidence? Maura doubted it, but the only alternative was that Helen had actually tracked her down, which wouldn't have been easy. She'd left Boston behind with no forwarding address.

Did Helen really want to fix things at this late date? Did Maura want to let her? Mick had given her permission to turn Helen away, as if she needed it. But she had to admit that she was curious. What had Helen done with her life after she'd bailed out on Maura? And what did Helen want now? Good God, now she had a brother and a sister. And a stepfather, too. Did any of them know about Maura? Did it matter?

Mick's breathing changed, and when she rolled over, she saw his eyes were open. "Regrets?" he asked.

"Hell, no. Thank you, Mick."

"Fer what? This?"

He ran his hand along her side, and Maura realized she wasn't wearing anything. "Well, that was nice enough," she said, smiling, "but I meant for showing up and sticking around last night. I guess I didn't want to admit that I was having trouble handling the whole mess. When you spend your entire life thinking of your mother as dead and suddenly she's sitting in front of you, it's hard to take. And I have no idea what she wants."

"Maybe it's as simple as wantin' to get to know you."

"Could be. I'm willing to hear her side of the story." She sat up abruptly, clutching the sheet to her chest. "Oh, shoot, I'm supposed to have breakfast with her in Skib in about half an hour, so I'd better shower. And you're supposed to be taking Bridget to church this morning."

"Damn, yeh're right. Is there room fer two in that shower of yers?"

"We can find out. And I think I've got an extra towel."

There was, and she did. Fifteen minutes later, Maura was headed out the door. But before leaving, she turned back to Mick. "We're not going to be all weird at the pub now, are we?"

"Will it be different?"

"How about we take things one day at a time? Oh, and let me tell the rest of the gang about my mother. Wow, saying that is going to take some getting used to."

"Get on with yeh and go talk to her. Yeh've plenty of time."

Maura stepped back in to kiss Mick goodbye. "Thanks again, Mick. For everything. See you later!"

ELEVEN

The short drive to Skibbereen didn't give Maura much time to sort out her thoughts. How had things gotten so complicated in a single day? John Byrne's death. Helen dropping into her life out of the blue. And then this thing with Mick — if it was a thing. Sure, they'd been circling each other for a while, but she hadn't wanted to start anything when she hadn't even been sure she was going to stick around. Even now that she'd kind of committed to staying, she had mixed feelings about getting involved with someone she worked with. Or more specifically, someone who worked for her. Of course, maybe "involved" wasn't the right word. Maybe it had been pity on his part and Mick hadn't meant anything more than to comfort her. She certainly wasn't the type to fool around casually, but she also didn't believe in instant happily-ever-afters. And if she was honest, even after a year of working side by side with him, she really didn't know Mick Nolan very well.

She took the back way to the hotel to avoid the church traffic and was lucky to find a parking space just past the bridge over the river. She hadn't given much thought to dressing up, either for the hotel or for Helen — could she have been a little distracted this morning? But she wasn't out to impress anyone. Let Helen impress her. Well, no, she'd already kind of done that by showing up wearing designer clothes and working alongside this now dead millionaire who was leader of some mysterious multinational business she'd never heard of. Okay, message received: Helen had done well for herself after ditching her immigrant mother-in-law and demanding child in their seedy Boston neighborhood. She'd made a new life for herself. But now she had a lot of explaining to do.

Maura had worked up a good head of steam by the time she entered the hotel. She marched through the lobby and spied Helen at a table for two in the restaurant, which was well filled. She looked like she hadn't slept well — she was pale with dark circles under her eyes. But her face lit up when she saw Maura hovering in the doorway. Helen waved her over and stood up to greet her but then seemed uncertain how to proceed. A hug? Maura would have rejected that. But shaking hands seemed weird under the circumstances. After some awkward hesitation, they both sat down. A middle-aged waitress appeared and filled Maura's coffee cup, then retreated.

"To tell the truth, I was afraid you wouldn't come," Helen began, clearly nervous.

"Why?" Maura asked bluntly. "There's nothing that says we're supposed to fall into each other's arms right now, but I know I have a lot of questions for you."

"You're angry," Helen stated. "You have every right to be. I was young and stupid and scared. What I did was wrong, and I was thinking only of myself. And once you've asked your questions, we can go our separate ways if that's what you want."

"Did you come over here just to make yourself feel better? Or to try to make up for what you did? To apologize? To ask my forgiveness?" Maura realized she was getting mad all over again and forced herself to stop. If there was a call of blood between the two of them, she wasn't feeling it, but she did want to know what had happened when she was a small child, and Helen was the only one who could tell her. "Does your family know about me?"

"My husband does. I've never told the kids — they're barely in their teens. Look, Maura, I want to make this right, as far as possible. No, I'm not a religious fanatic trying to atone for my sins, and I don't expect to carry you back with me for a happy family reunion. But I do want to apologize. Will you let me tell the story my own way? Then you can hit me with your questions."

"Fine. I don't have to be at work until noon." The waitress appeared again, and Maura decided to order the full Irish breakfast, while Helen asked for a plain omelet and toast.

When the waitress was gone, Helen took a deep breath and began. "I loved your father, you know. I was a kid from Southie, one of six, lousy at school, with no real skills. I was a waitress for a while, and I got by, barely. Then I met your father. You don't remember him, do you?"

Maura shook her head. "Nope. Or you either. I was, what, two when you split?"

"You'd just turned two when your father was killed. But let me back up. Did you ever see a picture of him?"

"Gran had a wedding picture of the two of you."

"He was a good-looking man, Tom —

sweet and funny and kind and pure Irish. Still living with his mother then. He had a job, off the books, so he had a little money. We started seeing each other, and a few months later, we got married."

"Were you pregnant?"

Helen looked sadly at Maura. "No. We married for love, if you can believe that. We stayed with your grandmother, saving up for a place of our own, and then I did get pregnant with you. We had some happy years then. What did your grandmother tell you?"

"Nothing. We never talked about you at all. She found it hard to talk about my father's death, so all I ever heard was that he died in an accident and you couldn't handle living with your mother-in-law and a baby, so you'd just left. Gone. Poof. But she never said anything bad about you, even when I asked what you were like. The whole subject was off limits, and after a while, I stopped asking."

"That story is pretty much right," Helen said, and she looked away before going on. "Tom and I were happy, and we had you, and then one day he died. No insurance, no money coming in. I could have gotten another crappy job, but you know your gran had to work, so there was no one to look after you. I was barely twenty then, and all I could see was a dead-end life in Southie. I panicked. I scraped together enough money for a bus ticket, and I just left while your grandmother was at church with you."

"No note? No call? No explanation?" Maura demanded.

"What could I say? I wasn't proud of what I'd done, but I couldn't see any other path. It took me a while to get on my feet. I kept heading west, picking up jobs along the way until I got to Chicago, and then I decided I needed a plan of some sort. So I dug in, got a better job, started taking classes at night. I guess it was my way of fighting my guilt: if I'd done such a lousy thing to you, the least I could do was work hard to make a success of my life."

"So, fine, you did. Look at you now," Maura said, trying to keep the bitterness out of her voice.

"You want me to apologize for doing what I set out to do?" Helen said with a spark of anger. "Sure, maybe I could have taken my hard-won successes and gone back to Boston and claimed you. And we all could have lived happily ever after. But I didn't. I met my husband, and we got married, and the kids came along. In case you're wondering, I do like kids. I like being a mother. I'm sorry you never got to see that."

The waitress delivered their meals, giving Maura a chance to control her thoughts — and her tongue. Being angry at Helen might feel good, at least for a while, but it wouldn't fix anything in her life.

"What about you?" Helen asked, poking at her omelet.

"What about what?"

"Your life after I left?"

"Boring. Work, school, repeat. I never figured I could plan a future, but then Gran died and I ended up here in Leap."

"Do you like it?"

"I guess. It's not anything I ever imagined, running a pub in Ireland."

"Is there anyone special in your life?"

Getting a little too personal, are we? "No. I haven't had time for that. I'm not even sure I want that. I guess I'd have to say I don't have a very rosy picture of relationships. Gran was a widow and never got involved with anyone again. My father died. You bailed out. Too many of the girls I went to high school with had a baby by the time they graduated. If they graduated. The guys were out for a good time with no strings. I didn't see anything I wanted there."

"I think I can understand that. But when your gran died, did you have a plan? I mean, any idea what you wanted to do with your life? Stay in Boston? Try someplace new?"

"I didn't really have time to think. I had to clear out our apartment by the end of the month, and Gran always said she wanted me to go to Ireland and tell her friends face-to-face that she was gone. I found a letter from her — she even left enough money for a plane ticket. And then I got here and found she had set it up that I would inherit the pub from an old friend of hers, plus his house. She never told me."

"I can't imagine what you must have felt then."

Maura sat back in her chair. "I think I just went numb for a while. But I kept it together enough to claim the business and the house. I thought I'd just sell both of them and go back to Boston, but here I am. Listen — how did you track me down?"

Helen tilted her head. "I always knew where you and your grandmother lived. I heard when she died. And yes, I could or should have reached out to you then. But you disappeared pretty fast — I guess to come over here. So I went through the few things of your father's that I'd kept and figured out where he'd been born, and then I started hunting. I have to say, there are a heck of a lot of O'Donovans in this neighborhood, but I figured it out. After that it was easy."

"Fine, so you knew where I was," Maura said impatiently. "Why did you come over here after you ignored me for years?"

"Oh, Maura, I couldn't live with myself any longer. I had to see you, if only once. I know I have no claim on you and you have your own life. So maybe I'm being selfish, wanting to know what kind of a person you are, what you've become without me. I was prepared to learn that you were a drug-addled hooker, and of course I would have blamed myself. But I needed to know. I am so proud of what you've done here, Maura."

Maura ignored that last comment, filing it away for later. "How did this whole hotel thing come up?"

"That was a gift from the gods. I took it as a sign. I'd been working for the company for a few years, and the deal for Crann Mor was already done when I got my last promotion to management. When I heard they wanted to send a team over here to get a feel for the area, I lobbied hard to be included."

"And your big pitch about including the pub in the plans? Was that your idea? And was it for real or just your excuse to snoop?"

"It was a legitimate proposal, Maura. It

still may be if plans for the hotel go forward, and it could benefit both of us. I'll admit I was glad of the opportunity to meet you without all this other baggage, but I can see that you might think it was kind of sneaky. Unfair to you. But I really didn't know how you'd react."

"So, let me get this straight. Your company just happened to buy a hotel in the same area where I inherited a pub?"

"Maura," Helen said wryly, "if you do the math, you'll realize that the hotel deal was in the works long before you arrived here. The two events were unrelated, unless you believe in fate."

"Huh," Maura said since she had no better response. What Helen said was probably true. Multimillion-dollar deals didn't happen overnight. Not that she believed in fate. It was just a strange coincidence. "So, okay, it happened and here we are. But why is your boss dead?"

Helen looked relieved that they had moved away from the personal stuff. "I have no idea. I've worked with John for years, and he seemed to be exactly what you'd expect: a good businessman who could turn on the charm when he needed to. Good at making money, but not by cutting corners or cheating anyone. A hard worker. A family man who valued his marriage, as far as I know. I don't know of any enemies he might have had at home or here. Are the police sure it wasn't simply an accident?"

"I told you, murder is rare here, so they're reluctant to call it a murder too fast. But that doesn't mean they're sitting on their hands waiting. They're investigating."

"That's good to know." Helen smiled. "May I ask how it is you seem so chummy with the local police?"

Maura forced herself to sit up straighter in her chair and looked squarely at Helen, even as she struggled to figure out what she wanted to say. This was not the time to get into how she'd gotten entangled with so many crimes in the short time she'd been in Ireland. "That's a complicated story. Let's say I've been on the fringes of a couple of recent investigations."

Helen seemed to accept Maura's evasion. "Is your pub a violent place?"

"No, not at all. But there are things going on around here, things I never knew about, like drugs and smuggling. I think I've gotten sucked into some of them because I'm American and I see things differently. The Skibbereen police department is small, and they don't see many murders or even much violence beyond the occasional pub fight. I can't say they ask me for help, but sometimes I hear things at the pub and help them put the pieces together. They'll treat you fairly, if that's what you're worried about. They're good people and not yokels. They aren't going to try to pin this on anyone just to close the case in a hurry. But you have to play fair with them too. Don't hold back any information or decide for yourself what is or isn't important. You don't know what matters. Just tell the truth."

Helen was still smiling. "Maura, you are one smart young woman, and I appreciate the heads-up. You're right — if you hadn't given me a heads-up, I might have dismissed them as unskilled rural cops. You're saying that would be a mistake, and I appreciate it. Thank you. But I'm still not sure where you fit with them."

Maura looked down and realized she was twisting her napkin into knots and made herself stop. "Think about it, Helen. I can help them because I run the pub, and people talk when they come in, especially about things like the unexpected death of a stranger. I listen, and I pass on anything that might be important but not so much that people who stop in won't trust me. Plus, this case isn't exactly typical. I'm involved because you're involved. If I've learned anything in my time here, it's that family comes first. You're family. I owe it to you to help figure this out if I can. So back to the question, why is John Byrne dead?"

TWELVE

"I don't know."

Was Helen hiding something? Maura didn't know her well enough to guess. "Do the gardaí want to talk to you again?"

"They did say what we said yesterday wasn't an official statement, right? I don't really understand how this all works. They can't investigate officially until someone else gives them permission? Or do they go ahead even if they don't really think someone killed John? I already volunteered to give them more details about the hotel project and its recent history if they want it. I haven't heard anything from them. I assume they'll talk to the hotel staff and get back to us later," Helen said.

"I don't get that whole business about the coroner, although I guess how they label the death is his decision. As for them not getting back to you, it may mean only that they're shorthanded. They've just added a new guy, but I don't know if he's up to speed yet."

"That large man from yesterday? He didn't seem to fit well with the others, I must say."

Maura nodded. "I had met him once before, but I did get the feeling he thought I didn't belong in the room. Did you kill John?" Might as well try a surprise attack and see how Helen reacted.

Helen looked startled by the abrupt question. "Seriously? No, I did not. He was my employer. We got along well, both professionally and personally. Why would I kill him?"

Maura took a bite of her breakfast — the hotel would probably want the table once the churches let out. "Frankly, I don't know you well enough to guess. Maybe you've been seeing him on the side for years. Maybe it was the only way he'd let you keep your job. Maybe you were allergic to his cologne and you snapped and shoved him."

"Maura, you're being ridiculous. None of that is true. Have your police friends told you any more about when and how he died?"

"No. You heard the detective — they had only a rough guess as of yesterday morning, and they don't call and give me daily

146

updates. If I have a question and ask it, they'll probably give me an answer, but I don't overuse that — I save it for important things. And I told you, I do share with them what I hear or learn from people at the pub or neighbors. You'd be surprised how many bits and pieces of information you can pick up in the pub, if you pay attention. Look, if you're going to confess to something, I'm going to tell them. Right now I owe the gardaí here more than I owe you. Sorry if that sounds harsh."

"I suppose I deserve that," Helen said quietly. "Why don't we start with what I do know? Which is what I'll be telling the — gardee, right?"

"Close enough. Okay, I heard what you told them, but there are other things I'd like to know. Let's start with when your group arrived in the country."

"We didn't all come together. There were four of us on this trip. John and his personal assistant, Andrew, came from Germany, I believe, where they were inspecting a potential property. They arrived at the hotel on Tuesday afternoon. My assistant, Tiffany, and I reached the hotel that evening. Tiffany called you at Sullivan's on Wednesday, and we all met with you there on Thursday. The rest of the time we spent touring the

147

grounds at Crann Mor, talking to the staff, observing day-to-day operations, and exploring local venues."

"Did you all stay together all that time?"

Helen nodded. "More or less. We all had dinner together at the hotel on Wednesday night to evaluate the chef and the service. You should be flattered that we all came to see your place — that wasn't true for all of our potential locations. As I'm sure you know, there are a number of nearby pubs, but yours offered the added asset of music."

"I still don't quite get what you want from me, but we can talk about that some other time. Anyway, you and I had lunch together on Friday. Did you see John after that?" Maura asked.

Helen carefully aligned the silverware on her now-empty plate. "We spent a little time together in the bar in the late afternoon — again, as a professional assessment. We're all familiar with the hotel on paper, but it's quite different when you're actually there. The local staff may report that they have high standards for cleanliness, but sometimes you get there and find spider webs in the corners. That kind of detail matters to our clients."

"Sure, fine. So John was still alive at, say,

five on Friday. And you didn't see him after that?"

"No. I went upstairs early, ordered a meal from room service — which should be on record — reviewed my notes, and went to bed. Oh, and I called my family on my cell, late-ish, to accommodate the time difference. There'll be a record of that too."

"And John was found Saturday morning with his skull bashed in," Maura said, almost to herself. "I wish I knew more of the details of where he was found, but the gardaí have no reason to tell me. Based on what Detective Hurley said, he was found outside of the hotel wearing nice clothes and shoes, so he it sounds like he hadn't changed after dinner. You said he was a sharp dresser?"

"It was more that he liked quality in his clothes — I think I told you that. I don't recall that I've ever seen him in jeans or a sweatshirt."

"So he doesn't sound like the type to take a walk in the dark after dinner to settle his stomach, much less dressed nicely and wearing the wrong shoes. Or at least, not past the garden. You've already said you don't know if he was meeting someone, either for dinner or after. I guess the hotel bills would show if he charged for more than a couple of drinks. Did he know anyone else around here?"

"If he did, he didn't mention it to me."

"Did you like him?"

Helen seemed startled by the abrupt change of tack. "Maura, why do you want to know that? We worked together well, as colleagues. I wouldn't say we were friends, exactly. If you asked him to give five personal facts about me, he'd probably get stuck at three. And I'd be in the same position with him. Married — yes, but I've never met her. Kids — I think so. Golf? He mentioned it occasionally. I don't know how much you know about the business world, but we're not all like the buddy-buddy California high-tech model, hanging out around the communal gym. We're more professional than that. Cordial. Polite. No shouting matches, no storming out of the room slamming doors. Nothing points to a reason for murder."

"Did he sleep around?" Maura asked.

"Not that I ever knew about, but why would I? As I said, he was a private man. Look, I've asked that the office forward to me a list of all the past employees at the hotel from the last five years, which is as far back as our records go. Just in case your police need them. They or someone up the line can check if any of them had any prior connections to John or this area."

"Okay, so as far as your tour of the hotel goes, everything was just peachy? Nobody found any dirty linens or fungus in the kitchen or anything?" Maura scanned the room again: more tables were filled now.

Helen cocked her head. "Maura, why do you keep looking around? Are you worried that someone will see or hear us?"

"No, not that. I know you manage hotels so you should get it. This is a small place. It's Sunday, and a lot of people come to town for church and maybe a nice meal. We're taking up a table."

"Goodness, I hadn't even thought of that. Should we go somewhere else?"

"I'd give it another ten minutes, and then we should leave." The waitress stopped by to refill their coffee cups, and Helen said, "Could you bring the check, please?"

When the waitress had left, Helen resumed. "To get back to your question, no, we didn't find anything objectionable about Crann Mor. It's a beautiful site, and the local management team is doing good work. There are a few structural issues with the building itself, but nothing that needs urgent attention. We want to take our time to assess the balance between maintaining the historic character of the place and allowing it to operate more efficiently in the modern world."

"Has your group done a lot of places like this?"

"A couple of dozen over time, I'd say. I haven't been directly involved in most of them. Do you want me to provide references? The majority of the places that we've worked with still retain us as consultants, so it would seem that they were satisfied with the service we provided."

"You make good money?"

Helen looked surprised at the question. "Do I personally? Or does the group? Yes, by most standards, to both. We also participate in profit sharing, so we have a stake in maintaining our reputation."

"What happens now that John is dead?"

A troubled expression crossed Helen's face. "I . . . don't know. I assume Andrew has notified the board of directors, and they will have to convene and consider the succession."

"Are you in the running?"

"Good heavens, no!" Helen said, laughing. "I've only just been promoted to my current position. And let me tell you, there are very few women in management-level positions in this kind of group. A fact that has always surprised me since women tend to be much more attuned to the smaller details that make a hotel or resort appealing and comfortable for its guests."

"So you don't benefit from John's death?"

"No. He was a mentor of sorts, based solely on my performance. I'm good at my job, Maura. I've worked hard to get here. I had no reason to kill John Byrne. His death doesn't help me in the least."

"And you don't know of anyone else who benefits either," Maura stated rather than asked.

Helen shook her head. "I'm sorry — I wish I could help. Could it be someone local?"

"Unlikely, I'd say, but I guess it's not impossible. We peasants don't wander around the grounds over there, even if they're open to the public. The gardaí are checking out the staff, which probably is local, but it's hard to think that any of them would want to kill someone they had barely met. Where was John from, originally?"

"I really don't know. Which sounds odd, to say it now. He never talked about his early years."

"Did he hit on women when he was traveling?"

Helen stared at Maura. "Seriously? No!

153

Are you suggesting that he was chasing one of the housekeepers around in the woods in the dark and she shoved him to his death?"

"It's been known to happen. I'm just asking."

Helen was silent for a moment. "You know, you're pretty good at this. Interrogation, I mean."

"I'm just asking logical questions. And I'm sure the gardaí will ask the same ones. Uh, you don't have to tell them we had this conversation — or at least, all the details. They might accuse me of helping you get your story straight."

"Your gardaí don't know I'm your mother yet, right?" When Maura shook her head, Helen went on. "So this is about that family loyalty thing? You'd try to protect me even though you just met me after all these years?"

"They might think so, when they find out about us."

The waitress returned with the check for breakfast, and Helen paid by credit card. When they had the receipt, Maura guided Helen out the door that faced the river.

"You want to sit for a minute?" Maura pointed toward the low wall on the river side of the driveway.

"Sure." They sat, and Helen looked out

over the river and the marshes beyond. Finally, she said, "You don't seem to like me much."

"I don't know you," Maura said. "And I've got a lot of years of resentment that I've been carrying around, so you're going to have to work hard to erase that."

"Do you want to?" Helen asked softly.

Maura hesitated before answering. "I don't know yet. Say we hit it off — what would happen? You'd invite me back to meet my brother and sister, and we'd all share holiday dinners? We'd send each other birthday cards once a year? What do you want?"

"Maura, you can decide what comes next. That includes telling me to get lost. I'd regret that, but it's up to you."

Maura nodded once. "Let me think about it. And let's get John's death out of the way. It's hard to worry about all this at once."

"Fair enough." Helen's cell phone rang in the depths of her purse, and she pulled it out and read a text. "Looks like your police are ready for me. It's at the other end of the main street from here, isn't it? I can walk it in a few minutes?"

"Sure. Get to know the town, even though most places are closed on a Sunday. It's a good place, although it may not be up to the standards of your people."

"Maura, my people, as you put it, want to see something real. People who can afford our hotels aren't snobs — they've got plenty of other places to go if all they want is parties and yachts. They would come here for different reasons."

"If you say so. So far they haven't come into Sullivan's." Maura stood up. "I'd better get over to the pub and see what's what. Thanks for breakfast."

"Thank you for being willing to talk to me, Maura. I'll let you know what happens with the police."

"Great." Helen stood up as well, then walked toward the center of the town, and Maura went around the side of the hotel to get to her car. When she got in, she sat for a few minutes without starting the engine. What did she think? For a start, she didn't feel any sort of kinship with the fairly polished, intelligent professional woman that Helen was now, even though she knew Helen had started from pretty much the same place that she had. Great, so now she knew that it was possible to remodel your life if you wanted to and tried hard enough. She wasn't sure she was cut out for that.

But then, she hadn't really considered a long-term plan for her life since she'd arrived here. How long was she going to stay? Forever? A couple of years? Not that she had anything to go "home" to in Boston, and life was cheaper here. And slower. And friendlier. She was in no hurry to leave, it seemed.

But right now, she had to get back to the pub and see what rumors were flying around. And deal with seeing Mick after what had happened the night before.

THIRTEEN

When she got to Sullivan's, it wasn't opening time yet, so she could take a few minutes to straighten the place up after Saturday night — and use the time to straighten her thoughts as well. A lot had changed in the past twenty-four hours.

First, there was Helen. Suddenly, she had a living, breathing mother, and she wasn't sure how she felt about that. As she started stacking up the chairs on the tables and retrieved a bucket and mop to swab down the old slate floors, Maura admitted to herself that she still had a lot of questions, some she couldn't even put into words yet. Her mother had been, what — nineteen? Twenty? Younger than she was now, anyway — when she'd had Maura. Her father had been killed about two years later. How long after that had Helen stuck around with Gran? Six months? Maura understood the feeling of being trapped in a life you didn't want, but she didn't have a child to think of. At least Helen had left her with Gran, who had been a decent, responsible person and Helen had probably trusted to raise her daughter right. Gran, who had had to work and manage a small child at the same time. Then Maura had started working as soon as she could pass for legal age — at least as long as it was dark — which had given her some experience with handing out drinks and now and then managing grabby drunks. There had never been enough money.

Helen, though, had found a way to move up the ladder, and now she had a cushy job and nice clothes, and Maura was still working in a bar. At least it was *her* bar, no thanks to Helen. But Maura still felt a spark of anger that Helen had moved on and done so well without ever looking back.

Floor: clean. Check. Maura moved on to unloading the glassware from the small dishwasher under the bar. Mick had had to take his grandmother Bridget to church this morning, as Maura had reminded him. When they were in bed. Wow, she hadn't seen that coming. Or maybe she had, but she'd buried it deep. She wasn't the kind of person to sleep around, and she didn't know what to expect now from Mick or even from herself. At least she didn't have to face him right away.

How did she feel about what had happened the night before? She really wasn't sure. Okay, over the past months they'd shared a couple of kisses. Two, to be precise. On separate occasions. Not exactly a steamy start. She had a lot of questions about him too — why was he so unambitious? He could be doing more with his life, so why wasn't he?

Maura, are you hung up on ambition? She didn't really have any herself, other than to earn enough to live simply and maybe have some control of her own life. The answer to that wish had kind of dropped into her lap when she'd inherited the pub and the house. But when Helen and her crew had waltzed in and more or less offered to make Sullivan's bigger and better, she'd balked. That wasn't what she wanted. She didn't want to be a corporate player. She didn't want to be her mother.

But what did she want? A day ago, she would have said she didn't want anything. She didn't want to depend on a man for her livelihood — especially given Helen's example. And speaking of her mother's example, a baby was nowhere in her sights, so she wouldn't find herself in the same trap.

The pub was now clean, but Maura still

had no answers. It was almost noon, and Sullivan's would open in half an hour to welcome those members of the church crowd who weren't rushing home for a big Sunday dinner with the family. Mick would be taking Bridget home before he showed up, so she had one more small reprieve before she had to face him. But she should tell Rose and Jimmy and even Old Billy about Helen in case they thought she was going nuts. She looked up to see Rose opening the front door, followed by Jimmy with his usual sour expression.

"You all right, Maura?" Rose asked as she hung up her coat on a hook behind the bar. "Yeh looked a bit off yesterday."

"I'm fine, Rose, but thanks for noticing. Morning, Jimmy," Maura added, which produced a grunt from him. "Mick was going to take his grannie to Mass, so he'll be in a bit late."

"I think we can manage." Rose smiled at her. "The farmers are busy movin' their cattle back to pasture, so it shouldn't be a big crowd."

"I hadn't thought of that. I don't know much about cow schedules."

"You've some herds up yer way, have yeh not?"

She shrugged. "I guess. I'm not usually

there by daylight, so I don't pay attention unless there's a cow in the road in front of me."

"Yeh've cleaned up the place," Rose observed after taking a look around. "I'd've done that fer yeh."

"I got in early."

"Anythin' new on the death of that man over at the fancy hotel?" Jimmy asked. Trust him to be looking for the gossip.

"Not that I know about," Maura told him. "What's it to you?"

"People ask when they come fer their pint. I like to be able to give them somethin' to talk about."

"Well, you'll probably know as soon as I do. Have you and Judith set a date yet?" Maura asked, changing the subject quickly to distract him.

"Her herd's calving season's about done, so she's pushin' for soon now." Jimmy looked glum at the prospect. Maura wondered if Rose would be joining them on Judith's farm or if she'd grab the chance to strike out on her own. But she wasn't going to ask in front of Jimmy. She'd find a quiet moment with Rose and find out.

It was still too early for customers, so she could afford to step away for a minute. "Listen, I need to tell you something. You're probably going to hear it soon enough, so I might as well share it with you now. Helen Jenkins, the woman who was in here with the Crann Mor people the other day, turns out to be my mother."

"Get on wit' yeh," Rose said, her accent thickening as she responded quickly. "I thought she was gone?"

"Yes, but not as in dead. She disappeared when I was two, and I haven't seen or heard from her since until this week."

"What's she doin' here now?"

"She works for the group that bought the hotel, but I guess she may have been looking for me. Kind of late."

"Ah, Maura, she's yer ma, and she's come back. Surely yeh're happy about that?" Rose demanded.

"I don't know yet. It's kind of complicated, and we haven't had much time to talk. She worked for the man who died, so the gardaí want her to stay around for a couple of days until they sort that out. I guess we'll have a chance to talk when they're done."

Unexpectedly, Rose threw herself at Maura and hugged her hard. "I'm happy fer yeh, I am. I'd give a lot to see me ma again." Then Rose let go, looking flustered.

"So that's why yeh were in a state yesterday?"

"Yeah. It was a surprise, for sure."

"Will the hotel project go on?" Jimmy asked abruptly. "Now that the boss is dead?"

"Jimmy, I don't think anyone has thought that far ahead. You'll just have to wait to find out like the rest of us."

"So we're done here?" Jimmy asked abruptly.

Maura stifled her annoyance. "Yes, Jimmy, you can go back to work now." He didn't notice the sarcasm in her voice as he left the back room.

In a low voice, Rose asked, "Does Mick know?"

"He does. I told him . . . last night."

"Ah," Rose said. "I'd best set up the bar, then."

Opening time finally arrived, along with a couple of men who had been waiting outside. Rose went behind the bar and started pulling pints for them. Maura spotted Billy as he slipped in and headed for his usual seat.

She caught Rose's eye and nodded toward him. "I'm going to go say hi to Billy." She went over to where Billy was settled in his usual seat next to the fire. It might've been spring outside, but the old stone building took a long time to warm up, and the fire felt good. The chair on the other side was empty, so Maura dropped into it. "Hey, Billy, how are you? Ready for a pint?"

"I'm grand, Maura, and I'd welcome a pint about now."

Maura signaled to Rose behind the bar, and she nodded.

"Big doin's over at Skibbereen, I hear," Billy went on.

"Yes, there are. The gardaí are calling it a suspicious death, until the coroner says otherwise."

"So the others from the States are stayin' around 'til it's settled?"

"So it seems."

"Includin' that nice older woman who came along wit' them?"

Maura turned to study Billy's face. Did he know something? But how or why would he? Or did all older Irish people develop psychic powers? "I think so. Why are you asking, Billy?"

He watched her face as he said calmly, "There was something about the lady that seemed familiar."

Maura shook her head but had to smile. In a village this small, there was no keeping a secret, although Billy could be discreet. "And why would that be, Billy?"

165

"I was in a good place to watch the two of yeh together. It's plain to see, although I don't know the whys and wherefores of her bein' here."

Maura sighed. "Okay, fine. She's my mother, the one who dumped me on my grandmother when I was a toddler and went off to seek her fortune. Which it looks like she found. So maybe now she's feeling guilty."

"Irish, is she?"

"Her maiden name was Lafferty, but I don't think her family comes from around here. Lots of Irish people in Boston, Billy."

"Will yeh be seein' her again?"

"Probably. I've got a lot of questions. But I'm still mad at her."

"That's yer right, fer now, but don't let it stand in yer way. She's family, like it or not."

Maura sighed. "And that's what I told her. Around here, family matters, whether or not you like the people."

"Did she have any part in this death?"

"Billy, I really don't know. She says she has no reason to wish the man dead, and I can't see why she would."

"Will yeh promise to listen to what she has to say to yeh?"

"Of course I will, Billy."

Rose delivered Billy's pint, and Maura

166

went back to the bar to serve the growing crowd. Cows or not, a suspicious death seemed to draw people to the pub, which she had learned the hard way.

Mick walked in shortly before one. "I took Bridget over to the church. She's met with a friend, and he'll bring her along after. I'll see her home then, if that's no problem."

Maura swallowed and looked up at him, trying to keep her expression neutral. "Sure, that's fine. Rose was just telling me the crowd should be smaller today because the farmers are moving the cattle around."

"Right so," he said but kept his gaze on her face, although his expression gave nothing away.

Or did she see a small smile? Odd — Mick rarely smiled. And not usually at her. Out of the corner of her eye, she noticed Rose turn quickly away, but not before Maura had seen a smile on her face too. So much for keeping secrets. Was she that obvious?

She slid behind the bar, and Mick followed. "Yeh're all right?" he asked quietly when nobody was paying attention.

"About . . . yesterday? Yeah, I think so." She couldn't think of anything more to say.

Mick smiled and turned to the next customer, making change for him when he paid for his pint.

Well, that certainly cleared things up, Maura thought.

A few minutes later, Maura watched Gillian come in. She wasn't waddling at this point; she moved more like a large ship, clearing everything out of her way before her. Old Billy stood up to offer his seat to her.

She sank into it with relief. Maura went over to her and asked, "Can I get you anything?"

"I'd give a lot to see my ankles again, but I suppose that's not what you mean. Would you have any juice?"

"I'll see what I can scrounge up. Where's Harry? I'm surprised he lets you out of his sight these days. You could pop any minute now, right?"

"Feels that way. I know it's Sunday, but Harry had a meeting set up with a possible client who was trying to fit in a round of golf at one of Cork's splendid courses and couldn't meet at any other time. No worries — he's not far away, and he has his mobile with him should anything happen."

"But?" Maura prompted.

"I worry about Harry more than myself. Me, I've plenty of friends who've had children. Even in Dublin, there've been nights when all the talk among us was about nappies and problems with finding reliable childminders. Harry hasn't had that experience, and I think he's terrified that I'll break. Or that he'll make a fool of himself during the delivery and spew all over the floor — or worse, the nurses. And that's just the birthing part."

"It's amazing the human race has survived," Maura said wryly. "I'll go find you that juice."

When Maura went looking behind the bar for some kind of drink, she noticed that Mick seemed to be avoiding looking at Gillian. "You think Harry's going to get his act together for this baby?"

Mick muttered, "I hardly know the man."

That was a non-answer. "But do you think he could do it if he wanted? If it mattered enough to him?"

"He might do," Mick said curtly.

Maura picked up a bottle of orange juice and a clean glass, then went over to where Gillian was sitting and snagged a chair. "Here you go. Are you really okay?"

Gillian's face tightened, and she laid a hand on her belly. "I think so. Harry's trying so hard. It's sweet. But neither of us has a clue what we're doing, and reading about it isn't much use. But we should be able to work it out. Anyway," Gillian said, cocking one eyebrow, "you and Mick, huh?"

Crap. So much for secrets. "I could say something stupid like 'What do you mean?' but that's not going to work, is it? Who blabbed?"

Gillian smiled. "Ah, Maura, I only had to look at you now to know that there's something different about the two of you together. Is it what you want?"

"I don't know what I want to do, Gillian. But you have to know that it was kind of wrapped up with something else that happened yesterday."

"Are you going to fill me in?" She took a sip of her juice but kept her gaze on Maura over the rim of the glass.

"Did you hear about the people over at Crann Mor, who seem to be part of the management team that bought it this past year?"

Gillian looked bewildered for a moment but evidently decided to roll with it. "Harry heard something. He was wondering if they were going to stick around and if they might have need of his services locally. He knows a bit about their Dublin hotel. Of course, that was before the death. Is this about that?"

Maura sighed. "Not exactly. It seems that

one of the management team members who came with them is my mother."

FOURTEEN

Maura's revelation stopped Gillian in her tracks, and Maura was almost amused to watch her trying to figure out which question to ask first. "You told me she'd left you when you were a small child."

"She did. Walked out and we never heard another word from her. Until now, when she walked back in."

"And she's part of this group of hotel investors or whatever they are?"

"That's what she says."

"Oh, dear God. And is she suspected of killing that man?"

"Her boss, you mean? The gardaí have only just started looking into things. They've asked the rest of the group to stay on for a few days."

"And have you talked with . . . your mother since her big announcement?"

"Yes and no. I had breakfast with her this morning, but we kind of avoided all the personal stuff. Turns out she married again and had a couple of kids, so I've got a brother and a sister. Well, half."

"But I'm guessing you didn't get into the stuff like 'Why the hell did you abandon me, dear Mother?' "

"Not a lot. We did talk about John Byrne's death, which may or may not have been an accident." Maura glanced around the room, but nobody seemed interested in their conversation. "You know, things like who worked for who, who had issues with him, that kind of thing."

"Who stands to gain, you mean?"

"Sort of. Look, so far we've spent maybe two hours together, so there's a lot we haven't covered."

"And will you?"

"I'll listen to her story. But that doesn't mean we're going to get all warm and fuzzy and fall into each other's arms."

"What's she like?" Gillian asked.

"She seems smart. She speaks well. She wears expensive clothes. I guess she's got to be good at what she does, or she wouldn't have her job. She didn't gush all over me, if that's what you're asking. She was very . . . careful, I guess I'd say."

"Maura Donovan, what would you expect from her? She's here, and she must have had to do some searching to find you. She hasn't seen you in over twenty years. She must figure she treated you badly, and she wasn't sure how you'd react. So she's being cautious, I'd say. At least give the poor woman a chance."

"That's more or less what I'd planned to do, Gillian. But I can't forgive her all that easily."

"Nor should you. But talk to her."

"Fine. Maybe tomorrow. Maybe the gardaí will have figured everything out by then."

But Gillian wasn't paying attention to her anymore. Instead, she seemed focused on something Maura couldn't see. "Maura," Gillian said carefully, "I think something's happening."

It took Maura a moment to put two and two together. "The baby."

Gillian nodded. "I've been having these odd feelings for a while now, but they're getting stronger rather than stopping. The midwife said there was such a thing as early contractions — I forget the name — but I didn't want to worry Harry, so I didn't say anything. Maybe I should have."

"This is early, right?"

"It is, but it's not like the date is chiseled in stone. It's not *too* early, which is a good thing."

"What're you supposed to do?"

"Wait a bit longer and make sure it's not a false alarm. Would you believe the instructions the hospital hands out say, 'You need to think positive thoughts'? Then at some point I have to get myself to the hospital in Cork."

"You should call Harry," Maura said firmly. "Unless you do think this is a false alarm?"

Gillian flinched again. "Maura, I think it's the real thing. And I'll call him now, but I may need a ride from you."

While Gillian called Harry, Maura hurried over to the bar to tell Rose what was happening. "You and your dad can handle the business for now, right? Mick will have to take Bridget home, but he'll be back after. I don't know how long I'll be."

"Don't worry yerself, Maura, we can manage. Where's the dad-to-be keepin' himself?"

"Gillian says he was meeting a client on a golf course somewhere. Before you jump all over him, remember that they need the money right now."

Maura looked back at Gillian to see her beckoning her over. When Maura was in earshot, Gillian said, "He'll meet us there — he's closer to Cork than to here. I'd call an ambulance, but they take a year and a day to arrive, and driving would be faster. Do you mind, Maura?"

At last, something practical she could do. "Of course not. I've been there before when Jimmy broke his arm, so I know the way. You ready to leave now?" When Gillian nodded, Maura added, "I'll go get my car."

She grabbed up her bag and fished out her keys on the way out the door. On the bright side, at least Gillian wasn't about to give birth on the floor of Sullivan's. That kind of drama she could do without.

At least the hospital was relatively close. Maura had heard stories about injured people in other parts of Ireland who had to travel halfway across the country to find the medical help they needed. She'd been spoiled by Boston, where there were top-of-the-line hospitals all over the place — luckily, she had never needed them, but it was nice to know they were there.

She started up her car, checked that she had gas, and drove to the front of Sullivan's. Before she could get out, Gillian came out the door, supported by Rose. Rose settled her in the passenger seat, then stepped back and gave Maura a thumbs-up sign as they pulled away.

"Everything okay?" Maura asked, praying for a positive answer.

"No changes, but I'm pretty sure these are labor pains. Little Darling here is ready to make his or her debut."

"Is Harry ready for all this?" Maura asked, heading east on the main highway toward Cork city.

"Who knows? Is anyone? So, talk to me, Maura. Take my mind off what's happening and what's to come. Anything new on the murder?"

Maura had to swallow a laugh. Gillian was about to birth a watermelon, and she wanted to talk about murder? "The gardaí haven't used the word murder. Yet." But they might if Sergeant Ryan had his way. Was he going to work out in peaceful Skibbereen?

"But you're thinking they will. Officially, I mean."

"They might. Depends on what the coroner says. Look, I trust the gardaí in Skibbereen to do their jobs. I'll let them decide."

"I won't argue with you. But why's the man dead? Why here? Who was he, and who wanted him dead?"

"Gillian, would your hospital manual say these are positive thoughts?"

She grinned briefly. "Let's say I'm happy to be distracted. It's better than staring at my watch and counting the time between contractions."

"Got it. I don't know a lot about the guy. Helen told me a few details, and of course I met him that once at Sullivan's."

"And as I recall, you didn't like him."

"Not much. Nice clothes, nice watch, nice haircut. But he was very self-important. You know, all 'Look at me — I'm rich and successful, and you're not.' "

"But he was rich and successful. Good-looking?" Gillian asked.

"Sure, if you like that type. What I didn't like was how his staff acted like a bunch of lapdogs around him."

"Including Helen?"

"Not as much, but it was clear she knew who was boss. Can we get back to whether this was murder?" Out of the corner of her eye, Maura could see Gillian's face tense, then relax.

"Right. So, John Byrne's group bought the hotel about a year ago, right? You know, I think I've been in his Dublin hotel — definitely top-drawer. Which doesn't explain what he's doing setting up business in this remote corner of the country."

"Maybe he got it cheap," Maura guessed. "Maybe he has insider info on the growth potential for West Cork. I don't know. But his company or group or whatever it is owns it now."

"This was his first trip here? I mean, he didn't take a look before he bought the place?"

"As far as I know. Before you ask, yes, it was also Helen's first trip." As far as she knew, Maura amended silently.

"How did he die?" Gillian asked.

"I don't have all the details. It was after dinner, that much I know. I think it was dark, or getting dark. He was still wearing his fancy suit and shoes — I'm pretty sure the gardaí will have checked if he ate with his team or with a guest by now."

"And if he stopped in the bar after dinner or went prowling the mean streets of Skibbereen looking for a drink and some company."

"He would have had to find a ride — a taxi or something. Helen rented a car, but I don't think John did. Maybe the hotel would have provided a car and driver. But it's pretty clear that he wouldn't have walked into the town — I don't think he was the type, and his shoes weren't meant for walking. The gardaí will check that stuff out."

Gillian was silent for several moments, her jaw clenched. Then she said, "But he died where he was found? On the Crann Mor grounds? Outside, not inside?"

"I think so. Remember, I didn't get to ask many questions, and all I got was hints. But nobody said he died somewhere else and was dumped in the woods. And I think it was just off a walking path, not a lane where anyone could drive to drop off a body. Have you been there?"

"A while ago. It's an impressive site. So, John had dinner, might have had a drink, and well after dark, he decides he wants to take a walk. Does the hotel have surveillance cameras?"

Maura zoomed past a slow-moving truck. "Gillian, how am I supposed to know? I've been there once, and I wasn't looking at the security. Nobody's mentioned cameras, and why would they tell me? So I can't say if he walked out of the hotel arm in arm with anyone, male or female."

"Are you thinking he was gay?"

"No, not really. Helen told me he had a wife and kids in a suburb outside of Chicago somewhere, but that's all I know. His personal assistant might have more information. Think the gardaí will ask him? About John being gay, I mean?"

"They're more open-minded than they once were, I think."

"By the way, there's a new garda — a sergeant. From Limerick."

"Really? He's bound to be bored in Skibbereen, then. Limerick would keep any garda busy. Though he has walked right into a suspicious death."

"I'm pretty sure he'd like to call it a murder. Maybe that's just what he's used to."

"Hmm," Gillian said. "But to step back, John, alone or with company, strolled along the garden path in the dark. Was he looking to smoke a cigar?"

"Gillian, I don't know!"

"Did he have a torch?"

"You mean a flashlight? Again, I don't know."

"Was he robbed?"

"He still had his watch and wallet on him."

"What were his injuries?"

Maura risked a glance at Gillian. She looked pale but focused, and she managed to smile at Maura. "I'm doing fine. Keep talking — it helps."

"Based on what little the gardaí told me, there were no injuries that could not have been caused by the fall down the hill. Mainly a blow to the head that did a number on his skull. Seems he fell quite a long way. That's why they've been careful about avoiding the word 'murder.' "

"Was he the type who liked to take rambles?"

"After hearing about the man's clothes from Helen, I'd say no. And why after dark? In an unfamiliar place?"

"Maybe he did know it — he'd sneaked in before in disguise when he was considering buying the place," Gillian suggested, stopping to pant.

"That's a possibility, although I don't think there was anything shady about the deal, but I don't know a heck of a lot about business. But why take a walk?"

"He needed some air after a big dinner? He wanted someplace private to think about what he'd seen and heard? Or he could have been meeting someone."

"In the woods in the dark?"

"Someone he didn't want anyone to see him with or to know about? Ouch!"

"You okay?" Maura asked quickly.

"Yes. Little Darling just kicked me. Impatient bugger. So what do the gardaí do now?"

"Talk to everyone around here who ever met the man, saw him from a distance, heard of him, had any connection to the ownership or management of the hotel before or after he took it over, or just hated guys with nice suits and shiny shoes."

Gillian laughed. "Well, that should cover it. And they talked to you? Which category do you fit in?"

"I did meet the man, although I doubt that he saw me as anything other than a rural pub owner who might be useful to him. He was on a fact-finding mission, checking out local resources that might appeal to guests. Plus Helen kind of dragged me in without knowing that I'd worked with the gardaí before. She wanted to come clean about being my mother."

"I suppose that was good of her. Did John know that Helen was your mother?"

"I don't think so. I don't know where that part fits. Pretty big coincidence, don't you think? I mean, Helen has worked for the man for a few years, she told me, but they didn't get this hotel deal set until maybe a year ago — I don't know when the earlier owners decided to put it on the market. So she could hardly have spent two years putting herself in a position to visit here with a good cover story just to check me out. Heck, up to a year ago, it would have been easy to find me in Boston if she'd wanted to. She could have written a letter or picked up a phone or jumped on a plane anytime without all this fuss. I mean, really — flying to Ireland just to get a look at me? That's a stretch."

"Maybe she was the person who identi- fied the property and pushed her boss into looking at it?"

"That's even harder to imagine, don't you think? I doubt she had enough influence at the company a year or more ago to get John to buy the place, even if she did suggest it to him. I'm not really sure what her depart- ment does, but I don't think it has anything to do with acquiring properties. More with spiffing them up after they've bought them."

"So, let's say we set your mother aside for a bit. Who else would want John Byrne to die? He was traveling with a small group, right? He didn't bring a huge team along?"

"Small. His personal assistant, Helen, and her assistant."

"Maybe someone back in Chicago was cooking the books and was afraid John would find out, so he killed him here to confuse things. Or had him killed."

"I suppose that's possible. Hey, we're get- ting close to Cork. You know where Mater- nity is?"

"I do. Keep going past the roundabout, and I'll guide you. Ooof!"

"How often are these pains coming?"

"About every ten minutes, more or less."

184

"Isn't that pretty fast?"

"Maybe. We're almost there. Turn left at the next corner, and follow the signs."

Fifteen

They both fell silent as Maura concentrated on navigating the roads outside of Cork city, and Gillian focused on whatever was going on inside her. "Park here?" Maura finally said.

"Yes. Fine," Gillian said through clenched teeth.

Maura found a space, pulled in, and turned off the engine. "Can you make it, or should I go get a wheelchair or a guy with a gurney or something?"

"I think I can walk as far as the door, Maura. It's only a baby I'm having. You'll come in with me?"

"Of course. But Harry should be here, right?"

"Yes. He will," Gillian said firmly.

Maura wondered if that was wishful thinking, but she wanted to give Harry the benefit of the doubt. "When we get inside, where are we going?"

"There'll be a big desk in the lobby. I'll be in their computer system. They'll know where to send me."

Maura looped her arm through Gillian's and kept her pace slow to accommodate her. Luckily, the parking lot was close to the entrance, and the desk was where Gillian had said it would be. And Harry was waiting in the lobby, pacing anxiously. When he saw them walk through the glass doors, he headed straight to Gillian and wrapped his arms around her.

"How are you, darlin'? When did this start? What do we do now? Are you feeling all right?"

Gillian smiled. "Slow down, love. It's only been an hour or two. Well, maybe more. I'm glad you got here. Shall we check in?"

Maura watched them as they made their way to the front desk. Harry started explaining things, waving his hands around when he wasn't fishing cards out of his wallet and dropping half of them on the floor. The receptionist stayed calm — she must've seen a lot of flustered pregnant couples in her job — and things were sorted out after a couple of minutes. Maura felt like a third wheel since Harry and Gillian were so wrapped up with each other and decided she really should get back to Leap now that

Harry could take over. She joined Harry and Gillian to let them know.

"I thought I'd head back now."

Gillian gripped her arm. "Maura" — she glanced at Harry, who nodded — "I know it's a lot to ask, but can you stay? Harry's not good with blood and stuff, and I'd really like to have another woman with me, and I can't ask my family."

Maura was touched, flattered, and panic-stricken. "Gillian, I don't know anything about having a baby!"

"You don't need to. There are nurses and a midwife and a whole hospital full of doctors to take care of that. I want you there to cheer me on. Will you?"

"Uh, yeah, sure, I guess. Will Harry be there too?"

"Unless I pass out," Harry said, looking relieved. "You're a good friend, Maura."

"Okay." What had she gotten herself into?

"Thank you," Gillian said. "Harry, tell the desk to add Maura to the partners list, will you? And then we're off to the races!"

What followed was a jumbled journey through halls filled with medical personnel wearing scrubs or white jackets, women on gurneys, and women walking the halls, hunched over their huge bellies and accompanied by men looking about as bewildered as Harry did. Maura could not have found her way out of the building for love or money and was wondering how she could smash out a window to escape when they finally stopped in what was labeled a delivery suite. The nurse who had escorted them there smiled and said, "The midwife will be here shortly," and then vanished.

A woman who Maura thought looked about twelve arrived next. "Hello, I'm Sorcha, your student midwife. I'll be here throughout your delivery. Your midwife will be along directly. Let me just take a look at your charts." She glanced over at Harry and Maura, who were huddled in a corner trying to stay out of the way. "You might as well make yourselves comfortable. This may take a while."

"What's 'a while'?" Maura asked.

Gillian answered, "I've been told first labors can take an average of eleven hours — that's what the book said. I have a feeling Little Darling here is on a faster track." She gasped as another contraction started.

Shortly after that, an older woman bustled in. "Gillian Callanan, is it? I'm Honora, your midwife. Let's see where we're at, shall we?"

"We'll be outside," Harry gulped and all but dragged Maura with him out the door into the hall. He leaned against the wall and took deep breaths.

Maura tried not to laugh at the poor man. "Harry, this is the easy part."

"Yeah, and it gets worse after this."

"You've had plenty of time to get used to the idea, you know. Having a baby — then having a baby around the house all the time."

"Look, I've had this thing about blood and ick since I saw my dog get run over by a truck when I was five. I'm not proud of it, but I'm stuck with it."

"Gillian knows this?"

"She does. That's why she asked you to stay."

"So it's not about the baby? You aren't going to walk away and disappear?"

"Hell, no! I've loved Gillian for years, even if I didn't manage to let it show. But we're in this together."

"Well, I'm glad to hear that. And I'm sorry about your dog. But I don't know that I'm any better with blood and stuff than you are. The worst I've seen is a couple of bar fights with knives back in Boston. And I watched *Alien.*"

Maura peeked in the door, but the midwife seemed quite busy poking and prodding Gillian, so she backed off again. "Gillian said you were playing golf with some corporate bigwig?"

"I know, poor timing. But it was the only time he was available, and his account could make a real difference to us."

"I'm not criticizing. Did the death at Crann Mor come up? I mean, had this guy heard about it?"

"Oddly, it did. Peter Flaherty said he'd met John once or twice."

So Harry was aiming high for clients. "Did he have an opinion of him?"

"He didn't say anything directly, but I gather he thought that John Byrne was very aggressive in his business strategies when he was buying the hotel."

Interesting, Maura thought. John must have wanted Crann Mor badly. "Gillian told me you were hoping to get some business from the new Crann Mor people?"

"I'd like to, but I don't think this is the right time to approach them."

Maura nodded. "That's pretty clear. Tell me, do you think the hotel is a solid business?"

"Financially?" Harry asked. "There's always an element of risk with a venture like this. On the plus side, the place has a long history and handsome facilities in reasonably sound condition. On the minus side, it'll take a big infusion of money to bring it up to current luxury standards, which is what I understood John Byrne was looking for. I'm sure he'd done his market research, scoped out the coming trends in regional tourism — that kind of thing — before he recommended buying it, but it's still a gamble."

"What will happen with it now, do you think?"

"I haven't enough information enough to say. They've already sunk a good deal of money in. It may depend on who's running the show now that Byrne is gone. You wouldn't know who'll be taking over, would you?"

"No, but I could find out. Want me to ask Helen?"

"Who?" Harry looked bewildered.

"Helen Jenkins, John Byrne's associate. And my mother."

"What? No, never mind — you can explain at some later time. Sure, go ahead and ask her."

The midwife Honora popped her head in and beamed cheerfully. "Everything's going just fine, but it may be a while yet. Do yeh want to sit with Gillian?"

Harry shook his head. "Let me know when things get closer, will you?" Honora nodded and disappeared again, and Harry turned to Gillian. "Don't worry — I'll be there for the important parts. Talk to me, Maura. Please?" They turned to other safer topics. The weather. Sports teams. How Harry's business was coming along. What he and Gillian hoped to do to fix up the old creamery — and how fast that would happen.

"How soon do you have to be out of Mycroft House?" Maura asked.

"Soon, I'm afraid — in the next month or two. I don't think the fact that there's a newborn involved carries much weight with the National Trust. We have an agreement in place."

"How's Mycroft House different from Crann Mor?"

"It isn't, really. A stately manor house belonging to an old family fallen on hard times. There's no shortage of those around. My family made the gift of the place to the trust with the agreement that Eveline could live out her days there. With Crann Mor, the family needed the money, pure and simple, and they weren't sentimental about it."

"Does this area need a hotel like Crann Mor?"

Harry shrugged. "I can't say. Even in my

lifetime here, we've seen big ups and downs in the economy and tourism. Like the Celtic Tiger economic boom. Now nobody knows what impact Brexit will have. You're well fixed — you have a business and a home, and you own the both of them free and clear. There's many that aren't so lucky."

At that moment, the head midwife stuck her head out. "I think things are moving right along. Will yeh come in now?"

Maura fixed Harry with an evil eye. "Man up, Harry. If you miss this, Gillian may never forgive you."

"Only if you come in too." Harry appealed to the midwife. "I'll take Gillian's upper end, and you can keep an eye on the business end. Will that be all right?"

"I've seen stranger things. But you'd better come in now before you miss the show."

SIXTEEN

Thank goodness the midwife had called the timing right. Both she and Harry had each ended up holding one of Gillian's hands — and Maura wasn't sure all her bones had survived intact — but it hadn't taken long for Henry Townsend Callanan to make his entrance into the world, weighing a healthy eight pounds, five ounces. Mother and baby were both fine, to everyone's relief. Gillian was going to stay the night, and Harry would see to getting her home in the morning, so Maura was free to go. She found her way out of the hospital by following the signs and stepped out into the fresh air, breathing deep. She was surprised that it was still light; in fact, it was barely six o'clock. She'd always believed that delivering a baby took quite a while. She thought for a moment about just sitting on a bench and absorbing what she'd seen and heard over the past few hours, but it would take her an hour to get back to Leap — more if traffic was heavy — so she should get on the road.

She made her way back to her car, then pointed herself westward. At least it was a road she knew as well as any in the area, because her attention was not exactly on her driving.

Harry had come through the delivery well. Squeamish though he might be, it was clear that he loved Gillian. Too bad it had taken the two of them so long to realize that they belonged together, but they'd finally figured it out. Where and how they'd be living was still an open question, but things like that had a way of working themselves out. She'd have to follow up on her idea of recruiting the guys at the pub to help out with the renovations at the creamery and get them to ask their wives to haul out their old baby furniture and clothes. Those were practical things that could be done quickly once she got the word out. Another plus of owning the pub: it meant she was kind of information central.

So why was she crying? She told herself that she was heading straight into the setting sun, but she knew she was lying to herself. Maura brushed away tears angrily, but it didn't help much. Seeing Gillian and

Harry with their child had been unexpectedly overwhelming. Why had Gran never told her anything about those first two years of her life, when she'd had a mother and a father? What had her father been like? She knew that Gran had loved him fiercely, and maybe that was why she never spoke of him. And Gran had already lost her husband when her son died. Maura had avoided thinking about all these questions, much less asking Gran, but now she had to face them. Why had her father married Helen? Where and how had they met? Had they been in love? Would they have stayed together if her father hadn't died? No way to know, not now. No one to ask.

Except Helen. That realization hit Maura like a physical blow. Helen was her only link to her father now, the only person who harbored any memories of him. And to get Helen to share those memories, Maura would have to work out some sort of relationship with her. She'd have to be nicer to her, open up at least a little. Which meant that she'd have to let go of some of the resentment and anger that she felt to get what she wanted. She could do that, right?

It was half dark by the time she arrived back at Sullivan's. She parked and walked toward the pub, and when she walked in, everyone in the place, staff and patrons alike, turned to look at her. It was almost funny.

"Healthy boy," she said. "Eight-plus pounds. Name of Henry Townsend Callanan. Mother and child doing fine. And the next round is on the house."

Maura's statement was met with cheers, although whether it was for the baby or the pints wasn't clear.

She moved behind the bar after taking off her jacket and took stock. Jimmy as usual was chatting with some pals in a corner, and Rose was already behind the bar handing out pints. Mick? She had to look around and finally located him in the far corner. At first she thought he was alone, but when he shifted, she realized that Helen was sitting at the same table facing him, and they were talking intently.

Maura wasn't sure how to react. Helen had every right to be here — or anywhere else, for that matter — but she hadn't given Maura any warning. Unless she'd tried to call Maura's cell phone, which she'd turned off at the hospital. What could she want? Had the gardaí figured out how John Byrne had died and decided everyone could go home? And what were she and Mick talking about?

Somewhere in the midst of her reveries, Maura realized that they were both looking at her, and then Mick came over.

"So all's well?" he asked.

"Fine and dandy." Maura nodded toward Helen. "Did she introduce herself?"

"She did that. Did yeh want her to stay in her room and hide?"

"No, I guess not. But what does she want?"

"Fer an intelligent woman, yer not very smart, Maura Donovan. She wants to talk to yeh. Why else would she be sittin' there? Surely the two of yeh have somethin' to talk about? The weather? The value of the euro? Where to buy fresh fish?"

He was annoying her, and Maura didn't like it. "Mick, it's not a joke for me. Of course I'll talk to her. I've got plenty of questions. And I won't yell at her or hit her or even throw her out of the pub. But I don't need you in the middle of things." There was already a too-long list of people who were trying to tell her how to talk to her mother. "You can handle the pub?"

He looked around at the sparse collection of patrons. "I think I can manage it. G'wan, talk to the woman, will yeh?"

"Fine." Maura stalked out from behind the bar and headed for Helen's table in the corner. Helen was watching her approach, and when Maura dropped into a chair opposite her, she said, "So, nothing new about John?"

"I wouldn't know. I've been . . . busy," Maura told her.

"You look exhausted."

That didn't begin to describe how Maura felt. She'd just helped deliver a baby. She was hip-deep in another investigation of a suspicious death. She was trying to figure out how to talk to the mother she had never known. She didn't know where to start, and what she wanted more than anything was some quiet time alone to give her brain a rest and then to try to sort through everything that she'd learned in the past couple of days. It didn't seem to be happening.

It occurred to her that food might help. "Have you eaten yet, Helen?" Maura asked.

"Uh, no. I came in looking for you and got to talking with Mick. Where do you want to go?"

Maura stood up again. "It's been a crazy day, and I just helped deliver a baby, and I'm crabby as hell. Let's go over to the bistro and see what the special is tonight."

"All right," Helen said, looking bewildered but game. "Lead the way."

Helen followed Maura out onto the street

and down to the corner, where they crossed and walked into a small restaurant with a pool table tucked into a corner. She waited until they were both seated and had ordered before asking, "You said something about a baby?"

"Yeah, a friend of mine just had one. Today. Her first. She asked me to hold her hand during the delivery since her partner was kind of squeamish."

"Oh, my!" Helen smiled. "I'm glad you have friends here, Maura. It must have been hard after your grandmother died and you ended up here, where you didn't know a soul. How did that happen?"

Safe ground, ground she'd covered before. "Gran rigged it with her old pal Mick Sullivan, who owned the pub. He had no one in his family to leave it to, and I was going to need a job and a place to live, so they fixed it up between them without telling me. I'd never known that she kept in touch with people here. And some of them still remember her. That makes me glad and sad at the same time."

"She was quite a woman," Helen said softly.

"I keep forgetting that you knew her."

"More than that — we all lived together in the same apartment for a couple of years, remember. Money was tight even with your father working. Then it got tighter, after —"

Maura stopped her quickly. "Let's not go there now, okay? There's a lot I want to know about my father, but I'll probably just bite your head off right now."

"I'd love to share it with you, Maura. He was a good man, and he adored you. I wish you could remember him."

Maura struggled to answer. "I'm glad to know that. But let's stick to a few basic facts for the moment."

"I'm sorry. Really. But this whole thing is such a mess! I never expected you to welcome me with open arms, but I didn't think we'd be in the middle of a police investigation. I thought we could ease into things a bit more slowly."

Maura smiled reluctantly. "It's not your fault — unless you killed John, and I don't think you did."

"Thank you for that, at least." Helen sighed. "What are the categories for deaths in Ireland? Apart from natural, I mean. Is it like in the States? Murder and manslaughter?"

"Helen, I really don't know. I could ask a friend if you like."

"Let's see how it goes. And if there's a suspicious death but not enough evidence to bring charges?"

That sounded all too familiar to Maura. "It does happen. Arresting someone and bringing that person to trial are not automatic — it's the coroner's decision. And in Ireland, if it's declared a murder, the case will stay open even if no one is convicted."

"So if the local police don't solve this fairly quickly, will they let us leave?"

"I guess. Unless they've got some pretty strong evidence, they probably will. How're you going to decide what to do about the hotel?"

"Well, at least it was functioning well enough when John died, so it'll carry itself while we consider our options. We'll have to get the management team together, look at where we want to go as a group — which projects look viable, which ones we should divest. That kind of thing. So the short answer is, we probably won't have an answer for a while. Tell me, is the hotel important to the local economy?"

Maura shrugged. "Look, I hadn't even heard about it until your crew called me, and I don't run in your circles. I don't think any of Sullivan's customers do either — they're mostly local farmers or shopkeepers with tourists added in the summer. But I think most ordinary people in Skibbereen are more likely to go to the West Cork Hotel or the Eldon Hotel down the street than out to Crann Mor. Skibbereen isn't exactly a fancy destination resort."

"From what little I've seen of the place, I think you're right. I don't really know what John was thinking when he went after it, but he didn't always share his brainstorms with the rest of us. But he was usually right."

Seventeen

Out of habit, Maura looked up when the door to the bistro opened and was surprised to see Sean Murphy. He scanned the room, lighted on their table, and came over quickly. "Mick said yeh'd be here. Can I have a word?"

"Hi, Sean. You've met Helen Jenkins, I know, but I don't think you know that she's my mother."

Sean's expression of shock was impossible to hide. "I thought yer mother . . . Oh, excuse me, Mrs. Jenkins, but Maura never said . . ."

Helen laughed. "She didn't know. And I didn't tell her until we met at that station of yours. Please, sit down — we're not in any hurry. Is this about the . . . death?"

"It is," Sean said, pulling out a seat for himself. "I'm glad to find yeh together, for it's the two of you I want to talk to. Mrs. Jenkins?" he began.

"Make it Helen, please," she protested.

Sean came straight to the point. "Helen, then. How long did you work with John?"

"About five years."

"And did you have a friendly relationship?"

Helen suddenly looked wary. "What do you mean?"

Sean looked perplexed, then realized what his question might have sounded like. He blushed. "I mean to say, did you talk about yer personal lives? Have dinner with his family? Send holiday cards?"

Helen relaxed a bit. "No, not really. It was a working relationship, no more."

The lone waitress arrived with Helen's and Maura's food, and Sean asked for a coffee. When she withdrew, Sean said carefully, "Did he ever speak of his early years?"

"Not that I remember." Helen paused for a moment to think. "Looking back, it was as though his life started at Harvard — that's where he went to college, and a Harvard degree means something in the business world. He never talked about his childhood or his parents. But most of us didn't — our interactions were always professional. We respected each other's privacy as coworkers. Why are you asking this now?"

Sean leaned forward. "We've found little

in his current life that might have led to his death. His employees, like yerself, haven't shed any light either. We've learned a bit about your company with the help of John's assistant, Andrew, but we've had no satisfaction there. So that got me to wonderin' if we might do well to look back a bit further."

"Why?" Helen asked.

"We're looking at all the possibilities, Mrs., uh, Helen. Seems yer boss didn't speak of his past to anyone, including yerself, as you've just said. Was he hidin' something?"

"I can't imagine what. I suppose he might have had a juvenile record, but that would have been expunged when he became an adult. That could explain why he never mentioned his past. Within our financial community, he was a very public figure. In fact, I'd say he thrived on the attention. I'm sorry I can't help you more."

Maura had stayed silent as Sean directed his questions to her mother, but finally she spoke up. "Sean, I'm guessing you've got an idea of some kind. Does this come from the inspector, or are you acting on your own?"

Sean blushed again. "The times we've worked together, you and me, Maura, have got me lookin' at things in a different way. Most of the crimes we see here are simple and easy to solve. But sometimes you have to look deeper — 'outside the box,' isn't that what you say in the States?"

"Yeah, okay. What are you thinking?" Maura prompted.

"That the man had somethin' to hide, somethin' he didn't want people around him to know about. We've dug through his present and come up dry. I'd like to see what we can find in his past. These days yeh can look up anything on the Internet, including the man's hat size and whether he has an ingrown toenail. But back when Byrne was a boy? Not so much, especially when we aren't sure of the dates and places we do have. We're doin' our job lookin' at the past few years, but before that won't be so easy."

"Where are you looking?" Helen asked suddenly. "You in the guards here can't exactly hop on a plane and do some research in . . . wherever he came from. Where did he come from, do you know?"

"His passport says he was born in New York — that'd be the state — USA."

"Hmm," Helen said. "I never knew that. I don't think he ever mentioned it. But that doesn't help you much, does it? I mean, if he was born in Manhattan, that's a pretty large place."

"It is that. We've only just begun our search, and it may not give us any answers, but I wanted to take a look at it."

"What about Harvard?" Helen asked. "That's the one thing he did talk about. Have you gotten in touch with them?"

Sean was staring at Helen. "Do yeh know, I never thought of that. How would I do it? Just ring them up and ask about one of their students from twenty-some years ago?"

Helen smiled. "Well, I doubt they'd share much with you. But listen — maybe I can help. I'll have to put together some sort of obituary for John, and I'm pretty sure they'd talk to me. Unless you'd rather handle it yourself?"

Sean looked momentarily confused. "I've no right or authority to contact an American university and ask for information about a one-time student who might or might not have been killed."

"So let Helen — she has a good reason. John must show up on some kind of college record that's available to the public, and Helen can find it faster than you could."

Sean looked back and forth between Helen and Maura and seemed to come to a decision. "Yeh're right. Helen, I would be grateful if you could ask your questions of

Harvard and pass on whatever you find to me."

"I'll call in the morning, then. I'm glad I can help."

Sean looked at his watch. "Sorry, ladies, but I promised me ma I'd be home for supper, and I'm already late. If you remember anything else, ring us at the station, will yeh? And I'll let you know if we learn anything new."

"Of course," Helen said, "and I'll call and ask for you if I learn anything. Do you have any idea when we might be able to go home?"

"That I can't say, but I'm hopin' it won't be more than a few days. Ta." He strode out to the now-dark street.

When he was gone, Helen commented, "My, they're making policemen awfully young these days."

"He's my age, more or less," Maura said. "He's been through the academy or whatever they call it here, and he's been working a couple of years already."

Helen sighed. "He still seems awfully young to me. Innocent, if that's possible. Or maybe I'm thinking that you seem older than he is, whatever his age."

"I've led a different life. And maybe you've noticed that there is a kind of innocence here in Ireland, even among the police."

"Interesting. No romantic sparks there?"

"I'm not looking for anything romantic. Not right now." And she was pretty sure if it ever happened, it wouldn't be with Sean, although she liked him as a friend. Mick, on the other hand . . . "Thanks for offering to help him with Harvard. I don't think it ever would have occurred to him, not that it's his fault. Look, I should be getting back to the pub."

Helen drained her coffee, then waved for the check. "You know, you really are a workaholic."

"Because I work hard to make my business successful? Isn't that what you do?"

"I suppose. I admire your energy, and I can only imagine what the place was like when you first arrived. But you have to leave a little room for other things. And people."

"I guess. I'm not sure what else I'd do if I wasn't working at the pub. It's mostly farming around here. Cattle, some sheep."

Helen laughed. "I'll admit I can't see you herding cattle, much less milking them. But surely there's something you care about?"

"I'm still looking. I've had a lot to sort out since I got here." *Including what happened with you and my father.* "I wasn't even sure I wanted to stay."

211

"Do you think you will?"

"Maybe. There's nothing for me back in Boston. Here I'm my own boss, and I think I like it."

Helen smiled. "Now that I can understand."

Helen begged off returning to the pub, saying she was tired, and Maura crossed the street and went back to Sullivan's. Sunday nights were always quiet at Sullivan's unless there was a big sports event or something like it. They didn't close until eleven, so she could put in a couple of hours tending bar before heading home.

There were few people in the pub, mostly a tight cluster around one of the corner tables, and when she came around to the back of the bar, one of her steadiest patrons, Seamus Burke, came over quickly, asked for another pint, then leaned an elbow on the bar while he waited. "So, what do yer gardaí pals have to say about the dead man at Crann Mor?"

Well, Sean had come looking for her at Sullivan's, so Seamus had made the logical assumption that the gardaí were talking to her. How long had he been hanging out waiting for her? "What're people saying?" Maura asked cautiously.

"That his death was no accident," Seamus

212

said quickly. "That his head was bashed in with — depending on who's tellin' the story — a rock, a tree limb, a shillelagh, or a hurling stick. There's some that say he was strangled and hittin' his head was just a bonus. Of course, there's always poison, which works with any of those. Maybe he was poisoned just so somebody could hit him in the head. I think we've put the heart attack idea to bed. Am I gettin' warm?"

Maura had to laugh. "So it's safe to say that everyone believes he was murdered?"

"Oh, we passed that point a while back. We know how the gardaí work, but they agree, am I right?"

"Officially? They won't say until the postmortem's done, but they're investigating as if it was a murder. Better safe than sorry, I guess. So, have you and your mates lined up assorted candidates for the killer, including somebody who plays sports with one or another stick? Man or woman? What's the betting?" Maura topped off his pint.

"Could go either way, could it not? A strong woman coulda done the deed with the rock or the branch. A man would more likely choose the shillelagh or the hurling stick."

Maura had to wonder how many people

213

went wandering around in the dark outside of Skibbereen carrying a shillelagh or a hurling stick. She'd never seen either one, as far as she could remember. "He wasn't robbed, you know," Maura said and wondered if Sean would approve of her sharing details. "He had a fat wallet and a nice watch on him."

"And what would you be meanin' by that? That the motive wasn't robbery but somethin' else?"

"I didn't mean anything! I just thought you should include that fact in your little betting pool. Seamus, have your pals talked about motive?"

"We don't know the man well enough to guess, and no one around these parts knew him. It's easier to talk about the 'how' than the 'why.'"

"I think the gardaí feel the same way. How many of you are in this betting pool?"

"Half a dozen, mebbe. Helps us pass the time. And it came in handy in that last case, wouldn't yeh say?"

Maura sighed. "Well, yeah, I guess so. Sometimes just talking about things kind of jogs people's memories. You all have any favorites so far?"

Seamus took a long pull from his fresh pint before reaching into his back pocket and pulling out a small battered notebook, which he opened with a flourish. "There's somewhere between six and ten possibles, dependin' on how we count 'em, we think. Are yeh wantin' to hear them?"

"Of course I am!" Maura told him firmly.

EIGHTEEN

Seamus settled back in his chair, clearly looking forward to explaining things to Maura.

Before he could start, Maura said, "Have you shared any of this with the gardaí?"

"Nah. It's just a bunch of the lads shootin' the breeze over a pint or two. Or mebbe three."

"Great." She looked around the pub: nobody was paying attention because there were no patrons except for Seamus's betting crowd in the corner, it seemed. She raised a hand at Old Billy, dozing by the fire, and he winked at her. Had he been part of this discussion? "Okay, I've got fresh ears, and I'm sober. Hit me with them."

"Well, if we're thinkin' it's really a murder, first on the list is yer ma, that Helen Jenkins. We set her aside pretty quick, out of consideration fer yer feelin's."

"Gee, that's nice of you. She had opportunity, at least — she was there, and she knew John better than anyone else around here. What's her motive?"

Seamus looked embarrassed. "Well, we though they might have been lovers, see, and somethin' went wrong. Or he wanted to have a bit of fun, bein' away from home and spouses and all, and she wasn't havin' any of it, so she shoved him away, and he fell down the hill, accidental-like."

Maura considered that. "Possible, although I'll tell you she denies it."

"Sure, and she would. Leavin' her aside, we next thought of one of the others in this Byrne's group. There's, what, two others still at the hotel, apart from yer ma?"

"Yes, his assistant and my mother's assistant."

"Ah," Seamus said. "They don't seem like the best of suspects unless they were lovers in one combination or another. Or there's this: mebbe their financial genius back home found out that John was dippin' into the till or had blown all the company's assets on the horses, and he got mad and had someone bash John. Maybe his own assistant, this Andrew lad?"

"I guess that's possible," Maura said amiably. "My mother says the financial officer in Chicago is very attached to his numbers.

But I've met both of the assistants, and I can't see either of them getting physical, especially not in a place they don't know in the dark. What about a hired gun?"

"There've been no strangers seen around the place," Seamus said dubiously. "And I can't say as I know any assassins fer hire in Cork."

"You know, Seamus, as far as I can tell, it would be hard for anybody to sneak in and out of the place without being seen, even in the back. A local would make sense since he'd know the lay of the land."

"Mebbe one of his colleagues from the company thought this deal would bankrupt them and that John had to be stopped," Seamus mused. "Killin' him here had the added bonus of puttin' a black cloud over the hotel. Although there's a problem with that one — the deal's already done, and a murder at the place would only drive down the sellin' price."

"I agree."

Encouraged by Maura's comment, Seamus picked up the thread again. "Might also be someone from back in the States, sneaked in under cover like and did the deed," Seamus said. "No one would be looking for 'im."

"Interesting," Maura commented. "Would

that person have been a guest at the hotel, do you think?"

"He might have done. How else would he have known the gardens well enough to meet up with John in the dark? He'd've had to check the place out first."

"Good point. I'll try to find out if the gardaí have looked at that angle. You have more ideas?"

"I do. There's the manager at the hotel, who might be worried about her job under new management. She's done a fair job, but she might not be refined enough for John and his lot with their big plans. They might have passed over her and brought in someone else," Seamus said.

"Good point. The gardaí are looking at employees. But would this woman care enough to kill John over her job?"

"Maybe they met up for a private chat, John gave her the bad news, and she just lashed out."

"Seems kind of unlikely, but I'm pretty sure that the gardaí have that covered. Any black marks on the hotel woman's record?"

"None that we know of, but people do manage to keep secrets now and then. Even in West Cork." Seamus grinned again.

"It's not easy, I know. Okay, more? We aren't up to eleven yet."

"I never said I'd finished, did I now? There's the last owner of the hotel. Maybe John stiffed him."

"What, never paid him? My mother said he played fair with money. And his financial officer would know."

"Unless they were in it together," Seamus said darkly.

"Ah, two for the price of one. Go on."

"Would there be another pint in it fer me?" Somehow Seamus's last pint had disappeared as they talked.

"Sure, why not?" Maura started another. "So, who's next?"

"We were thinking maybe John had his way with the gardener's daughter. Or the cook's daughter. Or the boatman's daughter. He was a good-lookin' man and rich as well, so the temptation woulda been there."

"Or son," Maura said absently as she thought about that idea. "Was it willing or by force? Because we know how it ended — with John dead."

"Even if it was willin', the girl might have told her da, and he might have taken it wrong. Or they could've done the deed together, the girl and the da."

"They'd've had to plan it. Is that all?"

"Unless the man committed suicide by hitting himself over the head and throwing himself down a hill in the dark, yeah, that's all we've thought of."

"Actually, I think you've done a great job, Seamus, although by my count that's only nine."

Seamus brushed away her comment. "Ah, go on — I'd count that angry father as three possibilities."

"You're just trying to pad your betting pool, Seamus, but I don't mind. Listen, can I share any of these with the gardaí? I don't have to say where the ideas came from."

"And you'd deprive us of our boasting rights? You tell them whatever yeh like as long as yeh add who gave it to yeh."

"Okay, then. I'd still guess they've looked at some of these possibilities already, like the hotel staff, but you may have added some new angles. Thank you, and tell your friends thanks as well. And before you ask, there'll be a round of drinks in it for you all — but only if one of your ideas turns out to be right." Maura grinned at him.

"Ah, yer killin' me, darlin'. But I'll hold you to it." Seamus picked up his glass and sauntered back to his pals in the corner.

Now what? Almost closing time. Helen had gone home, giving her a little space — thoughtful of her. Sean was going off on his own, pursuing new theories on his own time. Did his boss approve? Was he doing it to score points with his new sergeant or with Detective Hurley? She didn't want to see Sean walk into something unexpected, but she didn't think there was a crazed killer wandering in the woods at Crann Mor. It seemed to her that John was the actual target of the attack, if there had been one, but she had no clue who would have done it. And as Seamus had neatly outlined, there were a lot of possibilities, along with a lot of motives.

Mick joined her behind the bar. "I can cover if yeh want to go home."

"No, I should stay — I was out for a lot of the day. You can go."

"It was a slow day, and the evenin's no better. I'm not tired."

"Then send Rose and Jimmy home. I can't keep paying three people to serve pints to three other people. That's not good business."

"It'll be better come summer," Mick said. "What with the music now, it's better than it was under Old Mick at the end."

"Well, that's something. Did Bridget have a nice day? I don't see her in the village very often, much less in Sullivan's."

"She felt up fer it today, but she may pay the price tomorrow. It takes a lot out of her

222

these days."

"I can stop by in the morning. By the way, does she, uh, know about last night? Us, I mean. Did she say anything to you?"

"About what two people may do alone in the dark, yeh mean? She's lived a long time and seen about everything there is to see between people. If she didn't like it, she'd be one to tell you. She did say something about hearin' me car go by in the night. If she says nothin' to yeh, I'd guess she's all right with it. Will you be askin' her about what she thinks?"

His direct gaze — and the questions that came with it — made Maura uncomfortable. "I haven't decided yet. She's a friend, and I don't want to mess that up. And I don't want to talk about it right now."

Mick gave her a long look that she couldn't read, then gathered up his jacket and left. She still had no idea what he was thinking. If she was the type to bet, would she put her money on a one-night stand or the start of something more with Mick?

NINETEEN

Maura finally had to shoo Seamus and his cronies out of Sullivan's just past eleven, but they went without grumbling. She tidied up the main room and decided to wait until morning to do any real cleaning. It would be easier to see the dirt by daylight. It would also be more depressing. Maybe some kind leprechaun would show up in the night and make it all disappear.

She drove home carefully, keeping her eyes on the road. Spring brought out a lot of small animals, she'd noticed, and she didn't want to squish a lusty rabbit, or worse, a fox. She arrived home without mishap and let herself in. She'd left a dim light burning, but it did no favors to the old cottage. Was she going to let her mother see where she lived? It probably didn't resemble what a doting mother would wish for her darling daughter.

She climbed the narrow stairs and fell

into bed.

The morning sun woke her, and she lay in bed listening to the birds, plus some baaing of lambs and mooing of cows. Yup, this sure was Ireland. Nothing like Boston, with its constant traffic, round-the-clock lights and sirens, and airplanes flying overhead all the time.

She bounced out of bed and headed for the shower. She'd drop by and see Bridget to make sure she was all right after her excursion to Leap the day before and to tell her about Gillian and the baby. And if Bridget wanted to bring up the maybe relationship between her and Mick, so be it. She wouldn't lie, but she wouldn't start that conversation.

Chicken!

She followed through with her plan, but she found she was nervous when she walked down to Bridget's cottage. Bridget wasn't outside gardening, so Maura knocked. "Bridget? It's Maura." Was Bridget all right? Would she answer? Would she be angry?

It took half a minute, but finally Maura could hear Bridget's shuffling walk, and then the door opened. Maura was holding her breath until she saw Bridget's smile. "Come in, come in. I've just made a fresh pot of tea if yer thirsty." The old woman

225

stepped back to let Maura enter.

"Sure, that sounds good. I just wanted to be sure you were all right this morning — yesterday must have been a busy day for you."

"Ah, I can't spend all my time cooped up here, now can I? It was nice to be out and to see old friends. Would yeh pour, dear? The pot's full, and it's heavy fer me to lift."

"Sure." It was by now a familiar ritual for Maura after a year. Something she didn't want to lose, if Bridget was upset about her and Mick.

Bridget had settled herself in her favorite chair when Maura brought the two steaming cups of tea and set them carefully on the table where the sugar bowl and milk pitcher were already waiting. When Maura sat, she wasn't sure where to start, but luckily Bridget made that decision for her.

"Mick's told me about yer mother arrivin'."

Maura nodded. Of course he had. "It was really a big surprise. Since she arrived, I've been thinking about everything Gran ever said about her, and it wasn't much. Did Gran ever write anything to you about her?"

"We both had busy lives and not much time fer the writin' of letters. She let me know when yer father died, God rest his soul, and then when yer ma went off. I'd ask now and then if there'd been any word of her, but after a while I stopped askin'. Yeh never heard from her?"

Maura shook her head. "Never. And I guess I'm kind of mad that she just showed up here after all this time without trying to get in touch since she left."

"Mebbe she was afraid you wouldn't want to see her. Would that be true?"

"I'm not sure. And I'm also still not sure she would have told me who she was if the gardaí hadn't wanted to talk to her. She might just have gone home again. To her new family." Maura realized she was sounding bitter and stopped.

"Ah, Maura, let it go. Yeh won't be close, but try to keep her somewhere in yer life."

"I'm trying. The death of her boss has really messed things up. I hope the gardaí find out what happened fast so things get back to normal." With or without Helen. "The guys at the pub have started a betting pool about who killed the guy. They're convinced it's murder, but nobody's pointed to a killer yet."

"And I'm sure they've plenty of ideas."

"You want to get in on the pool?"

Bridget waved a dismissive hand. "I don't know many people around Skibbereen now.

So many are gone. But now that I think on it, my son Timothy's widow works at the hotel now — or did, last I'd heard. She started in the kitchens years back."

"She's still there?" Maura asked.

"She is. She's long since moved up from the kitchens, though. Some kind of manager, I'm told. I never knew her well — me son married late, and he's dead these ten years."

"I'm sorry. Not Mick's father?" She stopped: she'd been the one to bring up Mick's name. Should she backtrack now?

"No. Her husband, he'd be my second son."

Maura realized she'd never heard Mick talk about his family, apart from the one sister and of course his grandmother. What was it with all these closemouthed people? Irish folk either spent hours laying out their family tree for you, going back generations, or pretended they had sprung up like a mushroom with no family at all. Not that she was any better, but at least she had good reason to be clueless about her past.

"Does this woman go by Nolan now?"

"She never did, and she might have married again. Yeh'd have no trouble findin' out."

"Bridget . . ." Maura began but couldn't

find the right words to continue. She sneaked a glance at Bridget, who was watching her with bright eyes, a small smile on her face.

"If it's to do with Mick, it's not my place to tell you what you should do. Nor him. But . . ." Now Bridget was fumbling for words.

"I don't know that this is going anywhere," Maura rushed to say. "I mean, it kind of happened, but maybe for the wrong reasons. I'm not very good at these things. With men, I mean."

Now Bridget was shaking her head. "It's not you I worry about; it's my foolish grandson. He's a good man, but he's shut himself off since . . . Well, I've said it before, he's the one to tell yeh. Or not, if that's his choice. Just don't get in too deep, love."

More secrets. This was getting ridiculous. "But you're not upset with me?"

"And why would I be? I've known yeh all yer life, if only by mail. Yer grannie raised yeh, and yeh've turned out well, and Mick could do worse. Just take things slow, will yeh?"

Maura found herself smiling, if reluctantly. "I can do that. After all, that's how things are done around here, right? Slowly?"

"That they are. Now pour me another cup

and tell me all about Gillian and the baby."

"Well, I have to say it was interesting . . ." Maura began. Half an hour later, she looked at her watch and realized that she'd better head for the pub — she wasn't sure who was there to open today. It had been a rather jumbled week, and the scheduling had suffered.

"Bridget, I'd better get going. Do you want to see Gillian and the baby?"

"If she's up fer it. It's been some years since I saw one so young. When will she be home?"

"Today, I think. I don't know how long hospitals expect new mothers to stay these days. But the creamery is far from ready for the three of them."

"Ah, no matter. When babies're so little, they can sleep in a basket or a drawer, as long as they're safe and warm. They've a bit of time to get ready. Pity that Eveline never had a chance to see the child. She would have been happy."

"Even if Harry isn't married to Gillian?" Maura felt awkward asking, but she wanted to know.

Bridget brushed away the question. "Ah, Eveline wouldn't have minded. And times have changed. There's no shame in it now.

Did Gillian put Harry's name on the certificate?"

Did that make a difference? Maura didn't even know what the laws were in the States about who went on a birth certificate. "I have no idea, but I can find out. I'll ask Gillian when she's ready to come by."

"I'll see yeh out. If I sit fer too long, me joints get stiff."

Maura waited while Bridget pulled herself from her chair, then took Bridget's arm to steady her as they walked toward the door, tucking her hand under her elbow. When Bridget opened the door, she gave Maura's arm a squeeze. "Mick'd be lucky to have yeh, but only if it suits the both of yeh."

"Thank you, Bridget." Impulsively, Maura gave Bridget a quick hug, then turned and left quickly, relieved. Bridget was okay with her and Mick, whatever they had between them. If anything. But they were the ones who had to figure it out.

She felt much more cheerful as she drove toward Leap and realized that Bridget's approval must have mattered to her more than she had wanted to admit. Living in rural Ireland had pluses and minuses, and they were kind of one and the same: everybody knew your business — financial, romantic, and other. Mostly everyone didn't judge too harshly, and they were there for you if you needed help, but it was kind of claustrophobic. She was still getting used to it.

Of course, when she arrived at Sullivan's, Mick was the only other person there, but Maura felt ready to deal with their . . . whatever.

"Hey," she said. "I couldn't remember who was supposed to clean up today, so I came on in. Did we ever make up a schedule for this week?"

"Do we ever? Mostly it's not a problem until the weekend."

"True. I stopped by to see Bridget. She seemed to be in good form, so I guess she didn't overdo it yesterday."

"I'm glad to hear that. Thanks."

An awkward silence fell until Maura started giggling.

"What?" Mick asked, looking confused.

"We are ridiculous — the two of us. If this were a crappy movie, this would be the moment when we rip each other's clothes off and do it on the floor despite a crowd pounding on the door for their pints. Or maybe they'd be enjoying the show."

"That floor's pretty hard," Mick commented, smiling.

"What? You've tried it out?"

"That I have not. Are we good?"

"I think we are." For now, at least.

Twenty

Maura's cell phone rang before the pub opened. *Gillian?* Maura answered quickly. "Everything all right? Where are you?"

"Back at Mycroft House with my adorable squalling bundle. This is incredibly stupid, but I seem to have the wrong size of nappies. I hate to drag you away from your lovely pub, but could you swing by Costcutter and pick up some? I think I need the ones for three to six months since the newborn size is a joke on my little guy."

"Uh, yeah, sure. Monday's usually a slow day. Where's Harry?"

"He checked us out of hospital this morning and then he drove us here. He said he had to meet a client and he'd bring back lunch. I do hope this isn't a sign of things to come — I could really use another pair of hands here. I wouldn't ask you to run errands for me, and I promise I won't be ringing you every hour, but I don't feel comfortable driving yet. It takes a while to pack up the young master and install him in the car seat, which — by the way — we have only one, and it's a pain to swap it out. And who holds Henry while I'm fastening all the buckles and such?"

Gillian really was in a state and babbling. "Slow down, Gillian," Maura said, "and take a deep breath. I will go find some diapers, uh, *nappies,* for you and bring them by — shouldn't be more than half an hour. How many do you need?"

"Like I know!" Gillian's voice was tinged with hysteria. "Just buy as many as they've got that're bigger than newborn, and I'll figure it out later. Thanks, Maura. You're a lifesaver." At what sounded like a mewling cat in the background, Gillian added hurriedly, "Gotta go. See you soon!" and hung up.

Maura didn't know whether to feel amused or dismayed that Gillian seemed so unprepared for the messy tasks of motherhood. "Baby issues already?" Mick said with a half smile after Maura had put away her phone.

"We'll, she's new at all this. I've got to go find nappies for her. Him. Whatever. Can you cover?"

"Go on with yeh. I'll be fine here."

Maura grabbed up her jacket from where she'd thrown it over a chair and headed up the street to the Costcutter, where, thank goodness, they had diapers in a variety of sizes. She wondered what else Gillian didn't know she needed. Maybe Harry would be back soon and he could make the next supply run — he'd better get used to it.

Bearing her bulky prize in a large plastic bag, Maura retrieved her car and drove the mile or so to Mycroft House, where Gillian was waiting at the door.

"Thank God! This infant is leaking all over the place." Gillian snatched the bag from Maura, then went into the back parlor. While a couple of generations of Townsend ancestors looked on from the portraits on the walls, Gillian laid Henry out on a blanket she'd spread on the threadbare oriental carpet, stripped off his soggy diaper, and swapped it for a dry one. "There you go, my lamb. That should hold you for about an hour." Henry did not respond, unless blowing bubbles counted.

Gillian slumped next to her son. "Do I have to get up?" she whined.

"I don't care." Maura sat cross-legged on the rug. "I thought you had this figured out."

Gillian made an unladylike noise. "Does

any new mother? The ones who don't have a nanny waiting in the wings? Don't worry; I'll work it out. It's only that it's been so mad lately, what with the house, trying to get the creamery into some sort of shape, Harry trying to find himself work, and the baby coming. Oh, damn, now I'm crying again. I do it about every fifteen minutes. All those leftover hormones." Gillian pulled out her none-too-clean shirttail and wiped off her face.

"No word from your family?"

"Heaven forbid! I have heaped shame on the house of Callanan! Which is ridiculous in this day and age. Even the hospital has provided for unmarried parents — there's a separate line on the certificate for the birth father if you're not a legally recognized couple. It's not like the bad old days under the Magdalens."

"The what?"

"It was a group of asylums that took in so-called fallen women and made them do laundry while telling them they were criminals and evil, and most had to give up their babies. It only ended about twenty years ago. Not one of Ireland's brightest episodes. Oh, look, the little darling's asleep. That should last until the nappy fills up again. Tell me the real world's still rolling along out there?"

"The guys at the pub have started a betting pool on who killed John Byrne, assuming it wasn't an accident. Still no confirmation from the gardaí."

"How many choices are there?"

"About a dozen, at last count."

"You're kidding!" Gillian wasn't looking at Maura, but rather at the baby, who looked like almost every other baby Maura had ever seen. Which wasn't many. He had a full head of dark hair, and apparently all the other working parts.

"Nope." Maura proceeded to outline the list that they guys had put together. "And that list doesn't even include a random psychopath wandering in the woods in the dark with an itch to kill someone. Or an animal, for that matter. If a bull got loose from somewhere nearby, would it head for the woods? And if it did, would it charge anything that looked like a threat and knock him down the hill?"

"A guy in a nice suit? This is Ireland — I'm sure a bull would attack him without a second thought. Ah, Maura, you're cheering me up, at least."

"That's good. I should feel bad that we're making jokes about a guy who's dead, but it's not like it was someone we knew. Did you tell me you'd been to Crann Mor?" Maura asked.

"A while ago. I didn't exactly go exploring. No, wait, I remember — I was teaching a class one summer and I took a few of the students onto the public part of the property to try their hand at landscapes. There are some lovely views, but I had to ask the groundskeeper where and how to find them. The paths are well marked, but they don't say 'nice view' anywhere."

"Was the groundskeeper a local man? Assuming he's a he?"

"I think he was from around here. If you read the brochures, the former owners brought in a big-name landscape architect to redesign the place, but he wasn't about to dirty his hands with maintenance, so they kept on whoever had been doing it all along. The groundskeeper had a couple of people working for him — there's a lot of land there, not to mention the lake."

"You know anybody else who works there?"

"I had to ask the manager if my group could ramble about with me. She was helpful. She may still be there."

"Do you remember her name?"

Gillian was staring at the baby again. "What? Oh, her name. Siobhan something or other. It's been a few years. And she might not be there anymore. She was my mother's age."

Infant Henry was beginning to stir. "Will he be hungry, do you think?" Gillian asked anxiously.

"Gillian, I am so the wrong person to ask. You, uh, nursing?"

"If it works. The midwife said it would be best for the baby, and I don't have anything else to do. I assume I'll develop much greater sympathy for cows."

"Well, it is a dairy region," Maura said, grinning.

Gillian started laughing, and Maura joined her, and of course they woke up the baby, and then Harry walked in.

"This is a nice picture. All's well?"

"So far, so good," Gillian said cheerfully. "I think it's feed time. All the time is feed time, when he's not filling his nappy. I had to ask Maura to bring us emergency nappy rations. We really must get organized. How'd your meeting go?"

"Good, I think. I played the sympathy card — told the man that if I sounded incoherent, it was because you'd just had a baby. It seems to have helped."

Maura stood up. "I should get back to the pub — I left Mick there to open. And I'm sure Seamus and his pals are cooking up more crazy ideas. I hope they have enough sense not to go tramping all over the hotel grounds looking for clues or something. I'm not sure the gardaí would like that."

"Just keep filling their pints and they won't leave Sullivan's," Gillian said. Small Henry let out a whimper followed by a wail. "Oopsies, lunchtime. Thanks so much, Maura. I'll be bringing this one around to show him off as soon as the midwife says it's safe to expose him to all those grubby bar hounds."

"You do that. Oh, and Bridget would love to see him. She says it's been a while since she's held a newborn baby."

"Of course. I think we can do that. Right, Harry?"

Harry seemed mesmerized by the sight of Gillian, curled up on the floor holding the baby to her chest. "What? Oh, right, Bridget. Sure, no problem."

"I'll leave you two to deal with . . . whatever."

Harry and Gillian didn't seem to notice her leaving.

Back at Sullivan's, not much had changed. Rose had come in, but Jimmy was nowhere in sight, not that he was needed. Old Billy had arrived and was settled in his usual chair. Maura waved to Mick and Rose, then went over to sit next to Billy.

"I saw Bridget this morning. She's looking forward to seeing Gillian's baby."

"How's the new mother fairin'?"

"Frantic. Confused. Tired. She'll be fine. And Harry's on board, as far as I can see."

"There's many who've sorted things out before — nothin' new there. At least there's only the one child. Imagine yer cottage with only a smokin' turf fire to cook on or boil water and four or five small children underfoot. And yer man's out milking the cows or carrying the milk to the creamery."

"I don't even want to try. But didn't families help out?"

"That they did. And the neighbors as well. People got by as best they could."

"Aren't families in Ireland getting smaller?"

"They are." Billy sighed. "When I was a young man, havin' a lot of children was common, and the houses and townlands were filled with them running about. Now? The townlands are quieter."

Maura tried to remember the last time she'd seen a child near her cottage and came up blank. The world had changed, even here in rural Ireland.

"Do you need anything else, Billy?"

"Nah, I'm grand."

Back at the bar, there was little to do. Mick came out of the back room, which reminded her to ask, "We've got music this weekend, right? Friday?"

Rose spoke quickly. "We do, and I've already pushed it online and on social media."

Whatever that meant. Maura was glad that Rose had a handle on advertising. "Thanks, Rose. I've been thinking I should learn how to do all that stuff, but you beat me to it. Jimmy planning to come in today?"

Rose shrugged. "I've no idea. Judith's got him runnin' in circles, and half the time he hides where she can't find him."

Maura went into the back room, not because there was anything she needed to do there, but because she wanted to keep busy. The bar in that room needed some restocking, but she assumed Mick had noticed that. The place was reasonably clean and would get another pass before the event on Friday — not that any of the music lovers would notice dirt on the floor or cobwebs hanging from the balconies in the dim light. It was atmosphere. Maybe she should be adding spiders rather than swatting them to increase the "authenticity" of the space.

That thought brought her back to John

Byrne. Bridget and then Gillian had mentioned they had known some of the people who worked at Crann Mor. Surely the gardaí had looked at the staff, but it wouldn't hurt to double-check. She couldn't exactly ask an employee who was who at the hotel, but maybe her mother had gotten ahold of the staff lists, past and present? It wouldn't hurt to confirm. Before she could overthink it, she pulled out her phone and hit redial.

TWENTY-ONE

Helen answered quickly. "Maura? How are you? I was wondering if I'd hear from you."

"I'm fine. Look, I've got some questions about the hotel, and I thought maybe you'd have some answers. Can we have lunch?"

"I'm at the hotel now. Do you want to come here to eat?"

"Might as well, I guess. I didn't get much of a chance to look around the last time I was there."

"Twelve all right? I doubt we'd need reservations — things are pretty slow right now."

Gee, I wonder why? Could it be the dead body found on the grounds?

"Twelve is good. I'll meet you in the lobby."

Now Maura had an hour to fill before she was going to meet Helen at the hotel. She was pleased to see Sean Murphy at the door and waved him in. Maybe he had some news? She couldn't quite read his expression — it was kind of a cross between dejected and determined. She nodded him toward an empty table in the corner, where she joined him. "Can I get you anything? Are you on duty?"

"Coffee would be grand. Right now we're all on duty until John Byrne's death is settled, but I think I'm callin' our talks part of my investigation. Like with yer ma last night."

Maura turned back toward the bar and signaled to Rose to bring Sean a coffee. "Did she give you something to think about?" she asked as they sat.

He shook his head. "Her idea about this Harvard place was golden, but I haven't had time to follow up. We've been busy talkin' to the staff and guests at the hotel, but no one saw anything. No word from the coroner yet, but we could hear today or tomorrow. Not soon enough for the sergeant, though — he's after pushin' this as murder, and he's treatin' it like a crime. Tryin' to make his mark, I'm guessin'."

"He seems an odd choice for the Skibbereen station," Maura said carefully.

Sean looked around at the nearest tables, but nobody seemed to be paying attention to them. "I hate to be spreadin' gossip, but word is he was sent to us to cool down, not that we aren't glad to have another man. Seems he was a bit hard on a suspect back in Limerick with a bad outcome."

"Is that going to be a problem here? I mean, even in the short time I spent with him, I got the impression that he wasn't exactly patient and wanted to move faster with this investigation."

"So he does. I don't think he's ever lived in the country, so he doesn't know our ways."

"What does Detective Hurley think?"

"He's givin' him his head fer now. To be fair, the investigation would be little different no matter what label we slapped on it. We'd be doin' the same things, askin' the same questions of the same people. I'm only hopin' Sergeant Ryan doesn't make too many enemies in Skibbereen along the way by rubbin' people the wrong way."

Rose set a cup of coffee in front of Sean, dimpled, and went back to the bar. When she was gone, Maura asked, "So, no suspects?"

Sean shook his head. "Not a one. Still seems odd to me, though, that there's so little known about his past. Even by the people who worked with him. But I'm still lookin'. Yeh'll let me know if yeh hear anything?"

"Sure. Must be frustrating for you. I'd better get back to work — I'm heading over to have lunch with my mother at the hotel soon. Good luck to you!"

Once again she would be underdressed for the place, but Crann Mor would just have to take her the way she was. Besides, she wanted to get a look at where John Byrne had died three days earlier in relation to the building where he had been staying, and it was bound to be muddy. She wondered briefly if Helen had brought rubber boots with her and snorted. Not likely. But if Crann Mor was as a good a hotel as it claimed to be, surely they'd have some they could lend her. After all, they sent people out fishing on their little lake, didn't they?

Leaving Mick and Rose to deal with any customers who might wander in on a Monday at midday, she retrieved her car and drove to Skibbereen, or rather *around* Skibbereen, to get to Crann Mor. Who were the O'Donovans who had given it up? Any relation? At the moment, she didn't know any living O'Donovans with real money, although they were still mentioned any time the name of Leap came up in talk at the pub. The popular local mythology was that some long-ago O'Donovan had convinced his horse (*How?* she often wondered) to leap over the small river leading to the harbor in order to escape pursuing Englishmen. Maybe the river had been even smaller back then. Or it had been one really strong horse.

When Maura walked into the hotel lobby, Helen was standing in the middle looking critically at the space, and she didn't even notice Maura approaching.

"Sizing it up?" Maura asked when she was close.

Helen turned quickly and smiled at her. "I guess I was just fantasizing about what could be done with the place to bring it up to contemporary standards. I think the last remodel was about fifty years ago. I'm glad you caught me, though — since we talked, we've scheduled a meeting for this afternoon."

"Who's we?" Maura said, following her toward the restaurant.

"The JBCo people and the upper management of the hotel. I won't say we've made any decisions yet, but we're looking at various options."

"Your crowd does own the place, right?"

"Yes, we do, paid in full. We could probably unload it again without any significant financial loss, but we aren't yet sure that we want to do that." Once they were seated, menus in hand, Helen asked, "I assume you had something specific to talk about?"

Had Helen been hoping for girl talk? "Yes. I've been talking to some friends around here to see what they know or remember about this place, and I realized there are things I haven't asked."

"Does this have something to do with John's death?" Helen asked.

"Kind of. For example, I have no idea how many people there are on the staff or who's running what here. I know the gardaí have talked to the current employees, and I want to see if I know any of them or if my friends do. The other thing is, I'd like to take a look at the place where John fell. I've never taken the tour, and I don't know what the layout is apart from what you've told me. Will you have time to show me that before your meeting?"

"I think so — it's a large site, but there aren't that many paths. You weren't planning to take off through the woods?"

"No, I just wanted to get a sense of distances and things like that. Anyway, I know we ate in the restaurant here before, but I was kind of distracted. What else would you recommend to eat here?" Maura read the menu and had to stop herself from laughing. *Burnt Apple? Sprouting Broccoli?* At least the desserts sounded good — if they had time for that.

"You like fish? Because the salmon with asparagus is great."

"That works for me."

The waitress took their order and slipped silently away. "Anything in particular you wanted to know about the staff?" Helen asked.

"I guess I want to know more about how things are organized here. I mean, is there an inside staff and an outside staff, and are they run by the same people? Is the billing and accounting done in-house? How big is the kitchen staff? Is any group shorthanded or overstaffed? And I guess most important, is anybody worried about their job, or were they before John died, and will his death make a difference?"

Helen laughed. "Good heavens, Maura, you don't ask for much, do you? Luckily, you've come to the right person. I know the police have a current staff list, but it occurs to me that I can pull up the staffing reports for the past few years on my laptop — we put those together when we were considering the purchase and reviewing their financial status — and I can give you printouts and also tell you where we were talking about making changes to the current staff, which isn't on any list. Since we'd never been on-site before, we didn't get around to speaking with the managers or any other employees to ask them for their opinions. Hence today's meeting, although things will have changed since we first started thinking about it."

"You actually do that? Talk to staff, I mean?"

"Yes, we do. This is a relatively small operation here compared to some of our hotels. But the underlying philosophy is the same: we want our guests to feel welcome and comfortable, and that means our staff has to be happy with their responsibilities, pay grade, and job security. I do know that this part of West Cork is a fairly close-knit community with a lot of personal connections that we don't always see when we walk in cold."

Maura gave her points for having done her research. "Like the fact that half the people around here are named O'Donovan?"

Helen smiled. "Yes, things like that. We try to be sensitive to details, even though it isn't always easy. Otherwise we'd end up as no better than a decent Hilton or Marriott back in the States. We want to offer something more special, or at least that was the plan."

"That makes sense to me. So, who keeps this place running? Who's the top staff?"

The waitress appeared with their dishes, and Helen insisted that Maura take the time to really taste her food. Maura was glad she did, because she'd never met a piece of salmon that tasted anything like this dish. She'd always believed it was just orange chunks of blah the few times she'd eaten it before. This version was in a different league.

"You've got a very good chef here, if nothing else," Maura finally managed to say.

"I believe the owners have recruited regularly from the Ballymaloe Cookery School not far from here. Do you know it?"

"Seriously? I've heard the name, and that's it. So it's the real thing?" She remembered Rose mentioning it in a reverent tone.

"Definitely. You like your fish?"

"I think it's more than like. If I was a dog, I would be rolling in it."

Helen smiled. "That is high praise indeed."

"You know, I would love to bring Rose over to see the restaurant. She's worked in the pub for a couple of years now, but she'd really like to cook for more than just her father."

"Well, if we get things cleared up, maybe we can bring her over for a meal — on the company, of course. I know the prices are beyond the reach of most of the people who live here."

"They sure are." Maura decided to concentrate on her food and wait to try to figure out the administrative structure of the place. Helen would give her staff lists, old and new, and she could look them over later. Right now, it was more important to see the rest of the site. Even if that meant skipping dessert, she admitted with regret.

Helen was beginning to glance at her watch anxiously, so Maura said, "Look, you can give me the short tour of the grounds and show me where John died. I can figure out the rest for myself — it is open to the public, right?"

Helen looked relieved. "Yes, it is. Thanks, Maura. I wish I could tell you I knew the site well, but as you know, this is my first visit, so all I know is based on looking at diagrams and a quick walk or two. I haven't even been as far as the lake. But I assure you, it's very well maintained to prevent unfortunate . . . accidents."

"Don't worry — I'm pretty sure I can find my way around. You said there weren't a whole lot of paths. Anyway, I'm glad you could make the time for lunch."

"Are you ready to go now? It looks like you enjoyed your food." Helen waved at Maura's now bare and shiny plate.

"I did. I'm not much of a cook, and my place has about as little in the way of cooking options as possible unless I want to crank up the fireplace, which is about six feet tall and ten feet wide."

"I'd love to see that sometime," Helen said wistfully.

"Maybe later," Maura replied. She wasn't ready to let Helen invade her private space . . . yet.

"Shall we go?" Helen said, gathering up her bag.

"Sure. Lead the way."

TWENTY-TWO

Helen took Maura out the back entrance of the hotel. Once outside, she pointed. "This is the formal garden, and it's mainly for the guests. There's a gate in the left wall, and it leads to a walking path that loops around to the right, then veers left toward the lake. Eventually there's a path branches off to the right that would take you to the lake lodge, which also has rooms, mainly for dedicated fishermen. The lake will be to the left, and the land drops off fairly steeply."

"So it's hard to go wrong because this is really the only path in this direction, right?" Maura asked. "Where did John fall?"

"Off the main path, near where the lodge path branches off."

"How was he found? I mean, could you see him from a path?"

"I'm not sure. But he was wearing a dark suit, so he wouldn't be immediately visible in poor light. And it is a steep slope there, or so I'm told."

"Who found him?"

"The groundskeeper, I think — I've forgotten his name, if I ever knew it. Bernard something, I think. I understand he's been working here a long time. He was making one of his usual morning inspections when he saw John."

"How many people actually go walking here?"

"Maura, I have no way of knowing. I'm not sure who keeps records about things like that, if anyone, but I can find out for you if it's important. Or the gardaí will have those details. They talk with you, don't they?"

"Sometimes. And there aren't any security cameras or motion sensors or anything like that?" Maura asked.

"Apparently the prior owners didn't think they were necessary in this part of Ireland, and we haven't even gotten close to thinking about that. So the short answer is no."

Maura saw Helen check her watch again, and she took pity on her. "I'll let you get back to business, and I'll take a look around. I can come by and pick up those staff reports, if you want."

"I'll let you know when they're ready — I won't have time to print them until after

257

the meeting."

"Okay. Thanks for the lunch. It was great." Maura turned, walked briskly toward the fancy garden ahead, and spied the gate Helen had mentioned over to her left. She checked her watch: nearly two. She had no idea how far she had to go, but the place couldn't be too big, could it? She only hoped she could find her way back to her car when she was done.

She had to admit that it was a pretty walk, and it would probably be even nicer in summer. The path was roughly paved and wide enough for two people to walk side by side. There were tall old trees on both sides; the underbrush was low and had obviously been trimmed recently, and the brush had been cleared away. There was no way to get lost unless she deliberately left the path. If there was a moon at night, it might be possible to follow the path without a flashlight. Had there been a moon the night John died? She hadn't noticed.

If this had been back in the States, there would be flapping strands of bright-yellow police tape marking where John Byrne had left the path — forever. Here, there wasn't much to mark the spot. The dirt was churned up, and several branches were broken, most likely from the removal of

John's body, their raw wood showing white. The land sloped down fairly steeply on the left, toward what Maura assumed was the lake, invisible from where she stood. If John had lost his footing in the dark, he would have had a hard time stopping himself. Helen had suggested that he'd fallen quite a way. Had he hit his head at the start or later during his tumble down the hill? And on what? There was no railing, just lot of trees in different sizes. Had the gardaí examined every tree and rock on the way down the hill, looking for evidence?

What the heck was she doing here? Standing on the path, she turned in a full circle and realized she couldn't see any of the buildings on the grounds, including the main hotel and the lodge Helen had talked about in the opposite direction. This particular spot was isolated, all right. If John had not fallen accidentally — still a big if — then it was unlikely that he had just happened on somebody at this spot. More likely, someone had followed John until they came to a place where they would be unobserved, or that person had asked to meet him here — which mean his killer probably knew the path. So would this have been a spur-of-the-moment killing? Or had somebody planned it?

But Maura kept circling around to the "Why?" Why would anyone want John Byrne dead? Maybe he was arrogant and too smug, but not many people got killed for that. If it wasn't something in his current life, maybe the answer lay in his early life, as Sean had wondered. Who would know? Had the gardaí found out anything? She should talk to Sean again.

"Can I help yeh, miss?" The voice came out of nowhere, and Maura turned quickly to find a stocky man of late middle age, with a traditional Irish wool cap pulled low on his head and clothes that were shabby and not exactly clean, leaning on a rake. She hadn't even heard him coming.

"Uh, no, I was just looking around," she said.

"Sorry if I startled yeh. I'm Bernard O'Mahoney, the groundskeeper. I look after the place."

"By yourself?" A lot of ground for one man to cover.

"Nah, I've a crew of lads who help out in the warmer months. I can handle it on me own in the winter."

"I'm Maura Donovan. I run Sullivan's in Leap."

"The pub? Ah, yeh're the girl who got it from Old Mick. I've heard yeh're doin' him proud, with the music and all."

"I hope so — I've had a lot to learn. You're the one who found John Byrne's body, right?"

"I am that. A sad thing, it was."

"Was it near here?"

"Right there, in fact." He pointed to the scuffed patch Maura had been looking at. "He were down at the bottom of the hill there, all twisted up."

"Had you seen him out walking before? Because from what people have said, he wasn't exactly into nature walks."

"I seen him only from a distance, save the one time he introduced himself to all the folk workin' here."

"What do you think happened?"

Bernard shrugged. "No idea. He were hurryin' and he slipped? He coulda tripped over something, but there was nothing on the path that morning that coulda tripped him up."

"The gardaí already asked you all this, didn't they?"

"They have done. I couldn't give them much help. What's it to yeh? Did yeh know the man?"

"No, but I know someone who worked for him. I don't have to tell you that there aren't many murders around here, so I guess I was curious to see where it happened."

"So they're callin' it murder now? It's no surprise to me."

"Don't tell the gardaí I said so because it's not official and the coroner hasn't said it yet. Why wouldn't you be surprised?"

"The man didn't belong out here in the dark — he was a city man. Someone musta asked him out here, no? Someone who meant to do him harm."

"Any idea who?"

"I don't move among the guests and such, so I couldn't say who'd taken a dislike to the man."

Maura checked her watch. "Thanks, Bernard. I guess I've seen all there is to see, so I'd better get back to Sullivan's."

"Good luck to yeh with that."

"Stop by some time." Maura turned and retraced her steps to the hotel, but when she glanced back, Bernard was still leaning on his rake, watching her.

Back at the pub, Maura found that surprisingly little had changed. There were few people, but then, it was the middle of the afternoon on a Monday, and there was nothing new about John Byrne's death.

Billy was in his usual seat, right where she'd left him, dozing by the small glowing fire. Rose was behind the bar; Mick wasn't visible anywhere. Maura joined Rose behind the bar.

"Hey, Rose, did I miss anything?"

"I can't say that yeh did. Did yeh have a nice lunch?"

"I did. The menu sounded like a joke, but everything I tasted was wonderful. I'm just glad I wasn't paying for it! Helen said maybe she could find a way to treat us both to a meal there."

"Oh, that would be grand!" Rose looked like someone had just handed her a gift with ribbons on it.

"I'll hold her to it, then. She can probably call it a business expense anyway."

"And was business all the two of yeh talked about?"

"Pretty much. Look, I'll tell you what I told her: I can't deal with John's death or murder or whatever it is and her all at once. I know you miss your mother, Rose, but for all practical purposes I never had one at all. Helen is a stranger to me. We've got a lot of catching up to do."

"I didn't mean to set yeh off, Maura," Rose said stiffly. "I was only askin'. I hope yeh find the time to talk when this is over."

"I hope so too, Rose. But until the gardaí figure things out, it's going to be tense all around."

Rose looked up and smiled broadly. "Speak of the devil — here's the man himself."

TWENTY-THREE

Maura looked up to see Sean Murphy walk in, and he looked as though he was excited but trying to hide it. "Hey, Sean. Do you have news for us?"

"Mebbe. We've found nothin' more about John Byrne the man. Like I told yeh before, passport says he was born in New York, but it's a big place, I'm told, and some people can slip through the cracks. Plus there's no shortage of John Byrnes there."

"Hey, sit down for a couple of minutes, will you?" Maura said. "You've got more to tell, right?"

Sean pulled out a barstool and sat. "Could yeh do me a coffee, Rosie? I might. I'm workin' on yer mother's idea of his Harvard years. She said she'd see if she could get the people there to talk to her — I've had no luck gettin' personal information out of anyone there, but I've confirmed he was there, and that gives us a time and place to look fer the man."

She should check with Helen to see if she'd had any better luck with Harvard. "I saw Helen for lunch, and she said she'd have all the staff lists by the end of the day — she was tied up in a meeting at the hotel this afternoon. The company did their homework when they started thinking about buying the place. Maybe somebody was upset when the place changed hands."

"And maybe it's the wrath of the O'Donovans that John Byrne called down upon his head — the ghosts are still regrettin' they let the place go."

Maura had to smile. Sean was seldom fanciful. "I thought they hadn't owned it for years?" she said, placing his coffee in front of him.

"Oh, a century or more. Truth to tell, I'd have a better time investigatin' whether one of them rock stars who played here back a few years was outbid by Byrne's company and looked to get him out of the way."

"I suppose it's possible. But that list of Helen's could help. She said she'd give me a copy as soon as she got it printed out. I'll pass it on to you. I wish I could help you more, Sean. It sounds like you've covered most of the bases. Helen said her meeting this afternoon was going to be between

JBCo and the senior staff at the hotel. They want to kick around ideas about where to go from here, starting with whether to keep Crann Mor or cut their losses now. Nothing's settled yet, though."

"Will they hold on to the place and run it, do yeh think?"

Maura shook her head. "I can't say. I honestly think they don't know yet. Helen thought they could sell it again without losing money, but they don't seem to be in any hurry to do that. Maybe there are other issues."

"The bottom line's not just the money, then?"

Maura hadn't thought of that. "Maybe not." But what else could there be? Maybe Helen could fill her in about the early discussions about buying the place if she'd been part of them. But it sounded to her like John Byrne had told people only what he wanted them to know. "What happens next?" Maura asked.

"We keep talkin' to people. There's plenty of staff, and they have different schedules, so it might be somebody saw something but had the next day or two off and hasn't told us yet. Mebbe some staff will remember something they didn't think was important the first time we talked to them. Helen's lists might give us some more names."

"I went out after lunch and looked at where John Byrne fell. Tell me this, if you can: If the man was killed there, do you think it was planned or somebody just grabbed the chance?"

"Some part of it had to be planned, else why would Byrne and his killer be there at all?"

"True. Hard to just accidentally bump into someone on a dark path in the woods. Was it a meeting there, or did someone leave the hotel with him? Or follow him?"

Sean sighed. "Maura, I can't tell yeh what I don't know. If yeh've seen the place now, yeh'll know there's not much hope for evidence. The path is paved, and there've been gardeners tidying up the grounds, which they do often. Are we callin' in some great forensic expert from Dublin and askin' if he can look at Byrne's shoes and tell us exactly where he'd been in the last few days? No, for there's nothin' about this case that deserves that kind of attention, time, or expense. The simplest answer is that the man slipped and fell. Yeh can say that someone might have helped him fall, and we're doin' our best to look into that, but we've no motive and no witnesses and no evidence, beyond the man's body itself."

"I'm sorry, Sean. It must be frustrating. If I hear anything useful, I'll let you know." Not that she expected the people who came into the pub to know anything more than the gardaí.

Sean drained his coffee. "Right, I've got to be headin' back fer Skibbereen now."

"Before you go . . ." Maura began, then stopped, not sure what she was trying to say. "It's about your sergeant. He's the one who wants this to be murder, right?"

"That's what he's used to seein'," Sean agreed. "I guess yeh see what yeh want to see. But I can't say he's wrong either."

"I haven't talked to him much, but I have to wonder if his attitude is going to make people around here clam up instead of telling him what he needs to know."

"His attitude or the fact that he's not one of us?" Sean asked.

"Does that really matter? I mean, I'm an outsider, and people talk to me."

"Yes, but we know who yer people are, or were. That matters. And if we know yer people, we know who they knew as well. Do yeh see what I'm getting' at?"

"I think so. It's about the connections, isn't it?" When Sean nodded, Maura went on, "So if Sergeant Ryan saw a drug dealer in town, he'd recognize him for what he was, but if you introduced him to one or another O'Donovan in Leap, he wouldn't know where they fit."

"That's it. Of course, if yeh join the gardaí, there's nothin' to say you'll be posted back home. You could serve anywhere in the country. But servin' in a city with a lot of crime and servin' in a small station like Skibbereen are two different animals."

"Can he adapt, do you think?"

Sean considered for a moment. "If he wants, I'd say. He might come to see the good side of it. At least fewer thugs will try to kill him here."

"There is that," Maura agreed.

"I'd best be on my way. Keep yer ears open." Sean stood up and dropped some coins in the bar.

"You know I will. And good luck!" Maura called out to his retreating back.

Twenty-Four

Mick materialized behind her. "So he's no farther along?"

"No, he's not." Maura pivoted to face him. "Do you think the case will stay open forever? Like that last case in Schull? Or at some point do the gardaí label it an accident and close the file? And how long do they wait?"

Mick shrugged. "I've no idea. But no matter what, yeh've still got the question before yeh: What happens with the hotel?"

"I can ask Helen. She may know more later today — her people were having an all-hands meeting this afternoon with the staff at the hotel, and maybe they'll have a better idea after that."

Late in the afternoon, Seamus came in with some friends, and they settled at their favorite corner table. Seamus approached the bar to collect their pints. "Have we a winner yet?" he asked Maura, grinning.

"Let's say we've eliminated a few, but there's no horse leading the pack yet. Do you have a cutoff date for your pool?"

"We'll give it a few more days."

"If you're all wrong, do I get the pot?"

Seamus laughed heartily. "Mebbe we'll set up a fund for future rounds here. Would that suit yeh?"

"It might. I'll let you know if I get any news, but don't hold your breath. Sean Murphy was in just a while ago, and he had nothing new to say."

She slid four pints across the bar to him, and with skill born of much practice, he carried them over to his mates in the corner without spilling a drop.

The men didn't stay long, claiming farm chores and wives and kids waiting at home. Helen arrived around six and took a stool at the bar; from her expression, Maura guessed she had no secrets to share. "Can I get you something?"

"Coffee, I guess. I'm driving, and I don't want to find myself in trouble with the law for drink driving."

"How'd your meeting go?"

"Better than I'd hoped, I guess. There are some good people on the existing staff, and they've done a respectable job of running the place over the past few years with little guidance. Of course they'd like to keep their jobs, but I think they also care about how things are done, and they're proud of the results. I think they'd be on board with the changes we've suggested."

"Is that enough to convince you to keep the place open?"

"Not by itself, but it does matter. There are definitely things I'd like to see changed, but those aren't deal-breakers. You have to remember that the decision's not up to me. I can only make a recommendation to the investors. Oh, I brought you the lists I promised you — I thought I'd save you the trip." Helen reached into her shoulder bag and pulled out a large manila envelope. "I hope this helps."

"Can I share this with the gardaí?"

"Go right ahead — there are two copies in there. There's nothing confidential. In fact, they'll probably recognize a lot of the people on the lists because most of them seem to come from this area, and many have been there for years. I was somewhat surprised not to see more immigrant names on it, at least among some of kitchen or cleaning staff."

"You sound very American. Around here when there's a job open, people think of their relatives first and friends next. Not

273

that they'd put forward someone who wasn't right for the job, because they have to live with the results. It's a small community."

"I'm coming to appreciate that. You know, it's not what I pictured."

"West Cork? Skibbereen? The townlands?"

"Any of it. I'd seen Dublin, but clearly that's not typical. Your area is very different."

Helen looked tired, Maura thought. "Anything else come out of your meeting?"

Helen sighed. "It's no surprise that the people who work at the hotel want things to go on, preferably just the way they have for the past few years. But our investors usually demand a higher return on their investment than Crann Mor is producing."

That didn't sound promising. "What're the employees like as a group?"

"I'm not sure what you're looking for, Maura. If I was writing a report, I'd say they range in age from their twenties to their sixties. Mostly local with limited ethnic diversity, but you just told me that's typical for this region. Not a high level of education. And a lot of them are related to each other."

"Were there people from outside this area on staff?"

"A few foreigners, mostly kitchen staff and

housekeeping. Frankly, the whole atmosphere felt kind of like an overgrown bed-and-breakfast. It was clean and pretty and comfortable, and everybody was very kind and cheerful and helpful."

"And that's a bad thing?"

"Maura, you asked for my impressions, and I'm telling you what I thought." Helen was beginning to look annoyed. "Nice people, apparently working hard. Just not very polished."

Maura felt her own frustration beginning to simmer. "Then what did John Byrne see in it? And who did he think would want to come and stay here?"

Helen shook her head. "I still don't know. I'll admit that I have to adjust my sights a bit. It's kind of a Catch-22. If I upgrade the place to meet the standards of most of our company's holdings, then the guests will be isolated in their little luxury bubble."

Maura completed Helen's thought. "And that would make it like any other big-name hotel, except when you look out the window, you'll see cows, green fields, and maybe a rainbow if you're lucky. Otherwise it could be anywhere. Why did John Byrne want it?"

Helen sighed. "Maura, I have no idea what John saw in this place. John didn't share his reasons, but he'd usually been right about his acquisitions before, so we followed his lead. Now that he's gone, we have to decide whether it fits the consortium's needs."

"So sell it to somebody who wants that kind of thing. Like you said, your company could cut its losses and never look back. What's it to you?"

Helen seemed to deflate before Maura's eyes. "God help me, I don't know. I started out thinking that I respected John's business skills, and if he saw something here, he knew what he was doing. I thought if I looked hard enough, I'd see it too. But he's gone, and I haven't found it. Could I get a glass of wine? Something white?"

"Sure," Maura said, standing up. She welcomed the break. She stalked over to the bar. "Rose, can you give me a glass of the Chardonnay?"

"Fer yer ma? Looks like things aren't goin' so well," Rose said, reaching for a glass and a bottle.

"I don't have a clue where they're going."

Rose filled the glass and slid it across the bar. "Thanks, Rose," Maura said and went back to the table. When she'd sat down again, she said, "Nobody's forcing your group to keep the place. Maybe it would make a good mental hospital or a government office."

Helen looked blankly at Maura for a few beats, then laughed. "Oh, you're joking. Aren't you?"

Maura shrugged. "All I know is, it won't affect my business here. I told you once before: the people who come in here are local farmers, shopkeepers, tourists in the summer, and lately, music fans. We give them drink and good craic. No frills."

"Crack?" Helen cocked an eyebrow.

Helen really didn't know her Irish market, it seemed. "Talk. Fun. Friendship. You know that old show in the States — *Cheers*? And the theme song? 'Where they're always glad you came'? That kind of feeling. It's comfortable."

"Ah. Do you know, Maura, you're doing the same thing I do but on a very different level. Please don't take that as a putdown. You know your clientele. You know the strengths of this place. You don't try to fancy things up; you simply give people what they want. You may try new things — like the music — but if it doesn't work, you don't lose your shirt. You've got the right idea."

"Uh, thank you? I'm kind of making it up as I go."

"Don't sell yourself short. What you've got is common sense, and you're willing to learn, and to listen to people. And, I'd guess, willing to ask for help and ask questions if you think you need to. You'd be surprised how rare that is."

"Well, apply that to your place. Who do you want for customers? I'd bet it's not the same as for the people who stay at your Dublin hotel."

"And you'd probably be right." Helen drained her glass quickly. "You've given me a lot to think about. I want to sleep on this and talk to some of my own staff members back in the States, get them to look at our overall portfolio. They may not want to be flexible about this, but it might be worth it to try to persuade them."

"If you decide you want to keep the place," Maura said. "Have you?"

When Helen finally answered, she seemed to have changed direction. "You know, when I married your father, Tom, I knew he was a farm boy, but I had no idea what that really meant. From what he said, he and his family didn't get into town much, much less go to Cork or Dublin. When he felt nostalgic, it was the home farm he'd talk about, the people he knew back here. I was always amazed how often Tom found connections in Boston, even four degrees removed. You know, one guy knew the man who'd sold this other man the boat he used for fishing, and that man had sold the fish to a third man, whose sister ran a restaurant in town. That kind of thing."

Maura had to smile. "You've got that right. I've given up trying to figure out how they all do it, so I just listen and admire it. It's simplest to say that everybody knows everybody else — or at least a relative, which is good enough."

"Do you feel like you fit in here, Maura?"

Helen appeared to be serious, and Maura didn't want to give her a flippant answer. "It bothered me when I got here that everybody knew so much about me and I didn't know anything about them. But I guess I've come around, and now I appreciate it. It makes a difference that people accept me here. Welcome me, actually. Otherwise, I might have been on the next plane back to Boston."

"You're lucky. Your grandmother did right by you, I think, sending you here. She knew you'd need this kind of support. And don't tell me you're independent, because that's obvious. But everybody needs other people in their lives, whether they're family, friends, or lovers. You're lucky to have that. I wish I'd understood that better when I was your age."

"So do I," Maura said softly.

As Helen got up to leave, Maura remembered Harvard. "You didn't get a chance to call Harvard today, did you?"

"Sorry, no. It's been a busy day. The meeting ate up the afternoon, and now it's too late. I'll do it first thing in the morning. Good night, Maura." After an awkward pause, Helen laid her hand on Maura's arm, then turned and left.

Why do I feel so sad? Maura asked herself before pulling out her cell phone and calling Sean Murphy.

He answered after two rings. "Maura, have you something new?"

"Helen just dropped off that list she was talking about, and she made a copy for you. You want to come pick it up? Or I can drop it off in the morning."

"We're starvin' for any new facts — I'll stop by now if that suits yeh."

"Fine. See you soon." Maura opened the envelope and scanned the list, but the names didn't mean much to her. The surnames were familiar, of course, because a lot of people shared them around Skibbereen. The cover page was a summary of staffing numbers year to year without names attached, and it was kind of interesting to see how many people worked behind the scenes in a large hotel, even one that wasn't up to the snooty standard of JBCo.

Was there anything about the state of the hotel or its staff that could have led to John Byrne's death? Why had he been interested in a place that was so far outside his usual standard? It was hard to imagine that anyone who worked at Crann Mor could see any advantage to killing the man — he hadn't been acting on his own but for his investors, who without John to defend the place would be likely to turn around and sell it again. But how could it be something personal?

Maura shook her head. She simply did not have enough information to work with. Time to consult her secret resource: Old Billy, who knew more about who was who in West Cork than anyone else. Maybe he'd see something she hadn't. She made her way over to where he sat; he looked like an old dog, dozing in front of the fire, but she knew there was little he missed. He opened his eyes when she approached. "Yeh've had a busy day, Maura Donovan."

"Yes, and a confusing one. Too much information and not enough. Or maybe just not the right kind. Can I ask a favor?"

"Of course yeh may. I'm happy to help. What do yeh need?"

"Helen brought me a list of employees at the hotel for the past few years. If you've been listening, you know Sean and the gardaí have been through the current employee list and found nobody who had any connection to John Byrne, much less wanted him dead. I got to wondering if maybe there was someone who worked there a while back, who might have been fired or something, who might have a grudge."

"And yer askin' if I'd take a look at the names and see if anyone jumps out? I'm glad to, but I've had little to do with the grand hotel in the past. Will yeh let me take it home wit' me so I can read it over me supper?"

"Sure. Helen gave me a second copy for Sean, and he's coming by to pick it up soon. It doesn't really mean anything to me. I'm hoping you can do better."

"I'll do me best, but me memory's not what it once was," Billy said.

"Ha! You remember more about local history and families than the rest of Leap combined. But I won't be disappointed if nothing clicks for you."

Maura helped him out of his chair, wondering if it was time to get at least a new seat cushion. His favorite chair seemed to get lower every time she looked. Once Billy was up, she handed him a copy of the list and escorted him to the door. She watched as he made his slow way to his place at the far end of the building.

Twenty-Five

As Billy disappeared through the door to his home, Maura saw that Sean Murphy had arrived, so she stepped back. "That was fast!"

"I came by fer that list. We're that hard up for facts."

"Let's sit down if you have the time," she said and led him to the table that she and Helen had vacated. "You want something to drink, or are you on duty?"

"The inspector has given us the night off, seein' as there's nothing in hand to investigate at the moment. I didn't wait to see what the sergeant had to say to that. A glass of Guinness would suit me fine."

Maura signaled to Rose, who started filling two glasses. Maybe he was off duty, but Sean wasn't going to overindulge, asking for the smaller glass rather than the larger pint. Or maybe he was in a hurry to read the list.

Helen's envelope was still on the table where she'd left it, so she pushed it across to Sean, but he made no move to open it. Rose deposited the two glasses in front of them, then retreated quickly.

"So it's yer mother gave you this?" Sean asked carefully.

"Yes."

"Yeh're gettin' along, then?"

Maura almost laughed. Why was it that everybody was asking about how she felt about her mystery mother popping up in West Cork? Because they cared? Or was it just a good story? "We're doing okay. In an odd way, it's a good thing we have John Byrne's death to talk about — it's kind of neutral ground."

"But yeh're givin' her a fair chance?"

"Yes, Sean, I hope I am. I've only known her for three days now."

"Maybe yer showin' off, just a bit, with your helpin' the gardaí?"

That got Maura's attention, and she looked Sean in the eye. "What, you think I'm trying to impress her with my brilliant crime-solving skills? Look, Mom, the baby you walked away from now owns her own business and home, and by the way, she solves murders in her spare time. Aren't you proud?"

"Well, if you put it that way . . ." Sean looked down into his glass, and Maura suspected he was hiding a smile. She had to admit it did sound silly.

"Oh, all right," she finally said. "Maybe I'm trying to convince her that I've done just fine without her."

"And yeh have indeed. But let's keep lookin' at that death, can we?"

Maura sighed. "Sure. Nothing new since we talked earlier?"

He shook his head. "Yeh've looked at this list — do yeh see anything in it?"

"Not yet, but I'm the new kid here, remember? I gave Billy Sheahan a copy too. He's taken it home to read."

Sean nodded once. "Most of the time, I'd jump all over yeh fer handin' a civilian a piece of evidence, but I can see why yeh did it."

"Well, we still don't know it's evidence. It's just a few pieces of paper. But Billy knows half the people in Cork, and he's probably related to half of those." Then Maura stopped. Something Bridget had said earlier, something about a mother and a daughter . . . "Sean, can I run something by you?"

"Of course."

"You've told me you haven't had much

luck finding anything about John Byrne's background, right? Well, I was talking to Bridget Nolan yesterday morning. She said she'd never been inside the hotel, but that the wife of her son — the one who died, not Mick's father — had worked there and that she might be under a different last name than Nolan. And that gets me thinking — maybe John grew up under a different name? Maybe he was adopted or something?"

Sean rubbed his hands over his face, and Maura thought he looked tired. "So now yeh're tellin' me to look for a man whose original name we don't even know? Only his age, if he gave the right one, and that he came from New York, if he wasn't lyin' about that. Are yeh sure yeh're trying to help us? Let's hope that Billy will give us a push in the mornin'." Sean yawned, drained his glass, and stood up. "I'm desperate fer sleep — I should go."

"Of course." Maura walked him to the door. "Good night, Sean."

Maura picked up the two glasses from the table and delivered them to Rose behind the bar. "Where the heck is everybody?"

"On this side of the bar or the other? Me da's off doin' whatever, and I surely hope you don't pay him fer the time he isn't here.

Mick said somethin' about repairing somethin' at his gran's but promised he'd be back before the evening rush." Rose looked around the room and giggled. "I'm not sure if the two of us can handle this crowd." There were four men in the room and one woman who'd come in with one of the men.

Maura sat down on one of the stools. "I need a coffee, if you don't mind. And we should think about eating something."

"Of course, boss." Rose flashed a smile and started making a cup. "I'll pick something up soon as the coffee's done."

"Thanks, Rose." Maura hesitated, then said carefully, "I'm worried about Jimmy." When Rose flashed her a look, Maura amended that. "I mean, about replacing him. I don't expect him to want to keep working here forever. It's clear he's not exactly happy."

"Ah, that's just his way. He's no happier anywhere else," Rose said as she handed Maura the coffee mug.

"I don't doubt it. He's never going to make employee of the month here at Sullivan's. But I need a minimum number of people working here regularly — people who I can count on to show up and keep our patrons served and happy. And don't say you'll do it. I want to see you doing

288

something more with your life than handing out drinks from behind the bar."

"Oh, and now yeh've got me life planned out for me?" Rose said, raising an eyebrow but smiling.

"No. I can't tell you what to do. I just hope you can find something more . . . I don't know — rewarding? — than working here."

"I've been thinking . . ." Rose suddenly became very busy polishing the bar counter. "There's this place that's opened up in Skib, a combination restaurant and cookery school across from the Eldon. They give cooking classes, and I might like to try one or two. Mebbe learn a bit about how a real restaurant works."

"That's a great idea!" Maura said quickly.

"I could probably fit my schedule here around the classes," Rose added, looking hopeful.

"Rose, we can work it out. Just let me know what you need. But actually, I'm talking about a bigger problem than just your hours. We're going to need more staff here when the weather gets nicer and the tourist season starts, especially if the music takes off. But I haven't any idea how to recruit anyone. And I can't cover any more than I already am."

"I can ask around," Rose said. "Might be that you won't find the likes of us again — yeh know, the ones who stay around fer years for lousy pay — but there's plenty who'd like a job fer a while. Or there's visitors, tourists who want a way to just hang out here fer a bit, especially in the summer when yeh need help most. Anybody can pull a pint, and there's no call fer mixin' those fancy cocktails here. Maybe yeh'd like to find some Americans?"

Maura was staring at her. "Rose, you are wasted on this place. Those are great ideas. Anyway, this doesn't have to happen today, but if you run into anybody you think would fit, tell me, and I'll talk to them. And maybe we could do something with those rooms upstairs, if they need a place to stay, at least for a while."

"That's grand, Maura," Rose said enthusiastically.

Business picked up a bit after dark. Mick came in, and Rose went out to find something for their supper. Seamus and his gang were conspicuously absent — maybe they knew that John Byrne's death was still an open case, and they'd be sure to hear from someone if that changed. Maura guessed they'd be in fast enough once there was a solution, demanding their reward.

"No Jimmy today?" Mick asked when there was a lull.

"Not a sign of him. That's going to be a problem when we get busier. I was talking to Rose about it, and she had some good ideas about where to find more staff, or at least short-timers." She realized she'd created the perfect opening to ask Mick what his long-term plans were, but she didn't want to hear a negative answer, not right now. She shifted subjects quickly. "Rose said you were fixing something at Bridget's place?"

"I was, and just checking things out, now that winter's past. It's easy to forget how old the building is, but things keep wearing out and need to be looked after. Nothing big, though."

"She's still got the old stove," Maura commented.

"She does. And why not? There's little to go wrong wit' them, and she knows how it works. The kettle's always on fer a guest."

"Is it okay if Gillian visits her with the baby?"

"I told you as much, did I not?" Mick said, his tone surprisingly curt.

What was that about? "You know, Rose and I talked earlier about recruiting people to help Harry fix up the creamery so it's livable. We should be doing that sooner rather than later — they can't stay in Mycroft House much longer. Did I tell you about my idea of calling on some of the guys here to help out or chip in for what they need? I talked it over with Rose. What's the best way to do that?"

"Talk to Seamus. He seems to be the ringleader here. I'll do my part, but somebody's got to stay here and mind the pub."

"Of course. Well, let me know if you have any other ideas."

"I will." He turned away abruptly to serve a man at the other end of the bar.

The night remained quiet with few people coming in. She was lucky, she knew — the place was paid for, save for the lights and the heat and the taxes. She paid her staff only for the hours they actually worked, so during the slow times, she didn't need them. If some nights — or even some months — were slow, she wouldn't go broke.

Was that her life plan? To work here at the pub — *her pub,* she reminded herself yet again — serve whoever came in, and chat them up? In some ways, it was more than she had ever expected from her life, because she hadn't seen many choices in her path. But maybe it was time to rethink a few things. She liked living in this part of

Ireland, at least for now. She couldn't imagine feeling homesick for Boston, but that could change.

Maybe meeting her mother had shaken her. Helen had made some big choices twenty-plus years ago: to marry her father, Tom; to have a child; and to walk away from that child and start over. Did she regret any of those choices?

Maura shook her head to clear it. She spent the next couple of hours pulling pints and making small talk with the people who came in, but many didn't want to talk — they wanted to be left alone with their pint and their thoughts. She sent Rose home early and told Mick to leave too since he'd covered for much of the day while she was meeting with Helen. She closed up on time and drove to her house in the dark with no answers.

TWENTY-SIX

Maura woke up the next morning and lay in bed trying to figure out how she felt. Physically? Fine. Mentally? Confused. Too much going on, pulling her in all directions. What was she supposed to worry about first? Her mother? Gillian and her shabby and unfurnished new home — with a new baby, no less? Finding staff for the pub? Solving this flipping maybe-murder? The gods were not playing fair. Why did she have to deal with all these things at the same time?

Stewing under the covers was not going to help. She should get up, shower, eat something, and then maybe go see Bridget, who was always up early. Bridget filled a lot of the empty spaces in Maura's life — she was a friend but so much more. A grandmother, filling in for Gran. Someone who had known Gran a long time ago and held pieces of Maura's past that she hadn't even begun to explore. A treasure trove of local history, particularly the people in the area. Someone who had welcomed her with open arms.

Energized, she jumped out of bed, grabbed a towel, and went down the narrow stairs. She showered, then made herself a cup of coffee and toasted some slightly stale soda bread while trying to figure out what to wear. Her wardrobe was pitiful. Most of it was okay for the pub if she didn't want anyone to notice she was alive. She'd had to ask Rose for advice about what to wear on a casual date with Sean. She'd gone through a few of the Skibbereen thrift shops to replace things that were falling apart — she hadn't brought much with her from Boston. And that was about it. Helen showing up, looking professional and put together, had made her feel shabby, and she didn't like it.

No way was she going to ask Helen to go shopping with her. No matter what, she had no plans to be a girly girl. But as a pub owner and the face of the place, she really should step up her game.

With a sigh, she pulled on a pair of clean jeans and a shirt — checking to be sure there were no stains on the front — grabbed her jacket, and opened the door. Spring had definitely arrived. Even city-raised Maura could smell it in the air. She pulled the door shut behind her and strolled down the lane toward Bridget's cottage.

Mick's car was parked in front of the door, but he was up on the slate roof, doing something around the chimney.

"You're here early," Maura called out.

"The flashing's shot, and there's rain in the forecast. Won't take long to repair. Go on in."

Maura rapped on the front door, and Bridget opened it quickly. "Welcome, *mo chara*. Tea fer yeh?"

"Sounds great. How are you?"

"I'm grand, thank yeh very much. Mick's been pounding over my head for an hour or more, and yesterday as well."

"You're lucky he's looking after your place. If something goes wrong at mine, I'm clueless."

"Mick'll help yeh out if you ask, yeh know."

"I know, and he has before, but I hate asking people for help."

"Ah, Maura, surely yeh've noticed that around here people help each other?"

"Yeah, I've seen that. Not like living in the city."

"Pour yerself a cup of tea, why don't yeh?" While Maura poured, Bridget commented,

"Yer gran was always one fer helping others."

"That I remember," Maura said, locating a cup and pouring tea from a pot kept warm on the stove. "I never knew who I'd find at the table at supper. Mostly guys from Cork, I guess, looking back at it. Gran always gave them a good meal and told them who they should be talking to for a place to stay and a job. I guess it worked because I can't remember many of them coming back looking for help again, although sometimes they brought her a gift or some flowers."

Bridget smiled. "And is it only the Irish who do that in Boston?"

Maura shrugged. "I really can't say. I guess everybody looked out for their own."

Maura heard Mick clomping down the ladder leaning against the house, and then he walked in. "That should hold yeh at least fer a bit. I fixed the flashing, but there's a couple of roof shingles gone missing that should be replaced. I'll have to find some."

"Will yeh stay fer a cup of tea?" Bridget asked, beaming at him.

"That I will, if my boss here will let me." He glanced at Maura, smiling.

"Mick, it's not even nine o'clock," Maura reminded him. "We don't open for over an hour. Go right ahead."

He'd barely poured a cup for himself when they all heard the sound of a car approaching, its grinding gears hard to miss coming up the hill. "Who could that be?" Bridget asked no one in particular. "All the neighbors with jobs are long gone off to work."

The car stopped outside Bridget's gates, and then Maura heard voices — one male, one female — and the slamming of a door. "I'm going to guess it's Gillian. She said she'd bring the baby by."

Bridget got up from her chair more quickly than Maura had thought possible. "And her only just home! I'd best top off the pot." She hurried over to the stove to shift the kettle over the heat.

Maura glanced at Mick, who looked distinctly uncomfortable. "I should go so you can talk about woman things," he said.

"At least say hi to Gillian, Mick," Maura protested. "You haven't even seen young Henry."

"I've seen babies before," he said curtly, but Gillian was already rapping on the door and he couldn't escape.

Since Bridget was fussing with the teapot, Maura went to open the door. "Hey, Gillian! Are you driving now?"

"No, but Harry gave me a lift, and he'll

be back in a bit to collect me. Hello, Mick — I almost didn't see you there. Anyway, I couldn't stay inside that gloomy old pile on such a nice spring day. And of course I had to show off young master Henry here. Bridget?" Gillian called out.

Bridget came quickly to the door. "Gillian, yeh're looking grand. And this is the little one?"

"It is, Henry Townsend Callanan. Would you like to hold him?"

"Sure, and I'd be glad to, if yeh're willin'," Bridget said, her eagerness unmistakable.

"Of course I am," Gillian told her. "You've far more experience than I have with infants. Why don't you sit down first, and I'll hand him over?"

Bridget complied, settling herself in her upholstered chair, and Gillian laid the baby in her arms. He barely stirred, but Bridget was handling him like the mother she had long been, and there were tears in her eyes. "Oh, he's a handsome one, isn't he?"

In the moment of warm silence that followed, Maura happened to look up at Mick, who had been standing as if frozen since the door opened, and the expression on his face shocked her: his eyes were on the baby in his grandmother's arms, and there was so much pain in them that Maura wanted to reach out and touch him. And then it was gone, and his expression was carefully neutral.

"I'll be headin' out now. Good to see yeh, Gillian. Maura, see yeh in a bit," he said in a tight voice.

Bridget tore her adoring gaze away from the baby long enough to say, "Mick, remember what I told yeh."

He didn't answer but ducked his head and hurried out the door. Maura waited to hear his car start up, but she heard nothing. Where had he gone? And why in such a hurry?

"I'll take care of the tea," she volunteered. "Gillian, why don't you sit by Bridget? How's Harry holding up?"

"He's over the moon for now, but he's having issues with nappies. I tell him I'm doing the feeding, so he should deal with the end product, but so far he hasn't bought into the program."

"How's the creamery coming along?"

"Very slowly, I'm afraid. Between the packing and drumming up business for himself, Harry doesn't have a lot of time to work on it."

"I've still got that spare bedroom," Maura said, bringing the teapot over to the table between the chairs.

Gillian laughed. "And it's kind of you to offer, but can you see us jammed into that space with a baby? We'll work things out. And we have that nice beach overlooking the lough if Henry here decides to scream his head off. No neighbors to bother."

Henry was beginning to make cranky sounds. "I think he needs his feed," Bridget said.

"No doubt. Do you mind?" Gillian took the baby from Bridget, who seemed a bit reluctant to let go, then settled herself back in the chair. She pulled a shawl from her bag and draped it over one shoulder, guiding Henry discreetly beneath it for breakfast or lunch or whatever his nine o'clock meal was. Maura didn't know where to look.

But Gillian and Bridget seemed unfazed by a nursing baby in their midst. "So, Maura, what's new with the investigation?" Gillian asked.

"Not much. Helen provided a list of past staff, and I gave Billy a copy, and one to Sean last night. Bridget, didn't you say you used to know somebody at the hotel?"

"Ah, right, so I did. Me son Timothy's wife, Siobhan, used to work there, but I've no idea if she's there now. He passed away some ten years ago — pneumonia, it was,

301

after a hard winter — and I've lost touch with her. She never had the time of day fer me, though to be fair she was always workin', and I had no call to stop in to see her."

"And there's a daughter?"

"Yes, Ellen. Siobhan had the girl before she met Tim. They never had children of their own, sad to say. He loved that girl like his own, though, but the wife kept her from callin' me grannie. I can't say why. A spirited girl, as I remember. I haven't seen her since Tim's funeral."

Maura sensed there was more to the story, but it felt wrong to pry right then. Maybe Mick could shed some light — he would have grown up knowing this Ellen. Had he been close to his uncle Tim? Another family member he'd never talked about. Maura wondered how many more Nolans there were in the neighborhood that Mick hadn't bothered to tell her about.

Gillian shifted the baby to the other side. "How're things with your mother, Maura?"

"Well, warmer than they were. We're talking."

"That's more than I can say for my mother," Gillian said with a trace of bitterness. "At least my sister has stopped by, but she said she couldn't tell Ma she'd seen me.

Mick's got a sister, doesn't he?" Gillian turned to Bridget.

"He does, but I see little of her. She has the two small children and a job in Clonakilty, so she has no time to stop by and visit with an old woman. But Mick looks after me well."

The struggling engine was making its way up the hill again, so Gillian disengaged baby Henry and burped him. He didn't complain, his eyelids drooping already. While Gillian reassembled herself, Harry rapped on the door. When Maura opened it, he said, "Ladies? Have you had your fill of this fine young lad? Because Gillian and I have a lot of work to do."

"You know you can call on us if you need help, Harry," Maura said quickly.

"It's kind of you to offer, and we may need to take you up on that. But for now, we three are enjoying ourselves and packing a box now and then when he's asleep. Bridget, lovely to see you again. Gillian, are you ready?"

"I am. Bye, Maura — I'll see you again soon. And when we get settled down below, Bridget, I can pop up easily for a visit."

"Whenever you find the time. Take care, the three of yeh," Bridget said, her eyes damp again.

Maura walked them to the door, and as they were leaving, she noticed that Mick's car was still parked where it had been when she came in. "I should probably go too," she told Bridget. "Do you need anything? There's still tea in the pot."

"I'm well fixed, Maura. You've got a pub to run. But stop by again when you can."

"Of course I will. I'll shut the door behind me."

She left quickly, pulling the heavy old door to make sure it latched, and started up the hill toward her cottage. And stopped when she reached where the lane branched off: there was someone leaning against her door. When she came a bit closer, she realized it was Mick. What was he doing here?

"Hey," she said when she was in earshot. "Did you want something?"

"Yes," he said, avoiding her eyes. "We need to talk."

Why did that seldom mean good news? "Come on in, then."

Twenty-Seven

Disturbing possibilities raced through Maura's mind as she led Mick into her cottage. Top of the list was that he was going to tell her that Bridget was seriously ill or dying, which she refused to think about. Second was the he was quitting his job at Sullivan's. She struggled to come up with more options. *He* was dying? He had killed John Byrne just to see what a murder felt like? The pub had burned down while she was sleeping? No, someone would have called if that had happened. She was out of ideas.

"Coffee?" Maura asked as Mick wandered around the room, kicking at a pair of old rubber boots she'd left on the floor. "Or something stronger?"

He turned to her then. "Fer God's sake, Maura, it's nine o'clock in the mornin'."

She looked at him squarely, trying to keep her gaze calm. "I've known plenty of people who start that early, and I'm sure you have too. Come on. Whatever you want to say, spit it out. You're scaring me." She pointed to a chair on his side of the table, and he sat. She took a seat across from him.

Mick seemed willing to look anywhere but at Maura. "I, uh, don't often talk about a lot of things. Personal things."

Maura throttled her urge to give him a kick — anything to get him to talk.

Mick took a deep breath. "Bridget knows we've . . . been close. So she told me flat out if I'm even thinking about, well, being with you, yeh have to know what's gone on in my life. She said if I didn't do it, I didn't deserve you. And then she'd tell yeh herself, so you wouldn't think it was you who messed up."

"Okay," Maura said cautiously. She had no clue where this talk was going, but at least she knew now that Bridget thought it was important.

"I was married once," he said abruptly. "And we had a child."

It felt like a fist in her gut. It was the first time she'd ever heard anything about it, and she already could tell that things had ended badly. He'd never mentioned a wife, a lover, a girlfriend — or a child. And she flashed on the look that had crossed his face while he watched Gillian and her baby together. She didn't know if she was ready for what he might say next, and she couldn't think of anything to say that wouldn't sound silly and shallow. She kept waiting silently, watching his face.

He glanced briefly at her before turning away. "I got a degree, had a good job in Cork. We got married, Caitlin and me, had Sean a year later. We were the perfect young couple. And we were happy."

"What happened?" Maura asked softly.

"I started working too hard, spending too much time away. Sean was a fussy baby, and I left all the hard stuff of carin' fer him to Caitlin all day. We had a nice home, enough money. She had friends. I thought we had a good life. Except I wasn't there for more'n half of it."

"And?"

"When Sean was about one, she took him off for an afternoon with her friends and their kids. They went to a park together. He was just walkin', and he fell, hit his head. He seemed fine, she thought, but he wasn't. After a couple hours, she couldn't wake him from a nap, and when she got him to hospital, they told her his brain was bleeding, and there was nothing they could do for him. Just like that, he was gone. The doctors called me, but I was too late to see him — alive, anyway."

"How awful. For both of you." That went a long way toward explaining his silence about himself and his past. She couldn't imagine losing a child that way, and it was clear that he blamed himself in part. But there must be more for him to cut himself off from family, give up his work, and hide himself away in a small pub in a small village. *Let him tell you in his own way.*

He must have guessed what she was thinking. "It got worse. I'd say we both shut down rather than comfortin' each other. Caitlin was gutted, but she never said much. We went about our days like polite zombies — our talk was mostly 'we need more juice' or 'have yeh paid the electric?' I threw myself back into me work, never thinkin' that she had nothin' to distract her, leavin' her in that small flat with all the baby things still scattered about. Leavin' her alone because it was easier fer me. And one day I came home and found she'd killed herself."

"Oh, God," Maura whispered.

Mick wasn't looking at her, lost in his memories. "I never saw it coming. I never guessed. I thought I loved her, but I never knew her, never really saw her, and then she died."

"And you blamed yourself?"

"Who else? I'd been so wrapped up in me-self that I never noticed anything, and then, boom, in a matter of months, it was all gone. So I walked away from me own life. The job, the place, the whole thing."

"What about your family?"

"My sister had enough on her hands with the kids comin' and all, and I didn't want to see them, couldn't hear a word about babies. I guess I was worried that in her heart she blamed me too. My parents tried to help, but after a while they gave up — I wouldn't talk to them. I wouldn't visit for holidays. I just shut them out. I needed work just to pay for the simplest costs, so I started at the pub. Old Mick never asked any questions. Maybe he knew what had happened, maybe he didn't, but as long as I showed up and did the job, he was fine with it."

Well, that explained a lot of things — Mick's lack of ambition, his lack of connection with most people. His silence about his past. Like Old Mick, she'd never pried because she'd needed him to keep working for her, at least at first. "You said Bridget told you that you had to tell me. Why now?"

Mick shook his head as if reluctant to explain. "Because I've started to have feelin's fer yeh. You show up out of nowhere with nobody behind yeh, and I felt sorry for yeh. You were like a lost puppy, and you snapped at most people who only wanted to help. And I've been workin' alongside you fer a year now, and I've watched you change, open up — and I've felt what yeh might call jealous that you've been able to go on with yer life, make yerself a new one. When I couldn't."

"But you stayed on at Sullivan's."

"I didn't know where else to go."

"How long has it been?"

"Five years and some. Sure, I should have moved on by now, but it's easier just to drift along. Folk around Leap don't know the story, don't ask questions. They just take me as I am — the guy behind the bar, handy with the tap." He fell silent.

Maura felt lost. She sucked at heart-to-heart talks, not that she'd had many. She never knew what to say to people who were suffering. Bridget had given Mick his task: If he wanted to be with Maura, whatever that meant, he'd have to come clean about his past. And he had.

Bridget must have guessed that she might want the chance to think about what it might mean to have a future with Mick — she could end it now before anything even began. But it already had, hadn't it?

Could Mick stop blaming himself for the awful things that had happened and move forward? With her? She was so not the best person to help him.

But . . . he could have blown off Bridget, could have said nothing, could have gone on as before. He hadn't — he'd come straight to her, and here he was, clearly hurting. Which meant he did feel something for her, and he'd made an effort. Maura just wasn't sure what she wanted, but she knew she couldn't lie to herself or to Mick. She felt something for him too, something she'd tried not to look at too closely. He'd been kind to her from the beginning without expecting anything from her. He'd been there when she'd been totally upended by her mother's appearance — he'd actually seen how upset she was, even though she'd thought she'd hidden it so well. That meant something. He wasn't giving himself enough credit.

She'd be a fool to shut the door on him. But what could she say?

Oh, grow up, Maura. Mick's actually opened up and you're worried about yourself? Aren't you a better person than that? Yeah, one who's scared to death of screwing this up.

She took a breath to calm herself. "Mick,

it's not your fault. I'm pretty sure plenty of people have told you that, but you still don't believe it. But you have to. Life can be crappy, and there's no logic to it. Bad things happen. But you didn't do this to your child or your wife. I think you're right that you weren't there for your wife, but guess what? You've gotten better at paying attention to people. Like me. When I first showed up with no money, no place to go, and no plan for that week or the rest of my life, you helped me. You didn't know me, but you kept me from falling to pieces. I wouldn't have made it this far without you being there for me."

She paused; she'd startled herself. Where had that come from? *Okay, Maura, it's time to go all in.* "You said you feel something for me. You don't have to put a label on it. I feel something for you too, but I've been pretending there was nothing there because I didn't want to deal with it. Stupid, I know. But that's where we are. Two people with a load of problems that we don't know how to fix. But, Mick? I'm willing to try."

If this was a romance novel, Maura mused, waiting for an answer — any answer — this was when the music would surge and they'd fling themselves into each other's arms. The scene would fade to black, and roses would bloom, and bluebirds would fly, and . . . that was such a load of crap. They were two messed up people trying to find their way to each other across a minefield of issues.

Finally, Mick managed to smile. "Bridget's been after me fer a while to get on with me life, though she means it kindly. And I know yeh're right too. I've been feelin' sorry for meself, which serves no one. I loved Caitlin and I loved Sean. They're gone. Talk about God or the hereafter all yeh want, but they're still gone from my life. But I've got a life, and I'm not doing right by them by letting it just go by."

"So," Maura said. "What do we do now?"

"What do yeh mean?"

"I've shoved you onto the right path, so you'll pick up the pieces and go on with your life. Hooray. What do I get?"

"Me, I guess. If yeh think yeh want me."

"Do you want me?"

"Damned if we don't sound like a pair of schoolchildren: 'You go first.' 'No, you go first.' I thought we'd decided we're grown?"

"Okay, then kiss me."

"Ah." With great deliberation, Mick pushed his chair away from the table, stood, and walked slowly around it until he was face-to-face with Maura. "Yes?"

"Yes."

He took her head in both hands and moved in for the kiss. Softly at first. Maura found herself wondering, *Really? That's it?* But then things heated up, and all she could hear in her head was, *Don't stop. Please, don't stop . . .*

They pulled apart, their breath coming quickly. "Okay, good to know," Maura said. "But we're supposed to open the pub in fifteen minutes. Just remember where we left off, okay?"

"I will."

Twenty-Eight

They parted on weirdly formal terms, like they were trying to ignore what had just happened. As she drove toward Leap in her own car, Maura wondered exactly what had just happened. Sure, there'd always been some spark between them, but Maura hadn't been ready to think about a . . . what? Lover? Boyfriend? At least now she knew why Mick had been sending mixed signals.

So how's that working out for you, Maura? Could she actually handle a real relationship with Mick? Could he?

She arrived in Leap and parked up the road from the pub. She was walking toward the door when Billy's door opened, startling her. He peered out. "A word wit' yeh, Maura?"

She checked her watch. It was still shy of opening time, and Mick could cover. "Sure. Is something bothering you? Are you feeling all right?"

"I'm fine, but there's a few things I'd like to talk wit' yeh about." He stepped back, holding the door wide. "Come in."

She walked in. Much of the time, she forgot this little apartment existed, tucked away at the opposite end of the building from the pub.

"Please, will yeh sit? There's tea made, if yeh want," Billy said.

Maura sat on a sofa that had once been floral and now was just sort of . . . gray. "No, I'm fine. Tell me what's bothering you, please."

"Me mind's not as quick as it once was, so it took me a bit to work some things out. It was Dunmanway that set me to thinkin'," he said. "And I had to go back a long ways before I figgered out why. I don't get out as much as I used to, and I don't stray far from Leap and Skibbereen these past few years, but my memory's good for them earlier days."

Maura held her tongue. Billy had a fondness for traditional storytelling, and he was enjoying spinning out his discovery. She could wait.

"Has to do with yer John Byrne," he began again. "It took me a while to recall that there were once a few Byrne families up north of Drinagh, near to Dunmanway."

Once again Billy's endless memory amazed her — and then she realized what he was trying to say. "Hold on, Billy — are you seriously thinking that John Byrne came from there? I mean, Byrne's not a rare name."

"I won't argue wit' yeh on that point, Maura. But if it's true, it might go a long way to explain why the man chose to buy the hotel in Skibbereen." He fell silent, patiently waiting while Maura put the pieces together.

"I see your point," she said at last. "It's certainly not his typical kind of hotel. So, local boy makes good and buys up luxury hotel to impress anyone who might remember him? *Is* there anyone around who would remember him?"

"I'd put money on it," Billy said firmly. "See, there's more to the story if I've got it right. The Byrnes were dairy farmers, like so many around here. There were always too many brothers and not enough land to go around, so John's father, Paddy Byrne, got fed up and took himself off to New York to find a better life, leavin' young Johnny with his ma."

A common enough story there too, Maura recognized. Hadn't her grandmother done the same thing, packing up with her young son and heading off to Boston hoping for a better life? "What's this got to do why John ended up dead all these years later?"

"I'm tellin' yeh the story, aren't I?" Billy said. "As I remember it, turned out that John's father, Paddy, got himself mixed up with some shady business in New York. John was still livin' on the farm with his ma. Paddy was doin' real well at doin' bad things in New York, or so the story went. Mebbe he didn't exactly write a letter home each week, but people heard."

"Paddy Byrne was a criminal?"

"More than that, some said, though I've no way of knowin' how much was true. But there's those that claimed that Paddy Byrne was the last of the Irish bosses in the city there in a place called Hell's Kitchen. But then all these other people from other places came into the city and had their own gangs, and that was the end of it. Paddy's long dead."

Maura shifted forward on the lumpy couch and leaned closer. "So where does John come in?"

"Johnny's ma died when he was sixteen, and there was no room for him on the family land. So the uncles scraped enough money together to send him to live wit' his father in New York."

Maura didn't answer immediately, trying to make the dates work in her head. Finally she said, "So what you're saying is that John Byrne, Harvard graduate, rich developer, and business owner from New York City and Chicago, is the same Johnny Byrne who grew up on a dairy farm north of here, and whose father was a criminal?"

"Would yeh rather it was a blooming bunch of coincidences?" Billy asked.

"Of course not. You know, you've got an amazing memory, Billy. It's great that you figured this much out. But why would anyone kill him here and now?"

"Yeh're wantin' me to give yeh all the answers?" Billy grinned at her. "I've found out who he was fer yeh."

"I don't suppose there's any proof?" Maura wasn't sure she needed it: Billy's memory was definitely sharp, as he'd proved more than once. But the gardaí would want something to call evidence. She should give this to Sean quickly, so he could follow up on it.

"There's Byrnes up toward Dunmanway still," Billy said, "and some might remember Johnny. Some might remember his leavin' as well. Or even his da, Paddy."

There were still some gaping holes in the

theory. One of them was how a farm boy from West Cork somehow ended up at Harvard University. Where, admittedly, he'd done well in his own right at business school and also on Wall Street before creating his own company, which was apparently successful too. If he'd had a shady start, he'd kept his nose clean and worked hard ever since. "When did John's father die?"

"I couldn't say — I never knew the man — but I'd guess yer friend Sean Murphy could look it up on the computer. Paddy Byrne was well known in criminal circles in New York, or so the stories said. Mebbe it's true, mebbe not."

Did it matter? John Byrne had done well, maybe with some help from his shady dad. It wasn't a big jump to guess that he had come back to Cork for reasons both public and private. And he'd died. Why?

Maura shook herself. "Billy, you are amazing. I hope I remember my own past as well when I'm your age."

He smiled gently. "I hope yer mother will be part of those memories now. We've all done things in our lives that we regret, but yeh've still got time to fix 'em."

"I know, Billy. I know. We're working on it." Maura stood up. "I think I need to talk to the gardaí about all this. They may laugh at me, but at least there are details they can check to find out who John Byrne really was." Maybe a DNA test would prove something — if the Irish gardaí even used such a thing. No, it would be better if the gardaí just headed for Dunmanway and looked for relatives. "Will you be coming down to the pub later?"

"Do yeh need to ask? I'll let yeh make yer calls and see yeh a bit later. Oh, and here I almost forgot." Billy winked at Maura, then shuffled over to the table where he usually ate, came back with the list of hotel employees, and handed it to her. "I might have added a note or two, if yeh can read 'em."

"Thanks so much, Billy — you're amazing."

"Ah, g'wan wit' yeh. I'm just an old man with a long memory."

So much more than that, Billy! Maura gave him a final wave, then hurried down the sidewalk to Sullivan's front door, pulling her phone out of her pocket as she went. She stared at it for a moment, trying to make up her mind: Should she call Sean right now, or should she go to the pub and think about what she'd heard? There would be few patrons in the pub at this early hour. Would it be awkward to face Mick after what he had told her? Maybe. So it would be Sean first. She hit his speed dial.

"Sean Murphy," he answered briskly. "Oh, Maura, it's you. Everythin' all right?"

"Sure, it's fine. Look, Billy Sheahan just told me something that I think you might want to follow up on."

"Can yeh tell me on the phone?"

"I could, but I'd rather explain it to you. I'm in Leap right now, so it'll only take me a few minutes to get there if that works for you."

"Sure. Come straightaway — we've a meeting at eleven."

"On my way."

But her good intentions were diverted when she saw Sergeant Ryan walk into the pub. He looked grim, but then, he'd looked grim every time she'd seen him. Did he even know how to smile? "What can I do for you, Sergeant?"

"A word in private wit' yeh, Miss Donovan."

Maura checked out the empty room. But someone might come in, maybe. The sergeant radiated "angry cop" at anyone who looked at him with half an eye, so maybe it would be better for business if she took him into the back room. "Follow me," she said and led the way. She waited until he came in, then shut the door behind them.

He moved into the center of the room and studied it. "This where the music takes place?"

"It is."

"How many does the place hold?"

Maura was suddenly wary. Was he looking for faults? Something he could use to make her life difficult? "Our certificate says two hundred. Did you have questions for me now?"

"I do." He leaned against the bar and stared at her. She stared back. "How does it happen that yer mother's boss dies as soon as they get here? She'd never been to this part of the country before, am I right? Nor had he."

Maura debated briefly with herself about sharing Billy's theory, but the sergeant wasn't exactly inviting confidences. "That's what I understand. I gather John Byrne had visited his Dublin hotel but not Skibbereen. I only met the man a few days ago, and we never had a private conversation."

"And it's only a coincidence that this woman who says she's your mother happens to be travelin' with him?"

"She is my mother," Maura said, trying to turn off the alarm bells ringing in her head. Why would he question that?

"And who would yer father be?"

"Thomas Donovan, born a few miles from here. What does this have to do with anything?"

He ignored her question. "Where did they meet?"

"In Boston. Where I was born a couple of years later. Sergeant, what are you getting at? My mother isn't my mother? Just look at the two of us — clearly we're related. That the man I called my father wasn't? That's ridiculous. If you're trying to dig up a motive for John Byrne's death, you're definitely looking in the wrong direction. Is this how you city cops here operate? Try to piss off the people you're talking to?"

"Just lookin' at all the possibilities. Seems the Skibbereen gardaí are pretty soft on people they interview."

"Yes, because they know the people they're talking to. And from what I've seen, they've got pretty good instincts about people."

"They seem to trust you. And yeh're an outsider."

"Yes, they do, and I respect that trust — but I earned it. What is it you want from me? Do I suspect my mother of killing her boss? Hell, no. Do I know who did? Why would I? I had never seen Crann Mor until this past week. If you look around here, you can guess that I don't travel with that crowd."

"Are yeh hard up for money?" Sergeant Ryan asked without any expression.

"The pub? We get by. What, do you think I was hitting up Byrne for a loan? Or I wanted to sell him this place?"

"Did you?"

"No. I like it here. I still have a lot to learn about running a pub, but I don't plan to give up anytime soon. Look, Sergeant, you're barking up the wrong tree. None of us here knew John Byrne, and none of us gain anything from his death. And if that's not good enough, I have an alibi for the night he died."

"The whole night?"

"Yes."

"Yer mother doesn't," he said flatly.

Maura swallowed her bubbling anger. "Then tell me why she would want him dead."

"I don't know — yet. I'm only askin' questions. Yeh're right — I don't know the folk around here the way the others at the station do. Doesn't mean I can't take a hard look at the outsiders, because we're all on the same footin' with them. Byrne and yer mother don't fit, and one of 'em's dead." He gave her a long look and added, "I'll see myself out." He turned and left, leaving Maura fuming.

God, the man was infuriating. She gave herself a minute or two to calm down. Then she remembered that she had information she wanted to share with the gardaí, but Sergeant Ryan wouldn't appreciate what she had to say. Sean would, and young though he was, he would know how to fit it into the big picture. She fished out her cell phone and called him.

"Sean?" she said when he answered. "I'm running late. Your charming new sergeant paid me a visit, but I still need to talk to you. Can we meet somewhere outside the station? This won't take long."

"Apple Betty's around the corner?"

"Great. See you in ten."

TWENTY-NINE

It was still early enough in the day that it took only ten minutes to drive to Skibbereen and park in the small lot next to the garda station. No sign of Sean outside, so she headed down the street, turned the corner, and ducked into the small restaurant, where she spotted Sean sitting at a table in the back. She made her way through the tables to where he sat and dropped into the chair opposite him.

He cocked his head at her quizzically. "Good mornin', Maura. Yeh look like yeh're ready to spit nails."

"Still? Well, your new sergeant seems to have that effect on me. I swear, he asked me if I was sure Tom Donovan was really my father. And then he tried to pin John Byrne's death on my mother just because they were both outsiders."

Sean looked dismayed. "Yeh're not the first to report somethin' like that since he's arrived."

Maura leaned on her elbows. "I won't whine about him, but can you tell me if he's getting any results or just making people angry?"

"Mostly the second, so far. But it's early days. Yeh said yeh've got somethin' fer me? Oh, but I need to tell yeh: we've got the coroner's report now."

Maura looked at his expression, and she got a sinking feeling. "Isn't that good news?"

"Not when he couldn't reach a verdict. So it's not officially murder, just an unexplained death, and we're no farther along."

"I'm sorry, Sean. Does that happen often?"

"It's not rare. There's simply not enough evidence to make the call. So what do yeh have that's new?"

"I would have given it to the sergeant, but I don't think he would've appreciated it." She came straight to the point. "When I got to Sullivan's this morning, Billy Sheahan wanted to talk to me. You know he knows everything that's been going on with John Byrne's death. When he went over the list I gave him, it got him thinking, and he remembered that there were Byrne families up near Dunmanway. Is that in your district?"

"No, but I know it a bit, though I've never been involved with any business there. Why?"

"Billy said that the Byrnes had dairy herds up there, but there were too many in the family to make a go of it, so one brother took off for New York. Patrick — Paddy. Leaving a wife and young son behind. Billy thought that could be John. When the mother died, the rest of the family sent John, who was in his teens by then, off to New York to live with his father."

Sean was listening carefully. "It could fit, and there are facts we could check. But what would that have to do with the man's death thirty years later?"

"Billy didn't have any ideas about that, but he did believe that Paddy Byrne was some kind of old-style gangster in New York. Kind of the last of his breed. I know the story's kind of weak, but the timeline fits. John leaves the farm in Dunmanway in the nineties to go live with his father. Somehow after a couple of years, he gets himself into Harvard and proves he's a bright and hardworking boy and does well. And by the way, manages to lose his Irish accent. Then he goes to business school, works for big-name banks, starts his own company. And then he comes back here to show off what he's accomplished. Only he never tells anyone he's a local boy, as far as we know. Maybe he wanted it to be a surprise. Or maybe he told the wrong person."

Sean didn't look convinced. "I have to agree wit' yeh, it's pretty thin. What's yer point, Maura?"

"That if we have the right John Byrne, he does have a history with West Cork, and that opens up all sorts of possibilities, doesn't it? You can track down the Dunmanway Byrnes, if there are any left, and ask about their John and if they know where he is now. You can ask for records from New York, or Harvard, or whatever. All I'm saying is that you've got a reason to dig a little deeper into his earlier life like you were thinking, and you might just find somebody there who knew him — and wanted him dead. Have you got anything better to work with?"

Sean shook his head. "Fair enough. We've had no luck anywhere else. Thank Billy fer me, will yeh?" He lowered his voice. "And I'd say yeh're right not to hand it to the sergeant — he wouldn't give it much weight."

"That's what I was afraid of. You sure you don't want to make Billy an official consultant? He's got stuff in his head that there's probably no other record of, and he can put the pieces together."

Sean smiled. "If he was fifty years younger, we'd recruit him."

"So, will you bring it up to your boss?"

"I will, though maybe him alone fer now. I'll do a bit more digging on the American end unless yer ma comes up with something."

"Well, good luck. I'd better get back to the pub. Thanks for listening, Sean."

"I always listen to yeh, Maura. I'll walk you out."

Outside she breathed deeply — spring and auto exhaust. The town was waking up.

When Maura walked into Sullivan's, all eyes turned toward her. Except Mick's: he appeared very focused on lining up the bottles on the shelves. The rest of the crowd consisted of Jimmy, Rose, and Billy, in his usual chair.

"Hi, Jimmy. Nice to see you." Maura tried to keep the sarcasm out of her voice. "Why is everybody here so early? Is something happening?"

Rose dimpled. "It's spring, no more than that. We couldn't just sit in our homes stewing. Billy here's been tellin' us his ideas about John Byrne. Yeh've been to see the gardaí?"

"That's where I just was. I told Sean Murphy what Billy told me, and I think he's going to check out the things he can. Which still doesn't leave us any nearer to figuring out who might have killed John. If in fact he really was killed, which nobody's sure about."

"Odds are good that it's somebody from his past," Jimmy commented.

That was an unusually smart observation coming from him. "Seems likely," Maura agreed. "Although we can't be sure he didn't talk to other people here, he didn't have a lot of spare time, and nobody's come forward."

It was hard to read Mick's mood from the back of his neck. Maura went behind the bar and made herself a cup of coffee. While it dripped, she asked quietly, "Everything okay?"

He looked at her then and smiled. "So it is."

"Good," she replied, smiling back at him, and gathered up her coffee before turning to the others. "So, what've we got on for the rest of the week? We've got music on Friday, right? Are we ready for the band?"

"I told yeh," Rose began, "I put out the word on the Internet, and tickets are sellin' well."

"I'm impressed. We're actually selling tickets online now?"

"Sure and we are," Rose said firmly. "I asked some friends to help me, and we signed Sullivan's up for an online ticketing page. I was worried that the crowds would be so big that we might end up breaking local regulations."

"So we can look at how many people have bought tickets, and then we can plan our supply orders based on real numbers?"

"Of course. I've been lettin' Mick know the last couple of music nights."

"Well done, Rose!" *I really am behind the times, aren't I?* "Anyway, back to business. We probably need to give the back room a quick cleanup, right? Mick, I guess that thanks to Rose I don't need to ask how we're fixed for snacks?"

"Order's comin' tomorrow. Extra kegs in the cellar. We're good," Mick reported.

That took care of most of the business items that Maura could think of. Still no customers. Maybe it was time to look at that list of hotel employees that Billy had marked up. Sean had bought into her suggestion that whoever had killed John might have come from his past. Looking at an out-of-date but still fairly recent staff list was a long shot, but it couldn't hurt.

She sat at a corner table, pulled the folder Billy had returned to her out of her bag, and spread the pages on the table.

Maura glanced at the first page and smiled. No fancy yellow highlighter for Billy: his notes were chicken scrawls written in blunt pencil, and they were not always easy to read. But she could manage. Living in West Cork now, she was continually amazed that there were so few surnames — or first names, for that matter. Back in Boston, she'd thought it was something like a joke that all the Irish men were named Michael or Patrick and called Mick or Paddy, but here she knew plenty of both.

Focus, Maura! That same group of surnames dominated the hotel lists. No doubt some of them were related to each other. Probably most of the people on the list had stayed in the same job for the time period covered.

Maybe she should come at this from a different direction. Bridget had told her that her son's wife had worked at the hotel. No Nolans on any of the lists, but the woman might have taken her husband's name when she remarried. The only female manager on the earliest lists was Siobhan Buckley — and Siobhan was the name Bridget had mentioned. Two years ago, the name of the manager in the same position had changed to Siobhan O'Mahoney. Same person, new husband?

Farther down the list, Maura found the name Ellen Buckley. Bridget had said her former daughter-in-law had had a daughter named Ellen who worked at the hotel, and Ellen was the only other Buckley on the list. Farther again down the list, she found the name Bernard O'Mahoney, who was a groundskeeper throughout the entire period — he was the man she'd met in the garden. An older man. The one who'd found John dead? Was he Siobhan's new husband? The ages could be about right.

Maybe she'd better check with Billy before she went off in the wrong direction. She left the papers where they were and went over to sit by him.

"Young Murphy's on the scent now, is he?" Billy asked as she sat.

"I hope so." Briefly she wondered how Sean was doing with Harvard and asking about a student who had graduated twenty-odd years ago. On the other hand, John might have contributed money to the college and would be listed in donor records, which would more easily available. She should remember to mention that to Sean, who probably knew little about making big contributions.

"I see yeh're looking at that list I gave yeh?"

"Yes, and I have some questions. Let me run by you what I'm guessing, and you can tell me if I'm close to right. Siobhan Buckley — she's Siobhan O'Mahoney now?"

"That's right. Yer list goes back no more than five years, but she's been there far longer."

"And she's married to the groundskeeper now? Bernard O'Mahoney?"

Billy beamed at her. "Ah, Maura, yeh've a real gift fer this. And you not knowing them at all."

"Bridget kind of pointed me in the right direction, and you've helped a lot. One more question: Ellen Buckley is Siobhan's daughter?"

"Three fer three. Before yeh ask, back when Siobhan was married to Tim Nolan, may God rest his soul, she went by the name Buckley and kept it when she married, and that's how her daughter was recorded."

Was that unusual in Ireland? "Why'd Siobhan change her name this last time around?"

"Ah, and that would be because this time she wanted to do it right with a big fancy party. It'd be my guess that the hotel paid part of the cost of it fer the publicity, like. Things like photos in the papers. Good fer the hotel."

That made some sense. "Do you know Bernard?"

Billy nodded. "He's younger than me, but we've met from time to time. He knows the Crann Mor place up one side and down the other. First marriage fer him, brave man. Seems he'd been pinin' fer Siobhan fer half his life, but it took him a bit after Tim died to screw up his courage to ask the woman."

Another myth confirmed: Maura had always heard than Irish men were slow and late to marry. Poor Bernard must have been waiting for Siobhan for half his life.

So what had she learned or confirmed? A longtime employee at the hotel had once been married to Bridget's late son and was now married to the groundskeeper. And she had a daughter who also worked at the hotel. Bridget had said Ellen was born before Siobhan married Tim Nolan. Had there ever been a marriage to a Buckley back then? Had Ellen been born out of wedlock? Maybe people didn't comment on that much these days — Gillian didn't seem too concerned that she and Harry weren't married — but twenty years ago it might have been different. Siobhan might have had to choose between giving up the baby forever or toughing it out, bringing her child up in the face of nasty comments from the neighbors and maybe even family and friends.

Maybe she'd come to Skibbereen to get away from those nasty neighbors who knew the story. "Was Siobhan from around here?" Maura asked Billy.

"She came from up near Dunmanway, I recall. People didn't know her well."

Dunmanway. Where Johnny Byrne might have come from. Could Siobhan have known Johnny?

If she was going to string together wild guesses, she might as well jump in with both feet, Maura decided. Could Johnny be Ellen's father? Was it too much of a leap of logic to guess that Johnny Byrne of Dunmanway had gotten his neighbor, Siobhan Buckley, pregnant before disappearing to America?

She looked up to find Billy watching her with an odd expression on his face. "I don't know, Maura. Yeh'll have to ask Siobhan."

She stared at him. "Billy, are you reading my mind?"

"I can tell what yeh're thinkin'. I won't say I haven't wondered meself, but no one would have shared that kind of gossip with me back then."

Maura thought hard. "Even if it's true, I can't just hand this to the gardaí and have them asking embarrassing questions." She shuddered internally at the thought of Sergeant Ryan charging into a delicate interview like an angry bull. "That's not fair. But you think it's possible, right?"

"I do. Talk to Siobhan O'Mahoney, will yeh? Off the record, like. If yeh're wrong, she may be angry with yeh, but she doesn't need the gardaí knowin' all this unless there's a good reason."

"I don't even know her. How do I walk in and ask the kind of questions we're talking about?"

Billy sat back in his chair and looked at her. "It could be she's had a hard life. So have you. She stuck by her daughter, mebbe with no father. Yer ma didn't — so tell Siobhan she did right by her own daughter. If yeh've guessed right and she knows somethin' about Byrne's death and you do nothin', what then? Somebody gets away with murder, and that's not as it should be."

Billy was right, and she knew it. This was her theory, and it was up to her to ask Siobhan if it was true. "All right, Billy. I'll try to find her and talk to her before I tell anyone else what we think might have happened. It seems only fair."

"And yeh're fair woman, Maura Donovan."

At least she had Billy's approval. That was some comfort. "Any other interesting things you found in those lists?"

"Nah, I've given you the best of it. Might be it's time fer me first pint of the day, though."

"Coming up."

Maura went behind the bar to start Billy's pint, all too conscious of Mick's presence there.

"Everything all right?" he asked in a low voice.

"Billy's given me some ideas about John Byrne's death."

"And they would be?"

"I don't feel right talking about it yet. I need to check something out first. I'll tell you when I know more."

"Take care."

It hadn't even occurred to her that she might be putting herself at risk, but the idea seemed ridiculous. Siobhan had to be a middle-aged woman now, working at a large hotel with lots of people around — talking to her seemed safe enough to Maura. If she chickened out and told the gardaí instead about this possible connection, they'd probably embarrass Siobhan. She had to do this herself.

She looked around the still empty room. "I might as well go now. Who knows, we might get busy later."

In his corner, Jimmy snorted at that statement. No one else commented.

She gathered up the papers that she'd left on the table, stuffed them back in her bag, and went outside. It was shaping up to be a lovely day. Maybe that was where all the pub patrons were — out enjoying the spring, gamboling like lambs in the green fields. The image of Seamus and his gang doing that made her laugh out loud.

THIRTY

Once more Maura walked into the Crann Mor main building and immediately felt out of place. No one would mistake her for a guest. *Get over yourself, Maura!* she told herself sternly. No wonder Sergeant Ryan had had trouble believing that she and Helen were related: Helen was comfortable in her own skin in a setting like this, but Maura felt like a poor relation — or worse. She stood up straighter and approached the reception desk. There was a thirtyish woman standing behind it, starting intently at a computer screen discreetly embedded in the top of the desk. She looked up when Maura was a few feet away.

"Good morning. Welcome to Crann Mor. How can I help you?"

At least she didn't direct me to the servants' entrance, Maura thought. "I'd like to speak to Siobhan O'Mahoney. I understand she works here?"

The woman behind the desk beamed. "She does indeed. Would this be a business or a personal matter that you wish to speak about?"

"I'm not looking for a job, or trying to sell anything. It's personal. There's something I need to talk to her about."

The other woman's smile declined by about ten percent as she reached for a sleek phone. "Let me see if she's free to see you now." She turned away to talk, and Maura wondered if Siobhan would ask her under-staff person to send her on her way. If that happened, she'd have to enlist Helen's help to get her in to see Siobhan.

Maura breathed a sigh of relief when the woman turned back to her. "She'll be right out. Would you care to take a seat? Can I get you anything? Coffee?"

"No, thanks. I'm fine." Maura gave the staff points for polite treatment of anyone who walked in — that was good for business, wasn't it?

Three minutes later, a slender middle-aged woman emerged from somewhere in the back of the building. Since Maura was the only person waiting in the lobby, Siobhan approached her directly. "Good morning. I'm Siobhan O'Mahoney. I understand you wanted to speak with me?"

"Yes. I'm Maura Donovan. I own Sullivan's Pub in Leap, but that's not what I wanted to talk about. It's about John Byrne." There — she'd cast her bait, and she waited to see how Siobhan would react.

The woman's expression didn't change. "Ah. You're not from the gardaí, are you?"

"No, nothing like that. It's, uh, complicated."

Siobhan studied Maura's face and appeared to arrive at a decision. "Then perhaps you'll explain it to me. We can go to my office, or we can sit in the garden in back — it's such a lovely day."

"The garden, please." A place where no one would overhear their conversation.

Siobhan led her out through the back door to the elegant enclosed garden Maura had seen before with Helen. There was a sundial in the center of the intricate plant beds with a couple of benches grouped around it. They sat down on one of the benches, their backs to the sun.

"So, tell me, Maura Donovan, what's this all about?"

Maura realized that she hadn't planned any sort of script. She'd been focused on simply getting to the hotel and finding Siobhan. "First of all, thank you for seeing me. You don't know me, and you have no reason to talk to me."

"John Byrne asked about your pub, and after he'd seen it, he commented that it was rather charming. So I'll take that as an endorsement from him. What did you want to say to me?"

"I only met John Byrne that one time, but" — *Here goes nothing!* — "my mother worked with him. She's Helen Jenkins."

Siobhan tilted her head. "I do see a resemblance. She never mentioned she had a daughter in the area. I've a daughter of my own about your age."

"She didn't mention me because she hadn't seen me in over twenty years until she arrived last week."

"Oh, my," Siobhan said, not unsympathetically. "I'm sure there's a story behind that. But what does that have to do with me?"

"Did you know that the gardaí have still not said that John's death was an accident?"

Siobhan sighed. "Unfortunately, yes. There was an older man — a garda new to the town — who seemed sure he'd been murdered. I'll admit that we here at the hotel have wondered about it, but we've tried to downplay the unfortunate event to our guests. And I'm sure you know, the gardaí don't seem to have identified any suspects, much less arrested anyone. What is your interest?"

"I'll get to that. I apologize if any of my questions seem, well, too personal, but for my mother's sake, I'm trying to get to the bottom of what happened to John, and that garda you mentioned seems to think that anyone without an ironclad alibi is a suspect." Maura swallowed. "I understand you were originally from around Dunmanway before you started working here?" Maura asked carefully.

Siobhan seemed to stiffen just a bit, but she kept on her formal face. "Yes, from a townland on the south side of the town. You're familiar with the term?"

"Townland? Yes. I own a house in Knockskagh, north of here."

"I see. Do you know Dunmanway?"

"No. I seem to spend most of my waking time at the pub, and I haven't had much time to explore the area."

"What does it matter, where I came from?" Siobhan asked cautiously.

Here comes the curve ball. "It seems that John Byrne may also have come from Dunmanway."

"Ah," Siobhan said, then fell silent. Maura didn't add anything, watching Siobhan's face, waiting to see what she would say.

Finally Siobhan asked, "Who told you that?"

"A friend. Someone who's lived around here for a very long time and remembered the family. He's got a good memory."

"And who've you told this?"

"Based on what my friend told me about the Byrne families, I pointed the gardaí toward Dunmanway, but I never mentioned you or any possible link to you because I hadn't put it all together. And even if I had made the connection, it wouldn't be fair to you to tell them, especially if I'm wrong. You can tell me to take a hike if you want. Nobody's got proof of anything right now. But if they start looking harder at John's early life, what will they find?"

Siobhan studied Maura before answering. "There's nothing that puts the two of us together. No evidence, if you will. No history between us. No friends who knew about us because there was no us. No names joined on any pieces of paper. If I tell you what really happened, can you keep it to yourself?"

"As long as it has nothing to do with John's death, sure." Unless there was a whopping big motive involved, and in that case, Maura wasn't sure where her obligation lay.

Siobhan nodded as if reaching a decision. "Let me start by saying that I do not know how the man died. I didn't have a hand in it. You can believe me or not. Yes, John and I both come from near Dunmanway. We were neighbors of a sort in adjoining townlands. Farm kids and churchgoers, so we knew each other, as did our families. I was a bit older than he was. He was a decent boy — never in any trouble. But then his father took off to seek his fortune in America, and a couple of years later his mother died, and there was no one to take him in. So he was sent off to live with his father."

"That's how my friend remembered it. Do you know much about his father?"

"When he left here, Paddy Byrne was a dairy farmer. I gather he found . . . other employment in New York. It didn't pay to ask too many questions, and Johnny never came back. He kept in touch with his family here only when he felt like it, which was not often."

That much Maura had already guessed. It was time to dig a little deeper. "Tell me if I'm on the right track. John, a farmer's son, goes to New York and joins his father there. About two years later, he ends up as a student at Harvard, which wasn't then and isn't now an easy place to get into. So either he was some kind of genius or he had some help from his father and his New York pals — money, influence, whatever it took. Word is, they weren't exactly law-biding types. But as far as anybody knows, John Byrne grabbed that opportunity and ran with it, and he did himself proud. I've wondered if maybe he bought this hotel and came back to show everyone around here how well he'd done. Does that fit?"

Siobhan was looking past Maura, lost in her memories. "It does. Yes, he was smart, but only about some things. It'd be my guess that Paddy fixed it so he'd go to that fancy college — don't ask me how. John took what was offered and made good use of it. And the gangs or wise guys or whatever they were called back then were already on their way out, so none of them ever bothered John again. There were no favors to call in, no deals made."

"Well, there goes one theory," Maura said. "So we can be pretty sure that John Byrne was not killed in a mob hit by an eighty-year-old gangster," Maura said. Siobhan smiled faintly, and Maura went on: "Do you know if anyone else around here knew about his past?"

"I think there's still some family up in Dunmanway that recall him."

"Did he meet with you when he arrived?"

"I'm thinking you know full well he did and why."

"Look, Siobhan, I've got a pretty good guess, but I haven't shared it with anyone. All I want is to find out how and why he died. For my mother's sake, I suppose. In a crazy way, it was John who put us together after twenty years."

Siobhan looked away. "I suppose it's too late to end the story now, and I've trusted you this far. When Johnny was preparing to leave all those years ago, the families threw him a big party — that's an old tradition around here, if you don't know. Used to be that most people knew they'd never see the person again, so it was a send-off and a wake wrapped up together.

"There was plenty of drink flowing, and somehow in the night things got a bit out of hand. Johnny and I, we ended up in a grassy field doing what drunken kids do. Johnny left the next day, and I came up pregnant. I never told him. Hell, he was sixteen and thousands of miles away. What could he have done?"

Maura hesitated before asking her next question. "Did he know about the baby? None of the relatives ever told him?"

Siobhan shook her head. "I went off to

Skibbereen before it was obvious. My own family wouldn't have said anything — they were ashamed. That's the way it was back then. And Johnny's family was glad to be rid of him — one less mouth to feed. I doubt they ever wrote him a letter, much less mentioned a baby if they knew."

"What did you do?"

"I stayed with a friend 'til the baby came. She saw me through it."

"And you kept the baby. Ellen, right?"

"You have been doing your homework, Maura. Yes, I did. It wasn't easy. I'd no money and few skills. I found someone to look after Ellen, got a job at this place as a cleaner, and worked my way up. You know I was married to Tim Nolan?"

"Yes. His mother, Bridget, is a neighbor of mine, and we talk."

"She's a good woman, although we spent little time together, for with the child and my job, I had little time to spare. There were no more children with Tim, but Tim was happy being a father to Ellen. They got on well. We had a good marriage, and then he died. I'd a better job at the hotel by then, so we were pretty well fixed. Ellen started working here a few years back. And then John's company bought the place."

"That must have been a shock. You two

had had no contact in all that time?"

"None. What was the use of stirring things up? I never expected to see him again."

"When did you find out he was part of the group that bought the hotel?"

"I'm not at a level that anyone shared the sale details with me — I didn't recognize the name of the company, much less who was part of it. I didn't know until he arrived."

"What happened when you did finally see him?"

"Did he recognize me, do you mean? He didn't even remember that night. Not that I can blame him."

"So, did you tell him about Ellen?"

"Yes. I thought it was only right. I told him flat out that I didn't want or expect anything from him, financially or otherwise. I just thought he should know he had a daughter in Ireland."

"How did he react?"

"I'd say he kind of closed down for a bit. He had a good life in Chicago, a family and all, and he was looking forward to sorting out the hotel, and then I threw this at him. He was a careful man from all I've heard — he wanted time to think things through. But he wasn't angry, didn't accuse me of lying or anything like that. He'd already seen Ellen by then, not that they'd spoken."

"Does she know? About him, I mean — that he was her father?"

"I never told her. She always knew that Tim wasn't her father — at least, once she could do basic maths. I only told her I'd had a one-night stand that I regretted and I didn't even know the man's name. She wasn't exactly happy with me about that, but what could she do? Thank God she inherited John's brains." Siobhan turned to face Maura squarely. "So what're you going to do now, Maura Donovan?"

Maura looked at her squarely. "Siobhan, I believe you. Thank you for telling me the details. I won't go spreading it around, even to the gardaí. If you've told me the truth — and I think you did — you had no reason to kill John Byrne. I did wonder, though — on the staff list your last name used to be Buckley. You didn't take Nolan when you married Tim?"

Siobhan nodded. "Tim didn't care whether I changed it, and I wanted to have my daughter's surname. I changed it when I married my current husband, though — it's what he wanted. Bernard." Her expression softened. "He waited a long time for me."

Maura hesitated, unsure about whether to

go on. But what the hell — Siobhan had confided in her, and she felt that she owed her something in return. "This has nothing to do with John's death, but how did your daughter feel, growing up without her father?"

"You mean, did she realize that until Tim she had no father in the house? She was six when I married Tim, and he was the only father she ever knew. They got on well. You said you hadn't seen your mother for what must be most of your life. Did she give you up?"

"For adoption? No. My father came from around here, but when his father died, his mother moved to Boston with him. Then he died in an awful accident when I was about two, and my mother was still pretty young. She didn't want to get stuck with me, living with her mother-in-law, so one day she just disappeared. She left me with my grandmother. I don't have any memory of either of my parents. So I just wondered how Ellen felt about all that."

"She never asked, and I never volunteered — afraid of what more she might say, I suppose. It must have been hard on you, losing your mother and father before you could ever know them." They both fell silent for a few moments. Finally Siobhan asked, "So

354

what happens now? About John, I mean."

"Maybe you can answer a question for me. What was John doing out there on that path behind the hotel late at night? The gardaí said he wasn't exactly dressed for a walk, and he didn't have a torch. There was no sign that he fought with anybody. So why was he there?"

Siobhan looked around at the colorful, elegant, and very orderly garden. "He'd seen the place by daylight. When I told him about Ellen, I brought him out here to the garden to do it. It was daylight then, and we strolled a bit down that path, so he knew the lay of the land. We went a bit farther because I wanted to be sure no one overheard us. It was no one's business but our own."

"So he knew the path was there."

"Yes. And as I told you, he seemed to want time to think, to work things out in his head, although I can't imagine why he'd choose that path to do that. Maybe here in the walled garden, but not out there in the dark." Siobhan shook her head. "I've not found an explanation. I barely even knew the man after all this time, so I couldn't guess what took him out there. I wish I could be of more help to you."

"You've been more than fair just talking

to me." Maura stood up and held out her hand. "Thanks, Siobhan. I'll keep your private life out of it if I talk to the gardaí again. And that may not even happen. But thanks for all that you've told me."

Siobhan took Maura's hand and shook. "Good luck, Maura. I'm hoping that we can lay all this to rest."

"So am I. I'll find my way out."

THIRTY-ONE

Maura walked around the building rather than going through it to get to her car. She liked Siobhan. Her story seemed believable. On the other hand, Maura had learned that Irish people could nurse a grudge for a very, very long time, sometimes across centuries. Say John had known about the baby and blown Siobhan off. Her daughter, Ellen, was still part of Siobhan's life, a living reminder every day. Could Siobhan's resentment have festered for years and exploded when John stood in front of her, looking sleek and rich? Possibly. But Maura didn't want to think that.

Siobhan said she hadn't told Ellen about her father. Was she lying to protect her daughter? But if finding Siobhan and getting her to open up had been tough for her, finding Ellen and trying to learn what she knew without giving anything away would be next to impossible and might not turn up anything useful. Let the gardaí play the bad guys there if the issue came up at all — she could stay out of it.

Time to get back to Sullivan's and do her job.

She walked into the pub ten minutes later. The lunch rush had begun: there were five men scattered around with pints in front of them. One was Seamus. When he saw Maura, he stood up and came over to her.

"Do we have a winner yet?" he asked, grinning.

"No arrests yet. And the coroner wouldn't call it a murder — the evidence wasn't clear enough."

Seamus didn't look too upset. "Well, then, let me ask yeh, have yeh looked at John Byrne's ties to the mob?"

Maura stared at him for a moment, incredulous, then burst out laughing. "Where'd you hear that?"

"Are yeh tellin' me he wasn't connected?" Seamus countered.

"Seamus, just because I'm from America does not mean I know who the bad guys in New York or Chicago are or were. John may — may — have been related to someone with a criminal connection in New York, but no one has found anything criminal about John's business activities or even his personal ones."

"Ah, Maura, yeh're not tellin' me the whole truth, I can tell. But at least we know he's one of ours."

"What do you mean by 'ours'?"

"An Irish man from West Cork, come home again."

Maura was shaking her head and smiling at the same time. "Seamus, I don't know where you get your information. And I probably don't want to know. Another pint?"

"If yeh're pourin'," Seamus said.

Maura was filling a pint glass for him when she looked up to see a woman about her own age come in the door and scan the room. Her gaze landed quickly on Maura, and she walked quickly across the room to the bar.

"You're Maura Donovan?"

"I am. Can I help you with something?" Looking at the woman's face, she had an uncomfortable feeling she knew the answer already.

"I'm Ellen Buckley. Can we talk?"

Maura took a quick glance around the room. Rose wasn't in sight — she'd probably gone out to find lunch. Mick was talking to Billy, but Maura caught his eye and signaled for him to take over at the bar.

"Yes, I think we should. How about the back room? It'll be quieter there. And private."

"Fine."

Maura headed toward the back room. "Follow me," she said. After Ellen had followed her, Maura closed the door behind them. "Let's sit." Maura pointed to a table against the back wall with a couple of chairs. Ellen didn't say anything but took one chair and faced Maura, her expression a mix of curious and belligerent.

"You know who I am," Ellen began.

Maura decided it would save time for everyone if she came straight to the point. "You're Siobhan's daughter."

"I am. And John Byrne's as well." Ellen lifted her chin and waited for Maura's reaction.

"You know, then?" Maura said, trying to keep the surprise out of her voice.

"I've known for years."

"Does your mother know that?"

"We've never talked about it. She wasn't the one who told me. We've got relatives up in Dunmanway. Most of them stopped speaking to her when she got pregnant with me, but the rest filled me in years ago, probably out of spite."

"How did you feel about that?"

"You sound like a damn shrink. Obviously I knew I had a biological father somewhere, but Ma wouldn't talk about him, and I never saw anyone who fit the bill when I was young. When those cousins told me the story, it made sense, but there was nothing to be done about it then."

"You didn't try to track him down?"

Ellen shook her head. "What would be the point of that? I didn't want anything from him. We didn't need his money, and we certainly never expected him to buy the hotel and show up at our door."

Just as Siobhan had said. "Yeah, I can see that would be a shock. But why are you here now, talking to me?"

Ellen answered her firmly. "You're smart, you're not from here, and you've done pretty well figuring things out up to now. Figure this one out before things get any worse."

What would worse be? "You mean, whether John was murdered? Did you kill him?" Maura demanded.

"God, no."

"Do you think your mother did?"

Ellen shook her head. "She didn't do it. And it's not clear that it was murder, according to the gardaí. Maybe it was no more than a stupid accident."

361

"Assuming it was murder, who do you think might have done it?"

"I don't know. I'd never met the man before."

"None of those spiteful Dunmanway cousins in the running?"

"Not that I know of. They weren't exactly the brightest bulbs, but they usually stayed within the law."

This was incredibly frustrating, Maura fumed inwardly. Every slim lead she found went nowhere unless half of County Cork was lying to her. The best information she'd gotten in all of this was from two eighty-something people who had lived in West Cork for all of their lives. Without those bits, she wouldn't have known where else to look or what else to ask.

Ellen broke into Maura's pity party when she said softly, "I heard about your mother showing up with no warning. You could say the same thing has happened to me, only it was my dad, and now he's gone."

Maura sighed. "Thanks, I guess. It can't have been easy for you any more than it has been for me. Look, I'm not part of any kind of official investigation, but you must know that anyone who runs a pub hears things, so I'm part of it whether I like it or not."

"You've helped the gardaí before, I've

heard," Ellen said.

"Yes, but I never planned on that — it just kind of happened. Look, do you mind if I ask you a question? That doesn't have anything to do with your personal life?" When Ellen nodded, Maura said, "You might know more than you think since you work at the hotel and your mother does too. Were there people who would be angry if the Crann Mor management went in a different direction and put them out of a job? Who thought that stopping John would stop the changes?"

"There's few jobs around, you know. But I've worked with the staff for a while now and heard Ma talk about them for years, and I can't point the finger at anyone. Everyone knows that jobs come and go. We're used to it here."

"I understand. But it's good to have your perspective." Maura stood up. "I'm glad you came to talk to me."

Ellen smiled. "That's good to hear. You know, I think I like you. Sort out John's death and we can find out if we're friends."

"Right. Are you going to tell your mother you know about John?"

"Maybe. Maybe not right away, though. We'll see." Ellen stood up quickly. "I'd better be getting back if I want to keep the job

I've got, for however long it lasts. I hope I'll be seeing you again."

"Stop in here any time you want. There's music some weekends now." Maura led Ellen to the front door and watched as she walked up the street to where she'd parked. She turned back to the pub to find everybody in the room staring at her.

THIRTY-TWO

"What?" she demanded.

Seamus was grinning again. "Are yeh gonna fill us in on who she was?"

He seemed to see this whole thing as one big game, and that annoyed Maura. Plus Ellen's and Siobhan's secrets were not hers to share. "No. I don't have to tell you anything, much less everything. Ever heard about privacy, Seamus?"

"There's some would call it keepin' secrets." His smile faded just a bit.

"Well, I've got a right to do that too. Just to be clear: I do not know why John Byrne died or who might have wanted him dead. I'll tell you as soon as I do know and the gardaí say I can. Is that all right with you?"

"It'll have to do, now, won't it? No need to bite my head off."

"Sorry, Seamus," she called after his retreating back. Clearly this mess was getting to her. She'd collected a pot full of secrets, but she couldn't say whether any of them pointed to why John Byrne was dead.

Rose returned bearing food for everyone. "Thought yeh'd be hungry too, Maura, unless you ate at that fancy place."

"Thanks, Rose." Maura looked up to see Sean Murphy hovering outside. He gestured for her to join him outside. She waved to Seamus to catch his attention, and when he turned toward her, she said, "Seamus, I'll be talking to Garda Murphy for a few minutes if you want to press your ear to the glass and see if you can overhear anything."

Seamus grinned at her. "Ah, go on with yeh. Just report the good parts when yeh come back."

Maura grabbed up a sandwich and went out to greet Sean. "Sorry — have you eaten? I just got back from the hotel and Rose brought lunch."

"No worries," he said. "Go on and eat yer lunch. I wanted to let yeh know yer ma heard back from Harvard, and we talked with a few of our cop friends in New York, and it looks like we had most of it right, thanks to you. Harvard University reported that the young John Byrne was awarded the" — Sean pulled a small pad from his pocked and checked a note — " 'Hiberno-American Scholarship for Special Scholars.'

Created the year before John started at the college, and he was the first one to get it, though they're still handin' out money fer it. The college'll be checkin' the list of original contributors."

"Figures," Maura said. "I bet if anyone higher up in the gardaí looked into it, they'd find some of the donors were 'connected,' if you get my meaning."

"I've no doubt. But who's to say the scholarship was illegal? Surely John did nothing wrong."

"I know. And good for him — he might have had some help getting in with this shiny new scholarship most likely funded by his dad and his dad's buddies, but he seems to have proved himself."

"So it seems. And there's no police record for John in the States — not in Cambridge or New York or Chicago — save a parking ticket or two, which he paid. Have yeh anythin' new?"

Maura thought about what Siobhan and Ellen had told her, and her promise to keep that information to herself. "Sean, I'm not part of the gardaí, right?" When he shook his head, she went on: "Say somebody tells me something, and I promise not to share it with your lot unless I think it's really important. Is that illegal?"

Sean didn't answer immediately, instead studying Maura's face. Finally he said, "Are yeh tellin' me that you know something, but you've decided it's not important to this investigation?"

"Sort of," Maura admitted.

Sean didn't look happy. "If it was anybody but you, I'd be angry. But I've come to trust yer judgment. If it turns out yeh guessed wrong, yeh'll bring yer information to us, will yeh not?"

"Of course I will. By the way, Seamus in there is all over me to give him some hints or information or names. Can I throw him John's early story and the Harvard stuff?"

"No worries — it's all public information, if yeh know where to look. Maura, are yeh sure yeh've got nothin' to move this forward?"

"Mostly sure. Have you talked to the people near Dunmanway?"

"We've chatted with the gardaí there. Still, as best we know John Byrne had no contact with that lot on this recent trip. Hard to say if any of 'em knew he was around. Have yeh heard anythin' different?"

"No." Maura felt a stab of despair. "Sean, how long before you simply stamp this case as closed and walk away?"

"Maura, a suspicious death in Ireland is

never closed — yeh've seen that yerself not long ago. Call it what yeh will, people still talk about it for a long time. The gardaí won't let it go. We're nowhere near done with this death."

"I guess that's good. It means you can always hope for justice. I'll let you know if I hear anything useful." Maura refused to put Siobhan O'Mahoney's and Ellen Buckley's secrets in that category just yet.

"Thanks, Maura. I'll be on my way then. Take care."

"I will. Thanks, Sean. And good work with getting the info out of Harvard!" she called out as he walked away.

When Maura walked back into Sullivan's, still clutching her uneaten sandwich, she said quickly, "Sorry, folks, nothing new to report. Well, maybe a little. You knew that John went to New York to join his father there. Looks like Dad and his friends set up a scholarship for John to go to Harvard, but anything after that he accomplished on his own. Seamus, how are the odds on your betting pool?"

"Why, do yeh want a piece of it?"

"I could put in a bet just to throw you guys off, you know."

"Ah, Maura, yeh're breakin' me heart. Yeh wouldn't do that to us, would yeh? We're only after havin' a bit of fun."

One of Seamus's friends called out, "The butler did it." The others laughed, and Maura rolled her eyes.

"Guys, there is no butler in this," Maura told him. "But you've still got a lot of people at Crann Mor to consider. Maybe John was a lousy tipper. Maybe the whole staff got together and threw him down the hill because he was a cheapskate. Or say John was a bird watcher and thought he heard some rare Irish night bird in the woods and lost his footing when he was chasing it down. Chew on those ideas for a while."

The pub was not too busy for the rest of the day. Any unfamiliar faces might have been due to curiosity about John Byrne's death — maybe they figured they could pry more information out of people at a small pub not too far away from the scene. By mid-afternoon, Maura was flagging — she wasn't used to all this running around and trying to think of how to ask questions without making people angry. She made herself a cup of coffee and retreated to the back room and leaned against the bar. She couldn't say she was surprised when Mick followed her in, then leaned next to her.

"Are yeh all right?"

In what way? she was tempted to reply.

"Sure, I'm fine, except that it seems like it wears me out to try to talk and think at the same time. And then there's trying to figure out who I can tell what without messing things up."

"The gardaí are no further along?"

"Sean's found a bit about Byrne's time in the US, but it doesn't seem to move things forward. Seems like John caught a lucky break in New York, took off running, and never looked back. Now he's dead. As far as anybody knows, he hadn't been back here in over twenty years. Most of what we know comes from Bridget and Billy. Funny how long people around here remember things or people. Do you think that will last? That we'll know who was who, who was related, and what they ate for dinner in a couple of decades?" She waved her hand in front of her face. "Don't listen to me. I'm just tired."

"It's been only four days since the man died. Yeh can't say there's no progress."

"I guess not. But don't try to cheer me up." She paused. "I'm sorry — I guess this thing with my mother is still nagging at me, mainly because it's so unfinished. Maybe I'm using this blasted death as an excuse to avoid talking with her, at least about anything that doesn't involve the death. Does that make me a bad person?"

371

"No, it makes yeh human."

"You mean, if I want to I can just tell her to go back to wherever she came from so I can go back to business as usual?"

"Yeh can. Up to you."

After a long pause, Maura said in a small voice, "No, I can't. It's not that easy. She's my mother."

"I know," he said, looking at his feet. "Maura, I tried to walk away from me own life. Look where it's got me."

Maura couldn't decide whether to laugh or cry. "God, we're both messes. Maybe we deserve each other."

Mick smiled. "Could be yeh're right." He reached out and pulled her closer, mindful of the open door to the main room. "If I can help, you've only to ask."

Maura laid her head against his shoulder briefly. "I know."

THIRTY-THREE

After a quiet evening at the pub, Maura retreated to her cottage with a sense of relief. Back in her own place — alone, with only her thoughts to distract her — she paced around, looking critically at it. It was hers. She could do whatever she wanted with it. But in fact, in the year she'd lived in it, she hadn't done much of anything to it. She really wasn't into how things looked, which was okay since she rarely had visitors to impress, and most of them didn't care. Here she had only herself to please.

She guessed her mother would care. Helen would take one look at this century-old dump and feel sorry for her. She didn't want anyone feeling sorry for her. Besides, she didn't spend much time here, and rarely by daylight. Who cared if there was dust in the corners and she hadn't taken the trash to the dump for a while?

Gran would have cared. No matter how

little they had, Gran had always taken good care of their place and what was in it and made sure it was neat and clean. She'd always had enough food in the cupboards and refrigerator to feed someone who needed a good meal. She'd made sure Maura had decent clothes to wear to school, even if they weren't the latest fashion. Gran had had standards. Why had she herself tossed them all out? Maybe she needed to think about that. If this really was her home now, she should stop living like a squatter.

Too late — and too dark — to do anything about it that night. Maura went to bed.

She woke up with the sun and realized she hadn't talked with Bridget since her heart-to-heart talk with Mick, the one Bridget had insisted on. Who had Bridget been trying to help? Mick, because she knew too well he was stuck, mired in guilt for what he saw as his failure with his family? Or Maura, so she could get involved with Mick with her eyes open or decide now that it wasn't going to work before anything got started? Did Bridget want her to connect with Mick? For her sake or his?

Out of bed, into the shower. Maura dressed, ate some bread and butter, and marched down to Bridget's house. She wasn't angry with Bridget, and what she'd done wasn't really meddling — it was more like looking out for the people she cared about. So she couldn't exactly yell at Bridget, but did she want Bridget to back off? She hadn't decided when Bridget opened the door to her.

"*Maidin mhaith!* Come in. I wondered if I'd be seein' yeh."

"Why?" Maura asked, following her into the room.

"He's told yeh, hasn't he?" Bridget turned to face her. "Tea?"

"Please. You want me to make it?"

"No, but yeh can talk to me while I do. Have the two of you settled things?"

A fair question, but she didn't know what she felt. "I don't know. I wouldn't call anything settled, but we're trying. What he told me, it explains a lot of things I've wondered about. But he has issues, and I don't know if he's gotten past them, or will. And I've got plenty of baggage of my own." As seeing her mother for the first time had proved.

"We all need other people in our lives," Bridget said as she poured hot water into her teapot. "Without them, yeh'll just wither away."

"Do I need your grandson in my life?" Maura tried to smile but realized that it wasn't really a joke to her.

"Ah, Maura, he may need yeh more than yeh need him, but he's a good man. And that's all I'll say. Yeh have to live yer own lives, the both of yeh. But yeh needed to hear the whole story to make a fair choice."

There was a knock on the door, and when Maura opened it, she found Gillian standing outside with young Henry in some kind of sack thing hanging against her chest. "Hey, there," Maura said. "Everything okay? You're out early."

"As good as it gets. Morning, Bridget — sorry for just barging in like this. Harry and I were down looking at the creamery, and I couldn't take it anymore."

"Ah, it's always a treat to see yeh, and yer little one, Gillian. What is it that's botherin' yeh?"

"It's not that I mind hard work, as soon as I'm up to it, and I'm handy enough with tools and plastering and the like, but there's so much that needs doing! And we've next to no furniture, and what little money we have is going to this one here." Gillian dropped a kiss on top of sleeping Henry's head. "I'm just overwhelmed. I needed to get out and move, so I walked over the hill to see you. Please tell me there's something going on in the world apart from baby poo?"

"Uh, nobody's solved John Byrne's death yet, and my mother's still around," Maura told her. "That's all I've got. Is there something specific you need at your new place?"

"Apart from intact walls and ceilings and floors? No, I'm just whinging. We've got heat and water and light. Most of what we need is cleaning and prettying up the place. And furniture. It would be nice to sit on something that isn't the floor."

"When do you want to tackle the creamery itself, apart from the house?" Maura asked.

"Oh, that's months away. If I'm lucky, I might be able to handle giving some art lessons or classes in the summer, but no sooner. One thing at a time, Maura."

"I hear you. Look, I'd better get into Leap. Do you want a ride to your place?"

"That'd be a blessing. Coming up the hill really took it out of me more than I expected. Bridget, do you mind if I hitch a ride with Maura after I've only just arrived? I promise I'll come back again soon."

"No worries. I'm happy to see yeh any time, even fer a minute or two. Give my best to Mick, will yeh, Maura?" But Bridget wouldn't let Gillian go until she'd planted a kiss on baby Henry's head.

"I will. Bye, Bridget." Maura opened the

door and let Gillian plus baby go through, then followed them up the lane to her cottage to retrieve her car.

Gillian settled herself in the front seat, still cradling her baby. "If I'm going to ride with you often, you'll have to get a child seat."

"Oh, right, of course. I didn't think to ask if it was required in Ireland. If you're worried, you can walk instead."

"No, I'll give you a pass this time, but only if you promise to get one fast. Ask around — I'm sure there'll be secondhand ones available. And remember, you'll have to drive carefully."

"I always do." Maura pointed the car down the lane. "So, your life must be pretty busy these days."

"It is that, alternating with times when I'm afraid to breathe for fear of waking the baby. There's so much to learn."

"So I've heard." Maura turned left at the bottom of the hill, headed for the Drinagh road, and drove at a stately twenty-five miles per hour. Luckily, there were no other cars on the road.

"Still no conclusion on the death?" Gillian asked. "It's near a week now."

"I know. The gardaí have learned some stuff about John Byrne's early life. It turns out he actually was born around here up near Dunmanway, but he left when he was in his teens, and it looks like he never came back. His parents are both dead, and he didn't get along with any of his other relatives before he left. The gardaí are checking if he had any contact with them on this trip."

"How sad. Was he a bad kid?"

"No, but I gather there were just too many kids in the family to deal with them all."

"Not an uncommon story back in those days."

Maura turned left on the Drinagh road, then left again a bit farther on, on the road that led past the creamery and Ballinlough.

"Before you ask," Maura said, "I still haven't really talked with my mother. Maybe we're more alike than I thought — we both seem to be holding back, like we don't want to intrude on each other's lives. I appreciate that, kind of, but it feels weird. I guess biology isn't everything."

"Luckily not if you're John Byrne, I'd guess. Orphaned farm boy gets shipped off to the New World and becomes a millionaire. Sad that he had to die when he tried to come back. Do you think it was about his money? Or his family, maybe?"

"I don't know. Nobody outside of the hotel staff seems to have seen or talked to him last Friday night after dinner, and he wasn't exactly rubbing anyone's nose in his money once he'd bought that humongous hotel. As far as we know, nobody knew he was here, except his staff. Although I suppose the hotel people might have said something." Maura pulled into the graveled area in front of the creamery, but before getting out of the car, she looked at it critically. Sometime in decades past, it had been painted a cheerful shade of turquoise that was now faded and patchy. An old double door facing the road hung slightly askew on ancient iron strap hinges, and someone had painted it an unlikely shade of red. A lot of paint had simply fallen off over the years.

"You going to keep the color scheme?"

"Do you know, I haven't decided. It kind of grows on you. And if I'm trying to give directions to students, it would be so much easier to say, 'It's the big blue building by the lough.' "

"Good point."

Gillian gathered up the baby and got out of the car. "Thanks for the lift, Maura." Gillian waved as Maura pulled away and drove toward Leap.

As she drove, Maura reviewed her to-do list. Spend quality time with her friends Bridget and Gillian — check. Then there was Mick. They'd both taken a giant step forward after a nudge from Bridget, but there were still problems to be solved. But that was life, right? She'd never expected anything to be easy.

But this love stuff was confusing. Her grandmother had loved her husband, as far as Maura knew. Her mother had loved her father, or so she said. Maura had no idea how Helen felt about her current husband, but they had had two kids together, and they were still married. Gillian had loved Harry for years but hadn't ever assumed that anything permanent would come of it. Jimmy and Judith? That sounded more like a practical business arrangement than a grand passion.

Siobhan was a different case. She'd gotten pregnant after an unplanned night, but she'd accepted the responsibility, kept the child, and later married Tim Nolan. And once Tim died and a respectable amount of time had passed, Siobhan had married again. To someone she had known for years and had worked with. Someone who had loved her for a long time.

Maura suddenly pulled over to an open spot by the side of the road and stopped. Both Siobhan and Bernard O'Mahoney had said they'd known each other for years, and

Siobhan had added that he'd been sweet on her for a long time. While she was married to Tim? Before? After?

It had taken Bernard a long time to propose after Tim's death. And Siobhan had accepted, and they'd had a big wedding at the hotel. Now should be the happily-ever-after part. And then John Byrne had dropped in out of the blue. Had Siobhan told Bernard about Ellen's father? Or had he found out some other way? He was older than Siobhan, and he could have heard it from someone years earlier. Still, he'd married Siobhan and finally gotten what he had wished for. The perfect ending — until John showed up. Siobhan had met with John openly as a staff member. But she had also told Maura that they had met privately in the garden when Siobhan had shared the news about Ellen. Had Bernard seen them together? Had he seen his fragile happiness falling to pieces?

And when did you start thinking like a soap opera writer, Maura?

Okay, this new theory was loaded with a lot of what-ifs, but maybe it was worth talking with Bernard O'Mahoney.

Did she really think Bernard had killed John? Maybe. He was certainly strong enough, even if he was twenty or more years older than John. All that outdoor work — shoveling, chopping, sawing, and such — had to have kept him fit.

But why leave John's body where it was likely to be found? Bernard knew the property well, and there must be places to stash or bury a body. Maybe he'd wanted to be sure that Siobhan knew John was dead — after all, he was the father of her child. If he had been killed, someone had made some effort to make it look like an accident. Which meant that if that had been Bernard, he would have had to carry the body somehow to the lonely path where it had been dumped. Bernard was strong enough. And how very convenient that he'd found John's body. Maybe that was the point. Maybe he had tried to divert the gardaí's attention by getting his story in first. If he had killed John.

She pulled back onto the road and drove the last few miles to Leap. She parked in front of the pub and hurried in. Luckily, Mick was behind the bar, so she walked directly over to him. "Mick, can I ask you a really big favor?"

"Yeh may. Can I ask what it is?"

Maura glanced around. "Not in front of everyone. Come outside. Jimmy, can you cover?" she called out, raising her voice.

"Fine," he grumbled. "Fer how long?"

"I don't know. Thanks, Jimmy." She waited impatiently while Mick came around from behind the bar, and then she all but dragged him out the door.

"So?" Mick asked.

"I want you to come with me while I talk to the groundskeeper at Crann Mor."

"And why would that be?"

"I think it's possible that he may have killed John Byrne, but I'm not sure enough to go to the gardaí. If I'm right, he's a strong man, and he might be angry, and . . ."

"Yeh need me to watch yer back. We're goin' now?"

Despite her anxiety, Maura was warmed by his unquestioning response. "Please. And thank you."

Thirty-Four

"I'll drive — my car's closer," Maura told Mick. He didn't protest.

"How do yeh plan to find the man?" he asked.

"Uh, look around outside the hotel? That's where he works and has for decades. I talked to him once a couple of days ago, so I'd recognize him."

"And why is it you've landed on him as a suspect, all at once?" Mick asked as they walked toward Maura's car.

"It's only a theory, but here's what I've been thinking." Maura outlined the story that she'd strung together on her way to Leap. Mick didn't interrupt but listened carefully. "You think I'm totally off base?" she said finally.

Mick took a moment before answering. "I think it's worth askin' him about it. Though yeh'll have made an enemy or two if yeh're wrong."

"I know, and I don't want to do that. But isn't it better coming from me than from a garda? If I'm wrong, I'm the only one he'll be angry at. And I don't want to mess up other people's lives — Siobhan's, her daughter's — based on my theory."

"What is it yeh want me to do? Hide behind a bush?"

"No, just be there. You don't happen to know Bernard, do you? I mean, he hasn't ever been a regular at the pub or something?"

"I don't recall that I've met the man. Did yeh ask Billy about him?"

"Not about this. Billy told me about where he fit in the bigger picture and how he came to marry Siobhan. You think I should now?"

Mick stopped walking, so Maura was forced to stop and looked up at him. "Yeh're in a hurry, aren't yeh?" he asked.

"I guess I am. John Byrne's been dead for five days now. We've learned a lot about his history and maybe why he was here, but I still don't know who could have killed him or why. And now there's this new garda sergeant who's pushy and probably wants to start his time here off with a bang, and I don't trust him not to make things worse. And for myself, I'd really like to get this cleared up so Helen and I can have some time just to chill out and get to know each other a bit without all these questions hanging over our heads. So I guess you could say I'm in a hurry."

"Fair enough. So, if this Bernard tells yeh yeh're daft, what will yeh do?"

"Apologize and walk away, I guess."

"This is still about yer mother, is it not?"

He was being annoying, but he was probably right. "In a way. All these things — John's death, my mother being here — are all tangled together. But it's not just about me. Siobhan and Ellen deserve to know what happened to John and what's going to happen with the hotel and their jobs, and that's all bogged down in finding out why John Byrne is dead."

"Will this chat with Bernard be the end of it, then?" Mick asked.

"I don't know! I'm making this up as I go. I don't have any more ideas, so I'll have to leave it to the gardaí. Would you be happier if I left you here on the sidewalk and talked to Bernard by myself?"

Mick turned to face her. "Don't. Please. I couldn't forgive myself if somethin' happened to you."

Maura felt a spurt of shame: she hadn't given any thought to how he might feel. Did he really believe that Bernard would attack her? She really was bad with this relationship stuff. "Oh. Well, thanks for backing me up." Maura wished she had a moment to chew on what he had just said, but she wanted to get to the hotel and find Bernard. They had reached her car, so they climbed in and started for Skibbereen. A few minutes later, she pulled up in front of the main building at Crann Mor. There was no one in sight and no cars — business must be slow.

"The gardens are out back," she told Mick, "and there's the path where John died that leads from behind the building toward the lake. Might as well go around."

"Right." Mick followed Maura as she skirted the building and walked into the formal garden.

Maura breathed a sigh of relief: Bernard was there on his knees, weeding the flower beds. There were flats of plants next to him, ready to bloom. He looked up as she approached and then stood a bit stiffly, his expression wary. "Maura Donovan, is it? Were yeh lookin' fer somethin'?"

"Yes, Bernard — you. I wanted to talk with you. This is Mick Nolan, a . . . friend of mine." The two men nodded at each other silently. Then Mick retreated a short distance and sat on a low stone wall, watching.

"Can we sit then?" Bernard asked. "Me knees aren't what they used to be. What is it yeh're wantin' to talk about?"

"John Byrne."

"I've told you what I know. And the gardaí as well."

"Have you? I'm wondering if there's more," Maura said. "Please, sit down." She wanted to use the time it took to get settled to gather her thoughts. Of course, that gave Bernard the time to gather his own.

When they were arrayed on a long curved bench, Maura began. "You're married to Siobhan Buckley, right?"

Bernard nodded. "I am that, three years come summer. Yeh've met her, then?"

"I have. And her daughter, Ellen. Siobhan told me you'd waited a long time to marry her." Maura wondered if that was too personal to mention to someone she barely knew and was relieved when he answered her.

"I did. I'd known her since she started workin' here and before. What's that got to do wit' anything?"

"I know this is very personal, but did she tell you about Ellen's father?"

Bernard didn't answer right away but held

his eyes steady on hers. He looked sad. "It were her secret fer a long time, but she wanted to be straight with me, and so many years have passed . . . She still hasn't told Ellen."

Too late now; Ellen knew. But Maura didn't need to tell Bernard that. "Were you surprised when John Byrne showed up here?"

"I was. I knew some big company had bought this place a while back, but nothin' changed fer a time. And then these people show up, all high and mighty, and start talkin' about what they wanted to do with the place."

"Were you worried about your job?"

He shrugged. "I can't say that I was, not at first. I've taken good care of the place fer a long time now, even after that fancy garden designer came and went, so they can see what I've done laid out in front of them."

"Did you meet John Byrne then?"

Bernard sniffed. "He didn't dirty his hands shakin' with the likes of me. Not that I expected him to. He spoke to us all, gathered together, like, and then he spent a day or two, him and his people, lookin' in corners and askin' questions."

"Did he visit the garden here?"

"Must've done, mustn't he? He poked

around everywhere else. Yeh have to go out this way if yeh're inside the hotel and want to get to the lake and the other buildin's down that way. If yeh don't mind my askin', why do yeh want to know all this?"

Maura gave him points for being polite, at least. She would have been angry by now at this kind of nosy treatment from a stranger. But she hadn't learned anything new yet, and she hadn't asked the hard questions. She had to keep going. Bernard sat silent as a stone, waiting.

She took a deep breath. "You told me you were the one who found his body, and you didn't know why he would have been out here after it was dark."

"That's right." Bernard nodded, his eyes wary.

"The gardaí didn't find much evidence of the fall. No footprints and stuff."

"The path's paved, and there's brush alongside it. It hadn't rained much fer a few days. There'd be no footprints. Nothin' to see."

"Makes sense," Maura said. Then she said carefully, "What if he didn't die there, but someone killed him and dumped him there, hoping it would look like a fall? Did you see anything that would show that?"

"And what would that be?" Bernard asked.

"Extradeep footprints where they shouldn't be, maybe, like somebody was carrying something heavy. Scuff marks like he was dragged. Or" — her gaze fell on a battered wheelbarrow not far away, holding more flats of flowers to be planted — "a wheelbarrow, which would leave a deep tire track unless somebody was very careful to stay on the paved parts of the path. That person would have had to know the place pretty well to know that path and stay on it in the dark with a heavy load." Maura glanced briefly at Bernard, whose expression didn't change. He wasn't giving anything away.

Suddenly Maura was tired of beating around the bush. She had no patience left for this. "Bernard, I don't know you. I've talked to your wife, and I've talked to Ellen. I don't think they had anything to do with what happened, but maybe I'm a lousy judge of character. But let me just say this and get it over with. Were you involved with John Byrne's death?"

Bernard was watching her carefully. "And why would I be?"

Not exactly a direct answer, but she hadn't heard a no. "I can think of more than one reason." She ticked them off on her fingers. "You're trying to protect your wife, and maybe you were afraid John would accuse her of trying to shake him down for money — she told me he hadn't known about Ellen until he got here. Or you say Ellen didn't know he was her father — maybe you were trying to protect her. Or you wanted to keep your job. You wanted everything to stay as it had always been now that you'd married Siobhan. How'm I doing?"

"You've a sharp mind, Miss Donovan, but I think yeh might've missed a few." He almost smiled.

Am I getting warm? "Okay, how about these? You saw Siobhan kill him, and you moved John's body to try to cover it up. Or Ellen did it when he rejected her after she confronted him about being her father, and you wanted to protect her for Siobhan's sake. How's that?"

Bernard took his time answering. Finally he said, "I'm sure yeh mean well, but why should I say anythin'? I don't see any gardaí here. I told them my tale at the start, and they've let me be since. Give it a rest, Miss Donovan. The man's dead. I'm bettin' the official report will say John Byrne fell down the hill and died, and the dent in his skull could have come from any one of those trees on the way down the hill or mebbe a rock. Yeh don't know me, but others will tell yeh

I'm not a violent man. I don't drink, and I don't get into fights. I do my job and go home to my wife every night, and I stay out of trouble. What do yeh want from me?"

Maura felt deflated. She'd thrown all her ideas at him, and he hadn't bitten on any of them. Maybe she simply was wrong. Maybe she should go back and talk to Siobhan and Ellen again — maybe together this time. Or maybe she should just give up and get on with her life.

Mick stood and approached Bernard and Maura, then spoke up for the first time. "Bernard, there's many people here at the hotel that might've had reason to want John Byrne gone. Mebbe not dead, but they might've wanted to send him home and get on with things. And there's folk who don't like to see changes. Yeh've done a grand job here from what I can see, and yeh're right to be proud."

"Nolan, if yeh're trying to accuse me of murder, yeh're wanderin' all over the map."

"Did yeh kill John Byrne?" Mick said bluntly.

The question hung in the air, and Maura found she was holding her breath. Bernard looked out over the garden, which even in early spring looked lovely and must have given him great satisfaction. It was the result of years of care. His late marriage to Siobhan was the result of years of patient courting. Maura realized she found it hard to picture this not-young man acting on the spur of the moment, much less with violence.

After a long silence, Bernard sighed. "I might've had a hand in it, but not the way yeh're thinking. Will yeh listen?"

"Of course I will," Maura said.

Bernard began slowly. "Did yeh meet the man?"

"Briefly," Maura said, and Mick nodded. "Why?"

"Even a short meetin' would tell yeh what kind of a man he was. Pushy. Cocky. It got him where he was. But he rubbed a lot of the people here the wrong way."

"I felt the same way," Maura said. "Like Sullivan's was something he could buy and sell, not a real place with people."

Bernard nodded. "He came out around nightfall to look at the gardens or maybe just to get some air. He saw me, and we got to talkin'. First thing he tells me is that he wanted to move the path around so it would be easier to get to the lake, and he wanted put it straight through the trees, and put in some pretty flower beds alongside. Yeh could tell he was a city boy and didn't know his plants."

And John hadn't realized he was talking about trashing something that Bernard had cherished for years, Maura thought. "What did you do?"

"Kept me mouth shut. Nodded and smiled and said the right things. After all, he was just lookin' around, see? There was still time to change his mind. So he strolled about fer a while, mostly talkin' on his mobile phone.

"After a bit he calls me over. 'Bernard, is it?' he says. 'It's a beautiful place yeh've got here, but I'm thinkin', mebbe it's time to freshen it up.' Or some fool thing like that. I said nothing because I was afraid if I opened me gob, the wrong thing would come out. Then he looks me in the eye and says, 'Ye're married to Siobhan Buckley, are yeh not?' I nod, wonderin' what he's after. 'She's worked here for a good many years. And her daughter has as well, am I right?' And I tell him that's the truth. And I wait, fer I'm thinkin' he's still workin' up to something. Then he goes, 'Did Siobhan tell yeh that Ellen's my daughter?'

"And I say, 'Of course she did, years past. What of it?'

" 'She likes the job here, workin' with her ma and all?' he says.

" 'She does.'

" 'It'd be a shame if she was to lose that job, and her ma as well.'

"I look at him full on, and I say, 'Are yeh tellin' me that you'll look after them if I go quietly?'

" 'Yeh're a smart man, Bernard. I want to get this place off on the right foot. Siobhan's not young, and I might like a prettier face at the front desk. I'll admit yeh've done well with the garden, but yeh're gettin' on in years. Out of respect fer you and due to my connection with Siobhan, I'll guarantee her job until she's ready to go. And Ellen's. But not yours. Do yeh catch my drift?'

"So he's tellin' me I'm fired, but Siobhan can stay on if she wants. I could find work at some other place, no worries, but Siobhan might want to stick by me if she learns how it come about. She knows how much this place has meant to me since I was a young lad. 'Can I think on it?' I ask the man. And he says, 'No. This is a one-time offer.' "

"What did you do?" Maura asked softly.

"I was angry, wasn't I? He'd put me between a rock and a hard place, and it didn't sit right with me. I might have taken a step toward him, without thinking, to get in his face, and . . ."

"Did you hit him? Push him?" Maura asked.

Bernard shook his head. "I never touched him. He took a step back, not lookin' where he was puttin' his feet. So over there?" Bernard pointed to the far corner on the enclosed garden. "The man tripped on somethin' in those silly fancy shoes of his, and he fell over backward. Can yeh see that pump in the corner? It's iron — old, heavy — it's there because it's a handsome piece, not because it's easy to get water from. The man hit his head on the handle as he fell, and that was all. I was over to him in seconds, but there was nothin' to be done."

THIRTY-FIVE

After a long silence, Mick said quietly, "A doctor might've said different."

Bernard turned to face him. "Yeh're a local man, are yeh not? Yeh'd know how long it would've been to get a doctor here. Or to take him to hospital. Part of the man's head was bashed in like an egg — yeh could see it easy. He fell hard."

"Yeh could have tried," Mick said, "and explained what happened. It was an accident, right?"

Bernard straightened up to face Mick squarely. "I might've hit the man if I could, fer that's what I was thinkin' to do, and he saw that. But I never had the chance."

Mick was right, Maura knew. If Bernard had only left things alone after checking on John's condition and reported it immediately, there would have been no problem. A tragic fall, poor John, end of story. An accident. But Bernard had done his best to cover it all up, and then he'd lied. Why?

"So why didn't you call the gardaí and tell them what happened?" Maura demanded.

Bernard looked down at his feet. "Do yeh know, I really can't say. I knew I hadn't laid a hand on him. But he was rich and important, and I was the old gardener. Why would anyone believe me?" He looked up at Maura then. "And then I started thinkin'. There's plenty of people who had reason to do him harm if their secrets came out. Mebbe the world has changed, but there's still those who would think that Siobhan should have given her baby away and gone away herself. Could be Ellen wouldn't mind everyone knowin' how she came into the world, but it would still hurt her ma. I couldn't have that. Me job's not important, but Siobhan's is to her. I could've taken the man up on his offer and never told her, but I wouldn't want to lie to her. I was afraid she'd take my side and quit, and where would we have been then?"

"You told the gardaí you found John's body the next morning halfway down the hill. You moved him?" Mick pressed.

Bernard nodded. "I looked about and didn't see anyone — it was dark anyways, and there were few guests stayin' at the hotel, so none could see us in the back. I had the wheelbarrow close by, so I picked the man up and dumped him in it, then covered him with a canvas and shoved it in a corner where no one would look. I figgered I'd best wait until it was full dark to move him. I wanted folk to think he was alone."

"What about his phone?" Maura asked.

"Flew out of his hand when he fell and hit a rock. It was broken, so I pitched it down the hill after him. That's the truth. Figgered when he was found, people would think it had fallen out of his pocket when he went down the hill and might not even bother lookin' fer it."

"How long did yeh wait?" Mick asked.

"It was gone midnight when I shuffled him down the path and over the edge. Siobhan was coverin' the desk that night, so she didn't notice how late I was. It were early the next mornin' I called the gardaí, said I come upon Byrne at the bottom of the hill, and it was clear he were dead."

"Did you clean up the wheelbarrow?" Maura asked suddenly. There might still be evidence there, like John's blood. But did she want the gardaí to find evidence that pointed to Bernard? Or did she want to spare him?

She felt lost. Murder was a crime — but

this wasn't a murder, exactly. Bernard might have wanted to hit him, but he'd never gotten close enough, if what Bernard had told them was the truth. Was he lying to her? He'd only wanted to spare his beloved wife pain. Damn this love stuff. What exactly was Bernard guilty of? Threatening John? Concealing evidence? Were those crimes in Ireland?

What if John Byrne's death was officially declared an accident rather than a murder? It would be kinder to John's family back in the States. It would save Siobhan and Ellen possible embarrassment. Bernard would be in the clear, on record as the person who found the body. It might make a difference to the remaining members of JBCo — an accident on the grounds would be less damaging to its reputation than a murder.

But she would have to lie to Detective Hurley and Sean Murphy, or at least shade the truth, for the sake of someone she barely knew. And that would be wrong. The gardaí trusted her, and that mattered too.

What would Mick think? He'd heard what Bernard had said, and he knew Siobhan's and Ellen's stories. Would the idea that Bernard had wanted only to protect the wife he adored be enough to convince Mick to keep quiet? And did she have the right to ask him to do that?

Mick seemed to be watching her, waiting. Maura turned to face Bernard. "Bernard, I want to think over what you've told me and how it all fits together. You may not like it, but I think I need to tell the gardaí about what you've just told me. I believe that it was an accident, but that's not my decision to make."

Bernard's expression was grave. "I can respect that. I may not have liked John Byrne, but I never would've killed the man or let him die in front of me because I stood by and did nothing. I'd swear that on any Bible."

After a long moment, Maura said, "I believe you." She turned to Mick. "Let's go."

Mick didn't protest but followed her silently. Did that mean he agreed with her? Or that he was mad at her? How much did his opinion matter to her? How much was she willing to risk based on what was no more than her gut feeling?

When they reached Maura's car in front of the hotel, another car was pulling in — a garda car driven by Sergeant Ryan. Maura felt a chill in the pit of her stomach. Did he know something? Or was he just checking out anything and everything? He'd seen them, so they couldn't jump in the car and disappear in a hurry. So she and Mick waited in silence as the sergeant got out of his car and sauntered over to them. "Would yeh know where I can find the grounds-keeper?"

Maura bit back a flippant answer — she didn't want to annoy him. "I believe he's usually in the garden out back. Any progress on Byrne's death?"

"We're still making our inquiries." He turned without saying anything more and headed around the building the way she and Mick had done.

For a moment, everything whirled around in Maura's head. Bernard would think she had called the cops on him, which wasn't good. The sergeant was a no-nonsense guy and could be likely to jump to conclusions. The end result might be him dragging Bernard back to the Skibbereen station and accusing him of murder. She didn't want that, not without having a chance to explain. Which meant she had to talk to Detective Hurley before Sergeant Ryan did anything stupid. Would the detective accept her version, or would he have to side with his own garda?

"Get in," she ordered Mick. "We're going to the garda station." Mick complied.

It wasn't until they had pulled out of the Crann Mor driveway that Mick spoke. "Did yeh get what you hoped from the man?"

"Yes. Look, Mick, I've talked with Siobhan and with Ellen and asked them questions I had no right to ask and no right to expect them to answer. I don't believe either of them knew what Bernard did — or almost did. John died because he confronted Bernard and more or less fired him. That's a motive for Bernard, for sure. Would Bernard have fought with him, beaten him up, maybe killed him? I can't answer that. But my gut tells me I have to tell Detective Hurley what I know now. And I have to do it before Sergeant Ryan mucks it up." Maura tried to read Mick's expression, but he was good at hiding what he really thought. "Look, you're in this now — what are you going to do? You've every right to go to the gardaí yourself and tell them what you know. Or you can step back, Mick, and do nothing. This isn't your fight. I'll take it to the gardaí and leave you out of it."

He looked at her then. "And why should you do that? Yeh think I'd side with the gardaí?"

"You have no connection with the hotel, you don't know anybody there, and you spent the same amount of time with John

Byrne as I did, which is not much. Why should his death matter to you?"

"Because yeh're involved," he said. "And because it's the right thing to do."

"Is it?" Maura asked, hating the desperation in her voice.

"Do yeh doubt that? Maura, no one meant fer John Byrne to die. I don't trust the new sergeant any more than you do — he's looking fer a quick answer. He doesn't know the people here."

"I don't want Bernard to be hurt by this, but I still feel it would be wrong to say nothing. The gardaí need to know what happened."

"Look, Maura, yeh've got kind of a special relationship with the gardaí, even with the detective inspector. He's a fair man. Tell him what you know and let him decide. There may be charges filed, but I doubt he'd think first of murder. You trust him, do you not?"

"I do." Maura felt like a weight was lifted off her shoulders. How simple: let Detective Hurley make the decision. She knew from her own experience that he was a good man, and she did trust his judgment. "All right, I'll tell him. But we've got to give him our version before the sergeant drags Bernard in in chains. Or would you rather stay out of it?"

"I'm going in with yeh," he said and fell silent. And Maura was grateful.

Maura drove back into the town and parked, then marched to the garda station with Mick at her back. Inside she asked the person behind the desk, who she didn't recognize, "Is the detective inspector in?"

"He's here, but he's in a meeting. Would someone else do?"

Maura considered asking for Sean, but she needed a higher authority to handle this, and she didn't want to put Sean in a difficult position. "I don't think so. I can wait until he's free."

"Yeh're Maura Donovan, aren't yeh?" the young officer asked.

"Yes, I am."

"Why don't I let him know yeh're out here?" He got up and disappeared into the main room of the station, leaving Maura wondering what kind of a reputation she had here. At least the staff knew she wouldn't be here unless it was important.

Patrick Hurley arrived after another five minutes had passed. "Maura," he said. "Mick." Mick nodded his greeting. "Does this have to do with John Byrne's death?"

"It does."

The detective stepped back and ushered them through the door, then followed, directing them to the conference room. When he'd shut the door and they were seated, he said, "Tell me." Luckily, he looked concerned rather than annoyed that he'd been interrupted.

Maura swallowed. "I — we have some new information about John Byrne's death, but I'm not sure what laws might be involved, and I don't want to get anyone in trouble."

"Why don't you just tell me what you've found, and I'll tell you what I think?" he said gently.

So Maura launched into what she had learned from Siobhan and Ellen and Bernard. It took some time to present the bald facts, and she was careful not to reveal that Sean had heard any of it. Mick added no more than an occasional word. She felt drained by the time she was through. "So you see my problem? Bernard might have threatened the man, but I don't think he meant John any harm. The whole thing was no more than a stupid accident because of John's fancy shoes. I felt I couldn't tell you before because there were other people involved and I'd made promises to them, but when Bernard told me what had happened and the fact that he had tried to cover it up for what he thought were good reasons . . ."

Inspector Hurley held up a hand. "Please, Maura, take a breath. You should know as well as anyone that the gardaí are not ogres, and we do respect other people's confidences when we can. As you've said, it would have been better all around if O'Mahoney had told us right away rather than sending us off in the wrong direction, but he seems to have acted not in his own interests but to protect his wife. An understandable response."

"But isn't there some kind of law around here about concealing evidence or withholding evidence or something like that?" Maura asked anxiously.

"There is, and I think Bernard should be held accountable for that. But that's far better than accusing him of killing the man. What came after — the moving of the body — was poor judgment on his part."

More or less what she had hoped. Maura slumped in her chair and closed her eyes for a moment, then looked at the detective. "So what are you going to do about Bernard?"

"I'll have to think about the lesser charge, so I won't promise anything. I doubt he's going anywhere."

"Fair enough. I can live with that," Maura said firmly. "Did you already know all this stuff about John Byrne and his dad in New York and all that?"

"Sean Murphy pointed us in the right direction. It's an interesting tale, but as far as we've seen, Byrne moved beyond his past and did well for himself — there's no evidence of involvement in any sort of criminal activity later in his life. It's a shame his homecoming turned out as it did. Have you had any word about the fate of the hotel now?"

"No, but I'll ask . . . my mother. Are we finished here?"

Detective Hurley stood up. "I believe we are. Thank you for coming in, Maura. I'd like to think we would have arrived at much the same conclusions once we'd persuaded Bernard to tell us the facts, but you've saved us a bit of time."

They were on the verge of leaving when there was a commotion at the front entrance of the station. Maura froze, and Detective Hurley stepped forward. Then Sergeant Ryan came storming in, wrangling Bernard O'Mahoney in front of him. Both looked the worse for wear.

"Yeh need to arrest this man for murder," Ryan bellowed.

"Let him go, Ryan," Detective Hurley said in a quiet voice.

"What?" Sergeant Ryan protested.

"I said, release him. I understand what you're thinking, but I don't believe an arrest is warranted at this time. Mr. O'Mahoney, you won't be going anywhere, now, will you?"

"No, sir. I know I've done wrong and that you need to know about it, but I'd not leave my wife and my home. You may trust me on that, sir."

Sergeant Ryan spent a long moment looking incredulously from one face to another. In the end, he spat out something inarticulate and let go of Bernard before stalking out of the building. Maura let out a breath she didn't know she was holding. "Bernard, I didn't tell the sergeant anything."

Bernard nodded to her. "Ah, it would have come out in the end. Are yeh sayin' I'm free to go, Detective?"

"Give your story to Garda Murphy out there, and then you may leave. Just know that this isn't over yet."

"I hear what yeh're sayin.' I won't let you down." Bernard straightened his clothes, then turned and walked out of the room with slow dignity.

"Can we go now?" Maura asked.

Detective Hurley couldn't hide his smile. "You may. Though a word about Sergeant Ryan. He is a good and honest garda, but he's had a rough time. Be patient with him and he'll come around."

Outside, Maura took a deep breath. Doing the right thing felt good, especially when things worked out. "That went better than I expected," she told Mick as they strolled back toward her car. "At least until the end."

"I'd agree. And I'd trust the man to do right by Bernard. Let's hope the sergeant can come to terms with a different style."

"Not to mention the fact that a couple of amateurs like us figured out how and why John died simply by talking to people?" She grinned at him.

"Let's not rub his face in it if we happen to cross paths with him again."

They had reached Maura's car, but Maura didn't feel in any hurry to get back to work. She leaned back against the car, stretched her neck, and loosened her shoulders.

They'd done it: they'd figured it out. Let the gardaí clean it all up. She could finally relax and talk to Helen without the uncertainty of John's death hanging over her.

"We should be gettin' back to Sullivan's, if Jimmy hasn't run it into the ground." Mick nudged her. "What're yeh gonna tell

Seamus and the lads?"

"Oh, shoot, I hadn't thought that far. Was accident on their list?"

"Not that I recall — I think he tossed that idea early on. Does that mean yeh win the pot?"

"Let's hope so — I have a plan for my winnings."

"And that'd be?" Mick said.

"You'll see." Maura paused, struggling to go on. "Mick, thank you for backing me up, and thank you for giving me space, if that makes any sense."

Mick looked out the front window of the car. "It does. But it's not all my doin' — I've had more experience with the second one. Mostly too much space."

"I'm sorry — I didn't mean to remind you."

"It's part of me life — I can't undo what's happened. But I've been bogged down in self-pity fer too long. Yeh're a good example to me, yeh know. Life kicks yeh in the gut, time and again, and yeh just keep going. Yer mother vanishes, yer gran dies, yeh've no place to live, no job . . ."

"Jesus, Mick, next you'll start passing a can around for contributions. I don't want anybody's pity. And you forgot to mention the last part, when I showed up here and

413

someone I never met handed me a pub and a house. Problems solved. Did I deserve it? I don't think it's about that — it's just one of those weird things that happens. That doesn't make me a role model, just lucky."

Mick looked as serious as Maura had ever seen him. "But yeh don't quit, Maura. Yeh know what's right, and yeh can't seem to rest until yeh've fixed things. But on that subject, I don't expect yeh to try to fix me."

"And I don't plan to," Maura countered. "I'm still working on me. Now can we go back to Leap?"

"Yeh never said — what're yeh telling the lads?"

"Part of the truth: the case is closed."

THIRTY-SIX

When Maura and Mick walked into Sullivan's with Maura in the lead, Seamus and his pals turned in unison to look at her. "Any news?" Seamus called out.

"Yes, there is." Her statement created quite a stir among the seated men, and Maura felt bad that she had to disappoint them. But this was a game to them and far much more serious for the people actually involved. "I've just come from the garda station, and they have declared that John Byrne's death was an accident. He hit his head when he stumbled and fell" — she didn't have to say where and how he fell — "then went down the hill, and that was that. Things got muddied because the groundskeeper moved the body and concealed evidence. But there's no murder."

The group around the table groaned as one.

Maura grinned. "Don't worry, boys. You

made a good effort, and I'll buy you a round anyway. And if you remember, if none of you won, I get to claim a reward."

"The money in the pool?" Seamus asked, trying to look stricken.

"No, not exactly. Let me get your pints, and I'll explain."

She walked over to the bar where Rose had already anticipated her request and had the glasses lined up. "Did I miss anything?" she asked Rose.

"Just that lot." Rose nodded toward Seamus's gang. "They haven't been here long, though. They've had a grand time with their bettin'. Too bad no one won," Rose said as she topped off the pints.

"Truth and justice won, Rose," Maura said solemnly — then laughed at Rose's confused expression. "Really, it did. The gardaí figured it out in the end. With just a little help from all of us here." Close enough to the truth, Maura thought.

Maura picked up the tray of glasses that Rose had filled and carried it carefully over to Seamus's table. She placed it in the center, and the men helped themselves quickly. But they were surprised when Maura pulled up another chair to the table and sat down herself — surprised enough to hold off on drinking. "Guys, I want to talk about my winnings."

The men groaned again, sounding like a small flock of sheep.

"It's not that awful. Tell me, how many of you are married?"

Four of the six men raised a hand.

"And how many of you have kids?"

Three hands went up. "What's this got to do with anything?" Seamus asked.

"You know Gillian Callanan? My artist friend? She and Harry have just had a baby, and they've bought the old creamery on Ballinlough to live in. But the place is kind of a dump, and they don't have the time and energy to do much about it right away with a new baby and all. So I'm volunteering you lot to help out. Cleaning out trash, painting, whatever it takes to make it livable." When a couple of the men started to protest, Maura raised a hand to stop them. "If you don't like that, I'll call your wives and tell them to drag you over there — they'll understand. Look, it's only for a couple of hours. You can spare that, right? And those of you who don't have wives can haul away the old furniture and junk that's been left behind."

"Mebbe," Seamus muttered.

"Definitely," Maura said firmly. "If you all pitch in, it will go fast. And one thing more

— if any of you have baby stuff or clothes that you don't think you'll be needing anymore, Gillian would be very grateful to have them."

"When would we be doin' this?" Seamus asked.

"Saturday, mid-afternoon. Believe me, I won't cut into your drinking time. Most of you live up that way anyway, so it's not out of your way. Do we have a deal?"

"What happens if we say no?" one man asked.

"Then I might say no the next time you ask for a last pint in the evening, close to closing," Maura shot back.

Seamus looked around at his posse, then turned to Maura again. "My friends and I would be delighted to offer our assistance and support to our new neighbors. Possibly the prettiest of our neighbors." He raised his voice. "After you, of course, Rosie darlin'!"

"Ah, go on wit' yeh," Rose said in an exaggerated country accent.

Maura stood up. "Then I'll see you all on Saturday."

A second good deed done. Not bad for half a day's work.

She gathered up the dirty glasses and passed them over the counter so that Rose could wash them in case anybody else came in. Maura wasn't going to hold her breath on that. Thank goodness for her regulars.

Now there were only the issues with her mother to work out. Well, not exactly. Things to be done: Get Gillian settled with the bare necessities of equipment and furniture. Find new hires for the pub. Get Harry a job (yeah, like she knew where to look for someone who needed an accountant). Figure out where things might be going with Mick. Then settle things with her mother. Maybe she should try for world peace while she was at it.

Had she eaten today? She had a dim memory of breakfast, but that was a long time ago. "Rose, you mind if I go get something to eat? Want me to bring you something?"

"No, I'm grand."

"Billy?" she called out. "Have you eaten?"

He opened one eye. "I have done, but a packet of crisps would be welcome. I'll hear your story when you return."

"Deal," Maura said. Billy deserved to know since he was the one who had remembered the Byrne family. And Bridget had added her own pieces to the puzzle. Maybe someday she could sit down with Sergeant Ryan and explain how it was all the little details — and paying attention to the people telling them — that had solved the case. If he'd listen to an American publican — and a young female one at that. Maybe when pigs learned to fly.

Outside, everything looked normal in spite of the crazy week. Before stopping at the lunch place on the corner, Maura sat down on the bench that overlooked the small river — the one that O'Donovan's superhorse had leapt over — and called her mother on her mobile.

Helen answered quickly. "Maura? Is there something new?"

"Yes, I guess you'd say so. The gardaí have closed the case on John Byrne. They're calling it an accident." Explaining Bernard's role could come later.

"Oh, thank goodness. We've all been holding our breaths over here, waiting for word. Well, I have, at least. I think Andrew and Tiffany may be polishing their resumes. I'll send them home now because we need them at the office to coordinate conference calls and, well, a lot of other things."

"Do you want to get together and talk about it?"

"Certainly. Now? Where?"

"Today's good — things are kind of slow at the pub. Have you seen Glandore yet?"

"I don't think so. Should I?"

"It's a small town on the harbor, easy to get to from where you are. There are a couple of places to eat there, and I haven't had lunch yet."

"Sounds good. Tell me how to find it, and I'll meet you."

Fifteen minutes later, after stopping back at the pub to tell Rose her lunch might take a bit longer than she'd thought, Maura was leaning on a railing by the harbor in one-street Glandore, admiring the pretty boats and the pretty view, when her mother pulled up and parked. Helen climbed out of her car and joined her.

"I haven't been here before — it's charming. Sorry, that sounds condescending. I have to keep reminding myself that Ireland is not a cute theme park designed to provide tourists with nice pictures."

"Nope. It's full of real people with ordinary problems. Look, I'm starving. The Glandore Inn does some nice food, if that's okay with you."

"Fine." Helen followed Maura back across the street and into the restaurant. They found a table and ordered lunch, and when the waiter — who looked about sixteen and was probably the son of the owner — had scurried to the kitchen with their orders,

Helen turned back to Maura. "Why do I think you had a hand in the gardaí's decision?" she asked, smiling.

"I talked to them, sure. But the evidence showed that John fell. Off the record, it might be that he was startled by someone and slipped, but there was no harm intended."

"And that's all you're going to tell me, right?"

"Yup. Did that sergeant come after you?"

"He talked to me. Not a very polite man. Why do you ask?"

"He talked to me first. At least I had an alibi for that night. But he was looking hard to pin the death on someone, and he had you in his sights."

"He went away empty-handed. He's not typical of the local police, is he?"

"No, he just transferred to Skibbereen. I understand his bosses thought he needed some polishing, but it may take him a while to realize that around here people solve murders by talking. And remembering. Not bullying people."

"So we're free to go home," Helen said, almost to herself.

The food arrived, and Maura and Helen gave it the attention it deserved.

After a few minutes, Helen said tentatively,

"Maura, I know you've got your own business to run, so I'll get right to it. I've been trying to convince JBCo's investors that the hotel is worth keeping if we revise our original plans and projections. I've seen a bit of the area here and of course talked to you, and I think we didn't have a good handle on the local culture — we were overreaching. It was John's pet project, and he didn't want to hear any objections, but clearly there were things he didn't tell us. I get the feeling that this was more than a business decision."

"It was." Maura looked up. "Turns out he was born and raised about twenty miles from here."

Helen's eyes widened. "He was Irish? He never told us."

"He got shipped off to live with his father in New York when he was a kid. Looks like he reinvented himself."

Helen shook her head in disbelief. "Well, that would explain a lot. So am I to guess that his grand plans for the hotel were mainly to impress anyone around here who might have known him or maybe just to prove to himself how far he'd come?"

"Possibly. He never got in touch with anyone who knew him way back when" — except Siobhan, but Helen didn't need to know that — "so I think he did it for himself."

"Pride goeth before a fall," Helen murmured, then spoke more loudly. "Sorry, that's a terrible pun. I do think he cared about the hotel."

"What do you think your company is going to do now?"

"I'm hoping the group will give Crann Mor a chance, at least for the short term. I think it can work if we downsize our expectations. And what with Brexit and interest from the UK, it may yet prove to be a good investment. And one more thing." Helen hesitated. "The plan as I've presented it includes me as the project manager with a local assistant manager. I can make the argument that I have local ties. But I wouldn't be here often. Would that be a problem for you, Maura?"

"To have you popping in and out? No, of course not. Look, I'll admit I've had a chip on my shoulder, but for my own mental health, I have to let it go. You're still my mother, at least biologically. I need to give us both a chance. So if your plan works, I'll be fine with it."

"I'm so glad," Helen said and reached out and laid a hand on Maura's. And Maura didn't pull away.

She tried to figure out what she felt. Relieved, for one thing, because it seemed she had finally been able to move past her lifelong resentment of this mother she never knew. Hopeful? Whether or not anything ever came of it, she and her mother had made some kind of personal contact, and Helen might be back again. They would have time to work things out.

Before the silence could grow too awkward, Maura said, "There's music at the pub tomorrow night if you want to see the place in action."

"I'd like that. You know, the food really is good here. This area has a lot to offer to a particular kind of person, one who wants comfort but who isn't pretentious."

"That sounds about right. I can probably point you to other places you should check out."

"That would be great. I'd enjoy working with you — without intruding in your life, of course!"

"I think we can figure that out," Maura said, smiling.

THIRTY-SEVEN

"At least the house part is looking better," Maura told Gillian, taking a critical look at the rambling place on Ballinlough. The views would be great no matter how much of a pit it was, but you couldn't sleep and cook on views alone.

Gillian was bouncing the baby against her chest. "We're doing what we can. I can't believe you dragooned your pub friends into helping clear out the rest of the stuff here."

"Fair's fair. I won a bet. And promised them plenty of Guinness. Plus I threatened to get their wives to nag them. Did they bring along any baby stuff?"

"They did, and I almost kissed more than one of them. I don't know how Harry and I managed to stay so clueless when we had months to plan."

"It's been a confusing time for all of us. Let's hope things improve now. Is there anything out in the old creamery that you particularly want the guys to haul away? Or want them to save?"

"Good question, Maura. It's such a hodgepodge, like people have been dumping their discards there for years. If there are hidden treasures, I haven't seen them yet, but they could be under there somewhere."

"Want to go watch them work?"

Gillian looked down at her sleeping son. "Let's. I could use the air."

They walked around the corner of the building to where the old creamery stretched along the road from Leap. If Gillian wanted to use it as a studio and class space, there was certainly more than enough room. Seamus and his gang had arrived as a group, two of them driving battered trucks — clearly they knew what kind of a mess they'd be dealing with. They tipped their caps to Gillian and Maura but kept right on toting junk out of the interior. Maura saw a couple of orphaned toilets, some very rotten mattresses, a door, some old windows, and a cushionless couch go by. And a small, brightly painted rowboat.

She called out suddenly, "Hey, hold on a sec." She turned to Gillian. "You want to keep the boat? It looks like it might still float with a little patching."

"Well, there is a lake out back. Why not? Have them haul it around to the other side by the house."

Maura walked over to the two men who'd been hauling out the boat. "Guys, can we put that behind the house? Maybe Harry will take up fishing."

"Good place fer it," one of the men said cheerfully, and they pivoted and marched toward the water. The cleanout continued: piles of old rags or clothes (and Maura had to wonder if there had been squatters here at some point), old cans, bottles, and boxes. But an hour's work cleared most of it out, leaving only dirt and mold and some dangling wires.

"You know, if you're going to use this space, you'd better have the wiring checked out," Maura told Gillian.

"Of course, but that can wait. It may be a few months before I can think about that. What do you think of the house, now that you've seen all of it?"

"Well, it's in better shape than this side. You've got plenty of space. It's, what, three bedrooms? So that's the two of you, the baby, and an office for Harry?"

"That's right. We were lucky to get it well below the price asked. I guess the seller hadn't seen the shape it had fallen into."

"Does Harry have any leads on work?"

"He says he does, but none've come home to roost yet. But he remains optimistic."

"That's good. How's he enjoying being a dad?"

"More than he ever expected. More than I ever expected. Don't tell him I said so, but I think he's finally grown up. Maybe I'll tell him you thought he could learn to fish. Can't you see him, teaching our son to bait a hook?"

"That'll take a few years, but I do think you should keep the boat. Do you know how to row?"

"I can learn. You?"

"I'm a city girl, remember? I can tell you which end of a boat is the front, and that's about it."

"And here we are, living in the country. Me with a baby. Not what I would have foreseen a year ago, eh?"

When they walked around to the front again, Gillian peeled off to give the baby his latest feed. Maura kept going and saw an ordinary car parked in front with Sergeant Ryan standing beside it. Trouble? Maybe not — he wasn't in uniform. "Were you looking for something or someone, Sergeant?" she called out as he approached.

He looked oddly uncomfortable. "I heard

that yeh were askin' fer some help to get yer friends settled. I thought I'd come by and see if there was anything I could do. I'm on me own time now."

Wow — Maura hadn't expected that. "I'm sure we can find something. Do you know these guys? Most of them are regular patrons at Sullivan's. Do you have a wife or kids?" When the sergeant shook his head without commenting, Maura pushed on. "So I guess I can't ask you if you have a secondhand crib or toys. But there's still a lot of junk to be hauled away. Why don't I introduce you around, and you guys can work out what needs doing?"

"I'd appreciate that, Maura. I don't know many folk around here, and I seem to have gotten off on the wrong foot wit' some of 'em."

"Don't worry — they'll get over it. Especially if you buy 'em a pint at Sullivan's. Come on, I'll take you back to where they all are now."

After she'd handed the sheepish sergeant over to the work crew, she came back around to the front in time to see a car approaching along the road — usually a rare occurrence on this road, particularly in the middle of the day, but today it seemed to be more like a highway — and recognized her mother's rental car. She stepped closer to the road so Helen would see her and waved. Helen pulled in to the side of the creamery building near the house.

Maura walked over to join her. "How on earth did you find this place?" she asked.

"I'm learning my way around. And I asked someone how to find the old creamery near the lake. Besides, this road has a sign for Ballinlough, thank goodness." Helen took a moment to admire the view. "This is really nice, or it will be when it's fixed up."

"Come meet Gillian. She and her husband bought this place."

Maura led Helen over to where Gillian was still sitting. The baby slept on, but a slow, gentle rocking seemed to have become Gillian's usual activity. She turned when she heard Maura approach.

Helen stepped up quickly. "Please, don't stand up. How old?"

"We're still counting in days. You'd be Maura's mother?"

"Yes, Helen Jenkins. She told you about me? Not just the bad things, I hope."

"No, she's been fair to you. Welcome to my home — well, mine and Harry's. It's a work in progress."

"Is Harry here?"

"No, I sent him off to get more baby supplies. Amazing how fast a very small child can soil things."

"It is. Listen, if I miss Harry now, tell him I'd like to speak with him. We might be able to use a man with his financial skills at Crann Mor."

Gillian's face lit up. "He'd be more than glad to hear that! Wait, does that mean you and your people will be holding on to the place?"

"It looks that way. I must be more persuasive than I thought because I've convinced our investors to give it a try. I told them West Cork was an untapped market and definitely trending."

"Good for you!" Gillian glanced slyly at Maura. "Does that mean you'll be spending more time in this part of the world?"

"I hope so. We'll have to see how things develop. Maura told me you're the artist who painted some of the art in the pub?"

"I am — or was before this little one came along. Why do you ask?"

"I think the hotel could use something a bit fresher for the walls. I'd love to see more of your work."

Gillian stared for a moment, then burst out laughing. "Good heavens, woman, Maura didn't mention you're a miracle worker."

"She hasn't seen the best of me yet. Sorry I couldn't warn you, Maura, but the board only decided this morning on an emergency conference call. But once I had the go-ahead, I started bubbling over with plans and ideas — how to remodel without spoiling the place, how to find local staff, all that."

"I guess I can't complain." Maura turned and checked the progress the guys were making on clearing out the creamery. "You want to come see my place?"

"I'd love to. Is it far?"

"Just over that hill there. You up for walking?"

"I think so."

Maura turned to Gillian. "We'll be back in a bit. I'm sure the guys will be wanting their pints soon enough, but I've warned Mick and Rose to expect them."

"Take your time — I'm not going anywhere soon. Nice to meet you, Helen."

"Thanks. I'm glad Maura's got a friend in the neighborhood. Maura, lead the way!"

Maura checked to see that Helen was wearing sensible shoes because the road was a bit steep, then set off up the hill. She was relieved when Helen didn't start panting after the first few hundred feet. "Do you remember Gran or my father talking about

433

where they came from?"

Helen shook her head. "Not much. Tom was pretty young when they came to America, and he mostly remembered kid stuff like walking to school."

"We just walked past the school he was talking about — it's a private home now — and this was the road he would have taken. Gran lived the other side of the hill when her husband was alive. Old Mick lived near the top of the hill. Did Gran ever mention Bridget Nolan?"

"I can't say that she did, but it was a long time ago. She might have."

"Bridget lives just down the lane from me. She knew Gran and Tom when they lived here. She's in her eighties now, but her memory is good."

"You haven't told her I'm the witch who abandoned you and your grandmother to fend for yourselves?"

Maura stopped, and so did Helen, halfway up the hill. "No, but Gran used to write to Bridget. I don't know what she might have said. Still, Bridget's not one to judge. Times were different then, and people did what they had to do to get by. She'd like to meet you."

"Then I'll be happy to meet her."

After a few more minutes, they reached

the crest of the hill, and Maura pointed out the landmarks. "That's my place there on the left — you can just see the chimneys. Bridget's is the yellow house down a bit farther on the right. The road at the bottom of the hill is called the bog road, and there's a bog on the other side, where those horses are grazing."

"It's lovely," Helen said quietly. "Peaceful. So unlike cities and suburbs."

"That's very true. Come on, I'll show you my cottage."

Once again, Maura led the way, suddenly conscious of the overgrown ditches and various bits of abandoned dairy equipment, not to mention the long-empty house next to her own, now reduced to a stone shell. *Maura, listen to yourself. If you'd known your mother was coming, you would have cleaned the neighborhood?*

"This is it." Maura stepped aside to let her mother into the house, then followed her, leaving the door open. "It's not much, but . . ."

Helen laughed. "Maura, stop apologizing! Your father and I could never have afforded anything like this. After he died when I was your age, I was living in crappy apartments with multiple roommates, trying to get a degree and make something of myself. You have a home of your own here! With, what, two bedrooms? Views to die for? Neighbors who know you? You're a lucky woman!"

"Yeah, but I don't feel I've earned it."

"Stop feeling guilty. Look at it as compensation from the gods for what I did to you. It all evens out in the end."

"I guess," Maura said, smiling reluctantly. "Are you serious about making the hotel work?"

"You mean, am I going to get bored and leave if everything doesn't go my way? No. I've spent enough time here, talked to enough people, to know that it's going to take some serious effort and some money, but it matters to a lot of people. To the town itself. I'm going to do my damnedest to make it work. I'm not walking away again."

"I'm glad to hear that."

Maura was contemplating the idea of a hug when there was a rapping at the open door, and she turned to see Mick on the doorstep. "What are you doing here?" Maura asked. "And who's covering the pub?"

"Maura, half your patrons are down the hill there. Jimmy's at the place, and Rosie's keeping an eye on him. So I came up here to see what's what. I saw the two of you comin' up the hill and wondered if yeh planned to stop by me grannie's place. She said to tell Helen she has pictures that your gran sent her, from years back."

Helen replied quickly, "I'd love to meet your grandmother and to see her pictures. If that's okay with you, Maura?"

"Sure. I'm glad she asked. We should go see her now, because sometime today, I really should get to work."

"So let's go now."

"Both our cars are over at the creamery. We may need to hitch a ride from you to get back."

"Not to worry," Mick said, smiling. "It's this way, Helen."

He led the two of them down the lane and turned at the end. But he fell back just a bit to ask Maura, "Are the two of yeh good?"

She smiled up at him. "You know, I think we are. And you and me?"

"The same. Have you told yer mother about us?"

"I haven't had time. But I think if she sees us together much, she'll figure it out on her own."

"Then let's go down the hill before Bridget talks the woman's head off. And give Helen more of a chance to see the two of us together."

"Sounds good to me." Maura linked her

arm through Mick's, and together they walked down to Bridget's cottage.

ACKNOWLEDGMENTS

The Crann Mor Hotel in this story is based on a real place in Skibbereen, and it embodies the twists in Irish life. It's been a manor house for the local "big" family, a concert venue for rock bands, and more than once a hotel, under various managements. Its resilience is a tribute to the optimism of the Irish people as well as the complexity of their history. That's why I chose it as the catalyst for this story.

In this case the hotel is what brings characters from prior books together in sometimes surprising ways. As in so much of rural Irish life, there is a wealth of interconnections among people and places, and it requires the input of the entire cast to finally determine why someone was found dead in the garden of the hotel.

But some of the other people you've met in earlier books come together here for reasons not related to solving a crime. While

West Cork seems timeless, life does go on for its people, and there are some important changes for some of them in this book.

As always, much of my research for the County Cork Mysteries consists of simply talking to people in Ireland — in the pubs, in the villages, and now and then even to strangers on the street. What they see and what they remember from the past weave together to create a story in West Cork, even though they may now live in other parts of the world.

Thanks as always to Eileen Connolly Mc-Nicholl and her son Sam McNicholl for giving new life to Connolly's of Leap, the pub that's the model for Sullivan's: they've brought the music back, and the place is thriving. Thanks to Garda Sergeant Tony McCarthy, who is my go-to person for all things crime related in Ireland (any procedural errors are mine, not his!).

Of course I want to thank Matt Martz of Crooked Lane Books, who took on this series and moved it to the next level; his staff, all of whom have been so engaged in the shaping of this book; and my tireless agent, Jessica Faust of BookEnds, who brought us all together. Thanks as well to all my online friends and readers who have told me how much they enjoy my ongoing saga of modern life in West Cork. It is a special place.

ABOUT THE AUTHOR

Sheila Connolly is the *New York Times* bestselling author of more than thirty titles, including the Museum mysteries, the Orchard mysteries, and the Country Cork mysteries. She lives in Massachusetts with her husband and three cats and visits Ireland as often as she can. This is her seventh Country Cork mystery.

sheilaconnolly.com